CARNIVAL MAN

It took place at the kitchen table. A round, discarded antique, worn and scarred by pencils, cigarette burns and coffee rings. A pedestal table, surrounded by four mismatched oddly colored chairs. A centerpiece sitting in a well-worn rental house atop scratched linoleum in the town of Tolt, Washington.

Rosalene sat at the table; her red hair fell in spirals down her straight spine. Emma sat to her right, slouching and fingering her brown hair. Kimmy sat across from Emma, her blonde hair hitting shoulders that could not hold still.

"Let's try again." Rosalene held her palms high. "I feel the energy today."

"This is dumb," Emma said.

"Emma, I want to try. Your mama had the dream again, about my mom. I want to talk to her. Your mama has my message; she has to give her my message or I will die inside, again. Do you know what this means to me?" Kimmy's blue eyes were sharp.

"I'll do it for you Kimmy, but I hate this shit," Emma looked directly at her mother.

"Emma! Show respect for the powers of the universe, for the powers of the dead!" Rosalene shouted.

"Fuck the universe."

"Be Quiet Emma! Hold hands," Rosalene said.

ISBN: 978-1-63491-630-1

Published by BookLocker.com, Inc., St. Petersburg, Florida.

Printed on acid-free paper.

BookLocker.com, Inc.
2017

First Edition

Dedication

This book goes out to Greg and my mom, my family and my friends, who support me in all I do. Thanks to Susan Ross and Suzanne Sievert for your generous help. Thanks to Bob who wrote a novel and started the whole thing, even though we never found it. It is in the ethers. Thank you Kenya Dillon for the legal prowess. Thank you Race Dillon for the gorgeous photograph.

Chapter One: Emma; The High Priestess

If you've ever spent the beginning of summer in a river town, then you know what it's like. Everything changes. Everyone relaxes and gets pent up in a different kind of way. Like a mating season feeling. The river pulls you to it like a force and there you change into a completely different person. When your clothes are shed everything is exposed. School is out, so the person you were at school you can shed as easily as your pants or boots. The water, the incredible sound and the smell when you first come upon it, makes you believe that every moment is a new moment.

Maybe it was the river that made mama fall in love so many times with so many different men. And maybe that's why she fell in love with Carlos the carnival man over and over and over.

Mama fell for Carlos the first time he pulled up in his white truck with the ring of fire and the Bengal tigers painted on the door. The lettering above read "Ramos Brother's Carnival". There were no tigers and no brothers so I don't know what the painting was all about.

That summer the air smelled so good, it smelled like wild roses and grass clippings and fresh hay all rolled into one. Kimmy and I played each day in the hot sun and each night in the glow of a silver moon. Our friends came in and out and we made mud pies and forts and grass hills and went to bed exhausted, covered in those smells. And the carnival smells rose above that for three long weeks in July.

When the carnival rode into town we had two days of anticipation. The carnies were scruffy and colorful and they transformed the grassy field into a plethora of senses. Colorful awnings of red and white and flashing signs lit up the night sky and buzzed in the daylight. Sounds of shouting and laughter drifted over us like pink clouds in the wind.

Kimmy and I sat on the grass for three hours the day before the carnival opened, our legs stretched out before us, sunglasses on. We were eleven and we wore short shorts and flip-flops and talked about the boys we'd like to kiss. It seemed the carnival would never be ready.

The next day the carnival opened. Mama walked over with Kimmy and I. She wore a tight white skirt, sandals and a wide brimmed hat; her red hair tumbled down her back. I loved mama's hair. The air swirled with excitement. Red and white striped popcorn bags and hanging tufts of pink cotton candy were everywhere. Smells of elephant ears stacked row upon row, fresh sugary scones and roasting hotdogs swirled about me until I thought I would explode. I loved walking on the fresh straw. It felt good to be the first ones there, before any litter or trash had touched the field.

"Mama, let me have my money," I said.

"Listen baby, I don't want you spendin' all this in one day, you hear?" She handed me a ten-dollar bill so crisp I didn't want to fold it.

The day was magic and the colors and the sounds melted into the sky. The whir and grind of the rides, the low hum of generators and the "next" call of the carnies handling the rides were exhilarating. One thing at a time, I kept telling myself. Remember, you can come back tomorrow and the next day, but I felt like I wanted to open my mouth right then and there and take a big swallow of everything.

Kimmy and I spent hours and hours playing games and riding rides until we felt our feet grow swollen. It was time to find mama. She wasn't where she was supposed to be. Kimmy and I wandered around looking. We each had a cone of cotton candy that just about covered our eyes and it was hard to eat and look for her at the same time.

"There she is," Kimmy pointed to the milk can toss booth. Mama was sitting on the edge of the booth, her legs crossed, holding her hat and letting her curls roll about. Was she playing a game? Trying to win Kimmy and I a prize?

"Mama!" I yelled.

She turned and it was at that instant I got the sick feeling in my stomach. The feeling I got when mama was interested in something other than me. The feeling I got when we had an extra plate at dinner, or she put out a glass ashtray instead of a tin soup can because someone was coming over. I looked at Kimmy and she smiled as big as the summer day. She loved mama.

Mama waved us over, her smile as big as Kimmy's and I knew what she was about to say..."You all, meet so and so," and then he was going to end up over for dinner and he'd be there for breakfast and then dinner again and so on and so on, until there were days of empty whiskey bottles lying about. She'd forget to make my breakfast and forget to give me my lunch money and I'd do my own laundry. When mama had a man around she forgot about everything.

I've always had two mamas, an inside mama and an outside mama. The inside mama tucked me in at night and tickled me with her red curls when she bent over me. The inside mama read regular fairy tales, then reread them with changed plots and characters until they were silly and nonsensical. We performed them in the living room with the curtains wide open. We clapped and bowed for ourselves and fell into mounds of laughter.

"You and me Emma. We are like stardust, bright and shiny amongst the dirt of the earth," she said. The inside mama liked being with me when we were alone.

The outside mama I shared with everyone. Mama attracted people like insects to a light on a hot summer's night, especially men. People talked to her, cooed over her, walked close to her and stood by her in line. If they got a smile and a wave from mama they lit up like a sunbeam. She was an intoxicating scent and I watched those around her get drunk with the smell of her. They found her a mystery, a magnetic enigma and whether they believed in her tarot cards or not, curiosity lined their eyes.

That was the other mama. The mama that changed forms no matter how hard I stared. She faded further and further away until she became an unrecognizable figure on a screen, like a character in a love story at the theater. And there was no popcorn or juju fruits to go with that movie, only a sick feeling in my stomach.

"Girls, come here. Come over here, there's someone I want you to meet." She waved her arms in delight. Kimmy ran; I walked slow, dragging my feet through the straw. She hopped off the counter, wrapped an arm around each of us. We were her momentary prizes.

"This is my baby, Emma, and her friend Kimmy." She paused, flipped her curls, and smiled bigger. "And Emma, Kimmy...this is Carlos." Carlos smiled and flashed a gold tooth. His eyes were as brown as dirt.

"What beautiful girls." He reached out to touch my chin. I pulled away. His eyes locked with mine. "Ahhh, to have such a beautiful mother of course it would be as so." Carlos spoke with an accent. "You want to try the milk toss game?"

"Yeah," Kimmy shouted. I shrugged my shoulders like I could care less, but really, I did want to throw the ball and try to win a statue. I especially liked the pony. It was reared up and dazzling in purple and yellow and sparkly with glitter.

Carlos came outside the booth and put a baseball in Kimmy's hand. Kimmy threw three balls and did not hit a one of those milk bottles, but Carlos shouted anyway, "A winner, we have a winner!" He kicked the milk bottles over with his boot and handed Kimmy a small stuffed snake.

"Do you want to try Emma?" he asked.

"Okay."

He handed me a ball, looked me in the eye and winked. I took the ball and I threw it as hard as I could. I could pitch softball. Everyone in town knew I could pitch softball. I pitched that ball like I was Jim Palmer and then I closed my eyes tight.

"Emma, my god, did you just do that?" Mama looked down at me.

The ball had knocked down all six milk bottles, hit the side counter and bounced into the other stack of milk bottles hitting the three top ones.

"In all of Cuba, I have never seen a curve ball like that, in all of Havana...Saint DiMaggio of baseball saints protect us." Carlos dropped to his knees and gave himself the sign of the cross and I couldn't help but laugh. "Pick your prize," he said as he got to his feet.

I went home with the purple pony. Mama walked behind us and the world looked very good at that moment. Carlos came for dinner at eight, after his carnival game replacement showed up at the booth. Mama made pork chops with lots of gravy and after dinner, she got out her cedar box. She unwrapped her tarot cards from their white silk cloth and covered the kitchen table with a purple silk shawl. She held the cards in one hand and waved her other hand back and forth over the top. "God channel through me and protect me and let me see the truth delivered by yourself and your five hundred angels," she said with her eyes closed. When she opened them she smiled at Carlos. She shuffled the cards quietly, over and under, over and under. Carlos smoked. He was falling for it, the whole ceremony of it. I hated those cards.

The next morning I looked in mama's room. Mama laid all twisted up, her silk dragon bathrobe half open. Carlos had an arm splayed under her and he was snoring. I'd seen it all before.

I walked over to Kimmy's. She was dressed, watching cartoons on her color television. I loved Kimmy's house. She had everything. She had great art stuff, pens and paper and cutouts of ponies to trace. She had a Spirograph and plastic horses and a stereo for 45's and she had her own room with purple and pink wallpaper. I got her a butterfly poster for her birthday last year and we colored it together on her back deck. She didn't want to color anymore; she wanted to write the names of boys over and over again on notebook paper.

"Emma, you want to go to the carnival and see who's there? John Wright said he was going today." She chewed on her lower lip and stared at a Scooby Doo cartoon.

"Yeah, I want to go, but I just want to ride the rides," I said.

"Okay then, no games."

We walked to the carnival and as we approached the field I could see Carlos' booth. There was a woman working behind the counter. I let out the breath I had been holding.

"Yesterday you won a pony at the milk bottle toss," Kimmy said. "You think you can do it again?"

"They'll only let you win a prize once," I lied. "Besides it's stupid."

"Let's try it," she said. Before I could stop her, Kimmy had run to Carlos' booth and was digging in her pockets for change. I stood beside her and tried to focus on something, anything, but I couldn't get a take on one thing. All the colors of the carnival swam together.

I felt hot air on my shoulder, Carlos' voice, "Are you playing again or are you looking for your mama?"

I turned in time to see his gold tooth flash. He smelled like fresh soap and his black hair was slicked back into a ponytail. He wore a white undershirt and Kimmy stared at the tattoo on his bicep.

"Is that a carousel pony?" she asked.

"Yep. Do you want to see it move?" He flexed his bicep over and over and the carousel horse went up and down. Kimmy had her mouth open; even I was impressed.

She reached out and touched it. She stroked that horse up and down with her fingertips and Carlos smiled.

"Let's get out of here," I said.

"Are you going to play your game or not? You paid your money, do you want your throws or not?" The lady behind the counter was leaning forward holding out the three balls.

"Darla, this here is Emma. Emma has a baseball arm that the New York Yankees would buy in a minute. She can toss off the milk bottles from ten paces, can't you Emma?" He put his hands on my shoulders.

Before I moved, he had put a baseball in my hand. I wanted to throw it at him, but Darla in the booth was smiling real nice.

"No," I said, "I already won a big prize. Let Kimmy try again."

"Why, isn't that the nicest thing? Now how many kids do you know would do that Carlos?" Darla smiled even nicer.

"Emma's a special girl," Carlos said. He handed the ball to Kimmy.

Kimmy looked like she was going to bust open. She smiled and her body shook. "Here goes," she said.

Her throw was terrible again. It hit the side of the booth. Carlos winced and Darla flinched out of the way and covered her head with her hands.

"Shit," Carlos said. "Can we give a prize for over achieving?"

Darla laughed and she didn't have a gold tooth, but she had dimples in her cheeks and her eyes crinkled up. I liked her. She gave Kimmy a pony like mine and Carlos made a big production of handing it to her with a bow.

"Let's go Kimmy." I tugged at her arm. She wouldn't budge. "Let's go." I tugged harder.

"Bye…thank you, thank you so much. I mean really, really thank you." Kimmy held her pony like it was glass.

"I'll see you tonight Emma. Your mama's gonna read my cards," Carlos said.

She did that with every guy. Read their cards. They went all mushy about it, looked her in the eyes and thought she was so clever. Mama read the cards every morning. She spread the purple cloth over the scarred kitchen table, unwrapped the cards, said her hocus pocus spell and then shuffled them slowly.

She laid them out carefully, making sure they were evenly spaced, face down. She turned them over one by one. She kept her coffee next to her. The steam rose and mixed with the woodsy smell of her perfume. Mama always smelled like perfume, anytime of the day or night. She lit her cigarette in between cards and clucked her tongue or shook her head and mumbled to herself.

"There's magic here Emma," she tapped the deck of cards. I knew there was something, but I didn't call it magic. I called it her hocus-pocus and I didn't want to believe in it. It took mama away from me. I shared her with anyone who came close enough for her to cast her spell. She told me she saw things too.

"Emma, I can touch a person and see scenes of their life. It can be very disturbing." I didn't know what she meant, but I had seen her do it. Once at a garage sale, she stared and stared at a woman who wandered the driveway, picking up odds and ends and turning them over. Mama reached out and touched her shoulder and said, "Don't do it. Don't lie to save your love." The woman recoiled and turned her back on us. She pretended to be interested in a blue china bowl, her hands shook when she picked it up.

"Why did you scare her?" I asked her walking home.

"That woman will lie about a pregnancy, she will pretend to carry a man's child and when the truth is found out he will beat her to unconsciousness. I tried to warn her that's all. I just don't know." She shook her head and her eyes watered as she looked down at the sidewalk. "That's why I try so hard not to see."

I looked at her cards once, when she was working at the library book sale. I unwrapped them from the white silk handkerchief and I looked at each and every card. Some were very pretty and some were horribly ugly and frightening. How they could tell you what to do with your life I couldn't figure out. I laid them out like she did; then I held them in my hands like poker cards and fanned myself with them. I wrapped them back in the silk and put them in the cedar box before she came home.

Carlos came at eight and we had noodles with meat sauce on them. He smiled at me across the table. He told a dumb joke and mama laughed. I stared at him. It was kind of funny, but I didn't laugh.

After dinner mama told me to do the dishes and she cleared off the table. The purple cloth came out and it got real quiet in the room.

"Put on some music Emma," mama said.

I went to the stereo and started a record.

"Not that one," she said, "give me a Sinatra."

I put on a Frank Sinatra record. Carlos stood and wiggled his hips. I ignored him and mama watched him. She shuffled the cards real slow. She read his cards with her hypnotic voice. Carlos's eyes glassed over. They drank wine and smoked and the night stretched out like a cat.

Carlos kept coming for dinner and kept getting his cards read for three weeks, until the carnival rolled up its tents and folded up its awnings and tucked the ride buckets in tight.

The day the carnival left town, we walked to the field together to say goodbye. Mama wore a floral print dress and high heels and her floppy hat. I stood by the edge of the field and watched her say goodbye to Carlos. It was strange to see how the carnival turned into regular looking trucks and trailers. The only way you would know there was a carnival inside was by the paintings on the sides of each truck. Carlos scooped up mama and spun her around; she held her hat with one hand, the other hand wrapped about Carlos' neck. She laughed and tossed her long red hair in the sunlight. Her legs dangled as she flew round and round while Carlos' pony tattoo went up and down.

Carlos put mama down and walked toward me. He bowed at the waist making a big gesture with one arm. "Sweet Conchita, my beautiful sea shell, I will miss you terribly. Where else will I find a pitcher with such a great baseball arm, eh?" He smiled, his gold tooth flashed. "Take care of your sweet, sweet mama." He took my hand and pressed something into my palm. "For you." He turned back to mama and kissed her for a long time. Long enough for me to see two airplanes cross the sky.

Mama didn't cry after he left, she just acted like she always did. "It wasn't in the cards for us," she said. I opened my hand as we walked back to the house. It was a small chocolate bar, wrapped in fancy gold paper, just starting to get soft around the edges from the heat of my palm. The rest of that summer was hot and full of bugs.

Kimmy got a bra that fall. Her dad took her to the super mall in the city and bought her one. She showed it to me the next day. It was white and silky on one side, with white stitching of flowers and leaves around the edge. The inside felt like a soft silky towel.

"Why did you get it?" I asked her.

"I'm going to wear it, you dope. What do you think Emma?"

"I mean you don't need it, do you? Won't it just get in the way when you're running and stuff?"

She looked at me like I was the dumbest kid in school. "You wear a bra when your boobies are growing so they know how to grow right you dope. Otherwise they end up all long and saggy like National Geographic boobies."

"Oh."

I asked mama for a bra that night at the table. "We don't have the money right now," was all she said as she took a long drag off her cigarette.

Kimmy didn't have a mom, because she died when Kimmy was six, so her dad was always doing nice things for her. I think he felt bad that Kimmy's mom was dead. I once thought since I didn't have a dad and Kimmy didn't have a mom, her dad and my mama should get together. Then Kimmy and I could be blood sisters.

But when I told her she said, "My dad thinks your mom's weird."

Kimmy played the flute. It had been her mother's. It was beautiful silver; she kept it wrapped in velvet inside a black velvet lined case. She played songs that made me think of butterflies. The notes danced in the air and wrapped around me as soft as silk. She only played outside. "I try to get the fairies to come out," she said, "or my mom." But I knew she played outside because of Carl, her dad. The only time I saw Kimmy play inside, Carl stalked into the room.

"Stop it," his face was red and sweaty, "I don't like that." Carl leaned his body into the doorjamb and turned away. "I don't want to hear that."

Kimmy's mom had played the same flute. The sounds that washed over me broke Kimmy's dad's heart, I could hear it cracking in two.

The next time Kimmy's dad took us to the super mall I went too. I had my French poodle purse and wore my sandals with the black heels. It felt great to walk the mall with Kimmy. So grown up. Her dad let us go off by ourselves while he went into the Pizza Factory for a root beer. We went to Frederick & Nelson and tried on jewelry and watches, flung scarves over our shoulders and swung beads around until the saleslady scowled us at.

"I'll show you where I got my bra," she whispered.

On the second floor was the prettiest underwear I had ever seen. Pink and baby blue and frilly and lacy and silky and smooth. You could buy any kind of underwear in any color. If I got new underwear it was always packs of white with tiny flowers, three to a pack. They were pretty, but nothing like this.

"This is where I got my bra. I have it on."

We stood by the rack and I touched the bras, one by one. They were white and simple with tiny details, like ribbons or lace. I held one up that was silky, like Kimmy's, but with lace at the top edge.

"This is beautiful," I gasped.

"You should buy it," Kimmy said.

"I don't have any money. Mama said she doesn't have any money."

Kimmy looked at me. She didn't understand, because her daddy always had money. He was a logger and he went to work every day. He came home with wood chips around the bottom of his pants and on his boots and he always smelled like pine.

"I'll ask my daddy to buy it for you," she said. "He will you know."

"Don't."

Kimmy started to walk away. I don't know how I did it, even now, but I just slipped that bra with the lace on it right into my French poodle purse and left the hanger on the floor beneath the rack. I ran after Kimmy, my voice shaking, "Hey, wait up."

I put the bra in my underwear drawer, way in the back, so no one could see. I never wore it and I couldn't get myself to look at again. Thinking about it made my stomach feel sick. Two weeks later mama took me to the variety store and bought me one. It wasn't as pretty or as fancy, but I loved it. I loved the way it felt on and the way it made me feel. It made me stand up straight and tall.

Mama read my cards every other day, whether I wanted her to or not. "They keep the world straight for me," she tilted her head and smiled. She didn't know it, but I had my own magic, the river. The river swept through me. It made my soul burst apart and join it, flowing free over banks of silt and rocks. I walked to the river every day, by myself or with Kimmy, or with Marsha when she got off work at the 2 x 4. Marsha was a waitress there. "Pretty sassy," mama said, "that's why I like her." Marsha was ten years older than me, but she listened and she talked in a voice that I understood. Her life was fascinating.

"My mom was a lesbian and divorced my dad to live with her girlfriend." She flung her cigarette in the dirt. "She was a designer and was featured in Sunset Magazine. I'll show you, it's far out." She showed me the article. The rooms were decorated in reds and shades of green, lots of plaids and her mom's picture was in the corner. She smiled delicately and wore tiny horn rimmed glasses. "I think my dad was beyond jealous when he saw this," she laughed. Marsha's little house was at the end of Entwistle Street. It was colorful and full of exotic statues and findings from thrift stores and antique shops.

"I love this town," she said as we sat on a big log watching the geese fly over the river. They landed with dramatic splashes, their landings created ripples that lapped to shore. I closed my eyes and listened to their calls. "I moved here to change. To morph into someone nobody recognized, not even myself. You know what I mean?"

"Yes." I did. I wanted to morph every day.

"You can reinvent yourself. I don't have to be the lesbian's daughter anymore. I used to hear people in the grocery store say, 'Poor Marsha, her mom left her dad for another woman'. I hate being talked about when I'm standing right there. It was like I was transparent. I got so transparent, I disappeared and I ended up here."

Marsha wore her hair long, it was dark with streaks of gold and she never dressed in anything special but she moved like a princess. She smoked a lot of cigarettes. Her and mama smoked dope together and drank whiskey and talked in husky voices when mama read her cards, which was at least once a week. "I'm getting my cards read tonight by your mama. You're so lucky." She looked at me. "You don't know that yet do you?"

"I hate it when she reads the cards and tells me shit."

Marsha laughed. "Yes, I guess you would. I hated a lot of things my mom did too. Your mama's magic though. Magic. I'm really in love with her." The words hung in the air.

That winter when the leaves fell and collected on the slopes of the river, mama started dating a logger named Ned. Ned smelled like the forest, like wood chips, fresh and clean. Ned had sweet smelling earth beneath his fingernails and embedded in the cracks of his hands, old earth that had been around for hundreds of years. Our town was a logger town. The air smelled like wood chips and chainsaw grease, river and stone. The smell could fill a grocery aisle or permeate an entire café. I loved it and swallowed it in big gulps. Years later, the smell of fresh cut wood could make me cry.

Ned had dinner at our house every night of the week. Ned bought us groceries, the good kind of groceries too; not the kind that we normally got from the food bank. He bought ice cream and popcorn already popped in the bag and licorice and icy pops. Ned didn't drink whiskey. He drank tea while mama drank whiskey with tinkling ice. Ned didn't like having his cards read, instead he played solitaire on the living room floor while mama read cards at the kitchen table, drumming her fingernails on the wood and talking to herself. Ned paid attention to nature. He watched birds from the window and took long walks along the river. He spotted cougar tracks and deer tracks and we once followed a coyote's trail for two miles together. Ned understood the magic of nature and the magic of the river. He taught me more magic.

"Put your hands here," he said one day when we walked by the bank of the river. He wrapped my hands around the trunk of a birch tree. "Do you feel that?"

I closed my eyes. I felt something, a quivering. "Yes, I think so."

"It's going to flood. The trees vibrate when the river starts to swell, it shakes the earth." It flooded that night. The river swelled like a pregnant mother's belly and jumped its banks flooding the highway, barns and pastures.

"Ned knew, mama. He knew it was going to flood," I told her.

"So did I," she said. She let out a drag of her cigarette.

Ned and I hiked a trail on the bank of the river the next day to look at the wild water. "A logger can always tell a weather change," he said.

"How?"

"By the smell. I'll tell you." His breath came out in smoke puffs. "When the air smells sweet that means it is going to clear and get sunny. The warm air stirs the flowers and the herbs and creates a perfume." He grabbed a stick from the ground and twirled it. "And when the air smells like pine and fir it's going to rain." He stopped, put the stick near my nose. "Smell this."

"Mmm, that smells so good."

"That's the smell of rain I'm talking about."

"What about snow?"

"Oh that. That's not a smell. That's a sound. The forest gets quiet. It gets so still you could swear you're the only person left on the earth."

I remembered everything Ned taught me and held it in my heart like a perfectly round pebble.

Ned stayed through the winter. Life was good, sixth grade was easy. Kimmy let me use her lipstick on the corner in the mornings before school. We applied the color to our lips in rounded arches before we reached the playground. We were having junior high orientation that week and we wanted to look our best for the seventh grade boys. Kimmy had started wearing eye make-up and mascara and she let me borrow that too. In the bathroom that always smelled of little kid sweat, we would pucker our lips and stick out one hip and try on the make-up until the morning bell rang and ruined our trance.

"Who's your mom's new boyfriend?" Kimmy asked.

"Ned. He seems okay."

"He's cute," Kimmy said. "My dad said he knew him from the mill. My dad asked how many boyfriends your mom's had this year."

"I don't know," I said.

"Do you think hundreds, or maybe thousands?"

"It keeps her busy," I said. "I like Ned."

"Maybe he'll be your daddy." The second bell rang. Kimmy grabbed the mascara out of my hand and shoved it in her bag.

"I don't want a daddy."

"Everybody wants a daddy."

Truth was, I did want Ned to be my daddy. I felt like we belonged to each other. He spent time with me; he picked me up and twirled me when he came up the front walk, even if I was going on twelve.

One day, when the ice was starting to melt, Ned came home from work smiling wide. He lumbered up the walk, through the front door and said, "Hallelujah, get your clothes on".

"Oh, we've got our clothes on Ned honey," mama said.

"No, I mean get your good clothes on baby. I got lucky today and we're going to the city.

"The city?" mama asked.

"We'll go get a fancy dinner!" he laughed like a little boy with a new toy truck.

Mama danced around him and kissed him hard on the cheek. She put on a flowered dress and red high heels and danced some more. I put on the only dress I had, which was getting a little bit small so I wore cut-off jean shorts underneath. We drove in Ned's big white truck to Seattle and had dinner in a fancy restaurant by the water. The waitress told us her name was "Cecily" as she spread our napkins in our laps. Ned and I had big fat steaks and hot baked potatoes with sour cream piled in mountains on top. Mama had prawns with hot melted butter. Mama and Ned kissed in the red candlelight and I watched the ferry land at the dock, slow and majestic. I watched the people disembark with their satchels and their secrets, the city lights danced behind them like fairies.

Ned stayed through spring. He came to my baseball games and sat in the front row of the stands. He somehow got mama to come to some of the games; she had never come before. "I abhor organized sports," she said. Mama seemed to be pretty happy, though, sitting next to Ned in her tight Levis and peasant tops. She only brought her cards out in the mornings and on Friday nights and she hadn't done a reading for Ned yet. That wasn't too surprising. Ned didn't need the cards to be woozy over her. He touched her and stared at her loopy all the time. I swear she was afraid she would scare him off with her mumbo jumbo fortune stuff. Thank god. I was sick of hearing about my future in those cards. Ned cheered for me. Ned told me, "Great job." The coach asked if he was my dad.

"No," I said. "I don't have a dad." And that was the truth. I had never known my dad, I didn't know what he looked like or what he smelled like or what kind of car he drove.

One night mama was sitting on the back porch smoking and watching the night sky. Ned was inside doing the dishes. I sat beside her on the cold concrete step. I asked her about it, about him.

"Who's my daddy?" I asked.

"I don't know baby. I mean I know, but I don't really know, if you know what I mean."

"No."

She took a drag off her cigarette, let it out in a slow stream, it took off with the moon. "He was a looker, I'll tell you that. And look at you, it's pretty obvious with your long dark hair and green eyes, you are my star." She touched me under the chin. I looked at her and she was soft around the edges, like a painting in an old book. "Your daddy was only around for a few weeks, or actually it was me who was around for only a few weeks. He worked an arcade in Pittsburgh and he was something. He practically ran the whole show, and he with his great looks and the lights of the arcade and the smells of the cotton candy and the summer heat. Well, it was enough to make you pregnant; and it did. I left after three weeks. I left for the west coast."

"What about him?"

"Oh, he was traveling, they did shows all over the world, even in Europe. He didn't want a baby, but I did. I wanted you worse than anything. I had to have you. You were in my cards in a big way. I loved your daddy, but I didn't miss him. He was just one piece in the puzzle you know."

“Do you ever try to contact him? Does he write? Does he want to know about me?”

“Oh honey, he flew away with the wind.”

I was unwanted, unwanted by someone I didn't even know, someone who didn't know me. If you didn't know each other was it possible to want each other? "Is that why you like Carlos, because he works at a carnival?"

Mama laughed and looked me square in the eye, "Honey, Carlos doesn't work at that carnival; he owns that carnival." She took a drag, looked at the top of the apple tree. "Carlos keeps my feet on the ground, that's why I like him."

"Are you going to go back with Carlos?"

"It is in the cards. He's a prominent player, there's no doubt about that."

"What about Ned?"

"Honey, Ned's going to lose something very important to him pretty soon, so he will probably move."

"You don't know that." I wanted to plug my ears and scream at her at the top of my voice. Instead I asked her calmly, "Did you ever try to tell my daddy about me?"

"Nope," she stood up and stretched. "Don't have to."

And that was it. She kissed me on top of the head and went through the screen door, leaving me with the dark sky. I watched the stars take their place one by one.

Mama got a job that spring at the library stacking and recording books so I didn't have to go to the food bank for awhile, what with Ned bringing us groceries and mama's new job.

That was my job. Every Wednesday afternoon I walked to the food bank by myself. Every Wednesday afternoon the puckered faced old woman at the front table would say the same thing.

"Where's your mama?" she'd ask.

"At home."

"I'm not supposed to let you in without an adult."

I never answered, I just stared her down until her eyes crinkled up tight and she looked away. "I'll let you in today," she said every time, "but you tell your mama to come with you next time." I knew what the word "welfare" meant.

I walked the five blocks back to our house with bags of cheese and bread and butter, white rice and flour. Sometimes I'd get peanut butter and cereal, and once in a while stale cookies. Ned kept us well fed though, so Wednesday afternoons were my own, thank god. Mama still went to the clothing bank though, so my clothes were hand me downs and cast offs from other kids in the valley. I wore them, praying no one would notice me in the t-shirt or skirt they had just donated to the "needy", to me.

Everything was great until school got out and the summer stretched before me. I knew the carnival was coming back to town. My stomach hurt every day. I was afraid Carlos would come back and mama would pick Carlos over Ned and that would be the end of it all. Mama would quit her job so she could drink and smoke with Carlos and I would go back to the food bank and everything would be back just the way it was.

I went to the corner drug store a week before the carnival was due to unload.

"Where's your mama been Emma?" It was Jake McWeyer asking, one of the young pharmacists. He smelled of spicy aftershave. He was one of mama's audience members.

"She's got a boyfriend." I said it real snotty and turned away before I saw his reaction.

There were two carnival posters on the front window. "Excited for the carnival Emma?" he asked me.

"No."

"Let's go to the carnival Emma." Mama brushed her long red hair. She wore a pair of tight blue jeans and a blue gypsy shirt that flowed around her like holy water. Ned was at work. He left the house at five in the morning.

"Okay." This would be the worst day of my life. Ned was going to be gone that night; I just knew it. No more river walks with him, no more tracking coyotes or following squirrels, watching them hide their stash. No more rock hunting and stick gathering at the water's edge. I would be on my own again.

The morning was sunny and the carnival was setting up when we got there. The red and white awnings, the cotton candy trucks, the great trailers with the rides and the painted ponies, all the colors made me sick. I saw a truck parked on the edge of the grass. I looked for

Carlos. Then I noticed the door of the pickup. There were no tigers and no ring of fire painted on the door. There was a picture of a gypsy lady, and the words, "J&J Enterprises".

"Mama," I grabbed her arm and stopped her.

"What?"

"Whose carnival is this?"

"What honey?" She had her eyes shielded from the sun and was scanning the carnival horizon.

"Mama, where is Carlos? Is this his carnival or not?"

"No dear, Carlos is in Bellingham. They go where the best jobs are, you know that."

I felt a million sparrows light from my shoulders and fly away. "How do you know that?"

"I read it in the cards, he won't be here for another yearly cycle and besides, he writes to me." She grabbed my hand and we strode off toward the movement of colors and sounds.

Everything was all right for now. Seventh grade would start in the fall. The thought of it made me feel sick; at least I had Kimmy.

Kimmy and I spent our lazy summer days at the river. All we needed was a towel and a few magazines and we were content. We sat at the edge of the river and dug our heels into the silt, letting the water run over our legs. We swam and raced across the river to the bank on the other side. We dove for the bottom and let our bodies float the current. Sometimes it felt like Kimmy and I were one person, other times I felt a division growing wide between us. Kimmy wanted to move forward and become another person. I didn't want to be anything. I closed my eyes, breathed in the scent of the water and left my body behind, becoming a wisp of vapor, moving with the current far, far away. There were a lot of high school kids at the river and the smell of cigarette smoke mingled with the fresh summer air. Kimmy flirted with the boys. She talked different and jutted her hip out. I thought of mama. When the heat got to be too much we walked with our towels over our shoulders and went to the 2x4 café for diet cokes. Marsha worked in the afternoons and she gave us paper umbrellas for our drinks. "God, are you two jailbait or what?" she asked.

"What's that?" I asked Kimmy when Marsha was out of sight.

"It's a girl who is too young to fuck, but they want to fuck her anyway. Like me." She played with her blonde hair, stroked it up and down like a kitten. "If you're too young, they go to jail," she laughed. "I can't believe you don't know that, especially with your mama."

"How do you know that?"

"I read." And she did. So did I, but I read books from the library. Kimmy read fashion magazines, music magazines and gossip magazines.

One hot day Kimmy and I read each other's pebbles on the beach. We laid them out on a towel, just like mama laid out her cards and we told each other fantastic tales and predictions.

"This is the pebble of babies," I said with a mumbo jumbo voice. "You will have five babies and ten husbands."

She laughed, "No way!"

"And this is the pebble of baseball," she said, turning over a stone. "You will hit your dream lover in the head with a baseball, that's how you will know him."

"Right."

It was the summer of change. Our bodies changed, our friendship changed. Kimmy talked about boys and sex, even though we weren't sure how it all worked, and we spent all our free time at the river.

That fall Ned lost his job. It was a night when the wind howled about the small house. The wind blew in through the cracks of the house and tumbled through the air and circled the kitchen table where Ned sat, his head bent forward in his hands crying. Ned crying. I'd never seen a man cry before. I'd never heard a man cry before. Loud sounds came out in rhythms like a goat's bleat. Tears rolled out of his eyes and landed on the table. Mama sat quietly beside him. Occasionally she made purring noises and stroked his back.

The next morning while Ned was down at the union office, she took her cards out of the box and lit a white candle. She talked to herself. She waved the deck of cards back and forth in the air and chanted. I tried to ignore her and watch T.V., but I couldn't.

She shuffled her deck, cut it three times and slowly laid out a spread of cards that looked like a cross with a straight line of cards on the side.

"That's what I thought." She said this like she would have said, "The sky is blue." She picked up the cards, put them in a neat pile and put a white piece of paper over them. She sprinkled thick salt on the paper and said a bunch of words that didn't seem to go together. She took the paper with the salt and dumped the salt down the drain of the kitchen sink, and ran cool water down the drain. The cards got wrapped back up in the white silk and went back into the cedar box. This was nothing new. This was how she "cleared" the cards, she said, so she could get all the old energy off of them. I didn't see any old energy on them, and I didn't see anything going down the drain either. I never did.

When Ned came back from the union office, his eyes looked red and he had a file folder tucked in his armpit. “I got a job in Aberdeen if I want it," he said.

"You should take it," mama said.

"Aberdeen is four hours away." Ned hung his head and looked down at his feet, like a puppy dog.

"That's not so far."

"But I love you Rosalene."

There, that was it. That's what I wanted to hear, but I wanted to hear him say he loved me and that he wanted me to be his girl, that he wanted to be my daddy because I didn't have a daddy and he didn't have a girl and he'd always wanted a girl. Say it, I willed him.

"Come with me," he said. "We could all live in Aberdeen together. I could work and Emma could go to school there and it would be good. The water is not too far away, you know."

"It's really wet there," mama said.

"I don't care, we could be happy even if we were wet, you know that Rosalene."

"I may never find another rental that I can afford if I give up this one. And that's just a chance Ned, who's to say what you'll think of me in six months or a year."

"Damn it Rosalene!" He stomped his boot. “How can you give up so easily?"

"It's in the cards Ned."

Shit. Those goddamn cards! I slammed my bedroom door and crawled onto my mattress on the floor. I cried while I watched the clouds pass over the moon.

Ned took his stuff with him the next week. He wrapped me up and kissed me on top of the head twelve times. "You're going to come out and see me as soon as I get a place; you and your mama. We'll go to the ocean. You'll love it Emma. There is a lot of magic at the ocean. And I'll be back to see you soon baby." He pushed a folded piece of paper into my hand. "It's my address. I want to know what the coyotes and the birds are up to."

I couldn't say anything because I was trying hard not to cry. I didn't talk to mama for three days. I don't think she minded, in fact, I don't think she even noticed. She hummed a lot, played some old records, smoked five packs of cigarettes and drank two bottles of whiskey in the course of three days; so she didn't even notice that I wasn't talking to her. I didn't see Ned again until I was grown up and on my own. He wrote a lot and sent me funny postcards; he drew himself into the pictures as a stick figure. He always did something goofy in his drawings. I wrote him as much as I could. God I missed him.

By the end of sixth grade I began to figure it out. Mama could get men fast and she could let them go just as fast if she needed to. It was as if she was a keeper of birds. She'd feed them, love them, groom them, take their attention and then when the time was right, send them off to fly.

"I just love them all, whether they stay or go." That's what she told me when I asked her if she'd wished Ned had stayed, because I sure missed him a lot. She dated the guy at the dry cleaners, the pharmacist, the produce manager at the market, a truck driver she met on the bus, the driver of the library truck, and the barber on Main Street. The only guy she never dated was our landlord. "I never mix business with pleasure," she said. But he wanted to go out with her. He was intoxicated, just like the rest of them.

Carlos came back the next summer. The summer before Kimmy and I were going into eighth grade. He rolled into town with his tiger trucks and his pony tattoo and his gold tooth. He looked exactly the same. He smiled at me and tousled my hair. "Boy you've gotten pretty," he said. He lit a cigarette. "Where's your mama? How is she?"

"She's fine. She's got a boyfriend. She always has a boyfriend."

"Nah, she'll see me," he said. "We've been writing each other. She doesn't have a boyfriend. At least not after I get over there tonight." He smiled and looked me square in the eye.

Mama got off work at the library and headed straight for the fields where they were setting up. She saw Carlos and ran into his arms. He scooped her up and twirled her around, just like he had the day he'd said goodbye. Time moved backwards and I was eleven years old again.

Carlos spent every night at our house. He and mama smoked at the dining table and she spread her silk out and read his cards. They whispered and clinked their glasses together and I went to Kimmy's, leaving mama and Carlos alone with their drunken laughter.

I walked to Kimmy's house in the dark. I loved the way the night smelled. Like the smell of a perfect gentle old woman, fresh and clean with hints of flowers that are so intermingled you can't name the exact source. The mountains were the woman's dress, dark and silhouetted, and the moon, her tiara.

Kimmy's dad wasn't too hot about her going out at night so I threw pebbles at her window, progressively bigger until she heard. She crawled out the window in her cut off shorts and we walked around town. We hung out with boys at the market or got stoned behind the Texaco, and sometimes, if the moon were just right, Kimmy would bring her flute. We would walk to the football field at the high school and Kimmy would play music to the moon and then we'd lie down in the soft grass and stare at the night sky, just Kimmy and I and our dreams.

One night we walked to the cemetery. Kimmy had her flute under her arm. The moon was hidden behind a cloud. "Watch this," Kimmy said. She sat on a cedar stump and began to play. The notes sailed through the night, soft and grey. "Did you see it?" she asked when she had stopped.

"See what?"

"The dead dance. I can raise them all, but I can't raise my mom." Her head drooped and tears fell on the soft cedar.

We were smoking cigarettes and pot that summer. I stole the cigarettes from mama and Kimmy got the pot from a ninth grader, Jim Berry. He had a drum set in his garage. After school Kimmy and I hung around and listened to him play. He loved ACDC; we heard "Hells Bells" a lot. He wasn't that great, but he did sweat a lot and he could get us pot and he had the most amazing blonde curls. Kimmy made out with him one day in his basement. I felt jealous. Not because I wanted to make out with him, but because I didn't want Kimmy liking anyone better than me. I felt twisted up and mad inside. I hardly spoke to her walking home.

"He uses his tongue," she said.

"Gross. Wasn't it?"

"No," she said. "I kind of liked it. That's what they do in France you know." I didn't know that.

The carnival was nearly over and Carlos told us that he had time to stay. Oh boy.

"I've got a good three weeks between shows this summer," he announced, "I could stick around and help you out Rosalene. That is if you want me. I know you want me darlin'."

She pinched his butt. "Okay." That night we had chicken from one of the carnival vendors. He came over and gave it to Carlos.

"Leftovers man. Hey who's the chick?" He looked at Kimmy intensely, up and down.

Carlos put his hand on the chicken man's chest and gave him a little push. "Back off. She's thirteen."

"You're just getting too pretty Kimmy," he told her later. "You too Emma, I'm going to keep an eye on you both." Funny, I didn't think of myself as pretty. When I looked in the mirror I saw a girl with crooked teeth, green eyes, and brown hair with a little red in it, from mama I guess. I saw a baseball player with a mixed up face, a girl without a daddy. I didn't see a pretty girl. When I looked at Kimmy I saw beautiful blonde hair with beautiful blue eyes, eyes like a clear sky in the spring. She knew how to wear her clothes and she had boobs. No one else in our class had any to speak of, especially me.

Carlos stayed three weeks. While he was camped out in mama's bedroom he convinced her to start doing tarot card readings for money.

"You could charge fifteen dollars for a reading," he told her, he rubbed her shoulders at the kitchen table. "You're so good baby everybody will be clamoring to have you tell their fortune." They got drunk and wrote notes all over my flowered notepad doing their "business plan." That's how it started. That's how my mama became the fortuneteller of the Tolt valley. That's how I became the daughter of a witch. That's how the inside mama faded further into the distance.

"Are you going to write me?" Carlos asked me. He was packing his bag.

"I only write Ned. I don't have time to write anyone else." I said it to hurt his feelings. He looked at me with his head cocked. He didn't say a word. He finished packing his duffel bag and left, after kissing mama about five hundred times all over her face. Another bird flew away.

Chapter Two: Emma; The Chariot

These things I knew; I was going to turn thirteen, I played real good baseball, I had a best friend, I hated my mama most of the time and I hadn't gotten my period. Kimmy got her period that summer and told every girl in school.

Kimmy came over on a warm October night. The wind whipped up fallen leaves and it felt like anything might be possible, which I hardly ever felt anymore, unless I was at the river. That night, before we made a run for it and disappeared into the streets, mama called us into the kitchen. She had her purple silk cloth laid over the table. Two candles were lit, side by side, a white one and a red one and the cards were spread into a "T" shape with one card over the top of the "T".

"Sit," she said. She pulled out a chair for Kimmy. "We are going to do a special ceremony with the cards for Emma."

"Is it her birthday? It's not your birthday Em. What is it Rosalene?"

"We are going to bring on her menses."

"Oh my god." I dropped my head onto the table and moaned. Kimmy giggled.

Mama waved her hands over both candles and started to chant slowly. Kimmy held her hand over her mouth to keep from laughing.

My chest was burning. "Just stop. I don't need a ceremony."

"This will help your body to release itself into the next level baby. I feel your resistance. I think it has to do with all that baseball that you play. Now be quiet so I can concentrate. All I need you to do is be still and breathe. Try to let warm breath wash over you."

This is what happened. She chanted. She moved the cards around into a circle shape. Kimmy put her hands over her whole face because she couldn't stop laughing. I pressed my fingers to my temples and breathed like a hot dragon.

I laid my head back against the chair and waited, waited until I heard mama pack the cards away and slide her chair from the table.

"There now," she said. "That should do it." She rubbed the back of my head. "Anything for my baby."

The next morning Kimmy and I laid in sleeping bags on the back porch. “Is your mama absolutely nuts?” she asked. I felt something wet between my legs.

Mama started making money. Real money. She gave me ten dollars and told me to go out and buy some make up. Two months earlier we didn't even have extra money for underwear, even though she worked part time at the library. Mama did the "readings" in our kitchen. The downtown paraded through our kitchen. The bold ones came through the front door and the shy ones through the back. Marsha came every Friday, and mama did her readings for free. They drank wine together and smoked cigarettes on the back step. I loved talking to Marsha. She came into my bedroom and laid on the mattress with me. “What's jivin'?” she asked one day. Her voice was light as a bird's song.

“Do you sing?” I asked. She sat up and started putting my nail polish on her toes.

“How do you know?” She looked down at me.

“Your voice is just so…so pretty.”

“Yea, I sing. I sang in the high school choir and I tried to go to community college. I wanted to join their choir, but I never made it to the audition. My mom would have paid too, I just, I just had to skip town. I hated myself.”

“Do you hate yourself now?”

She laughed and fell back on the mattress. “Only on Tuesdays.”

“Tuesdays?”

“That's when I have to clean the bathrooms at the 2x4. I think, what the hell? I could have been a contender!”

We watched T.V. together. We laid on the mattress and watched my little black and white set that sat on the floor in the corner. "Maybe your mama will be on T.V.," Marsha said. "I saw a psychic on a T.V. show, she solved crimes for the cops. She was finding dead people. Maybe your mama will do that." She flashed her red toenails. “Your mama's psychic you know.”

"Great."

I hung around if Marsha was having her cards read because I liked her, but anyone else, I was out of there. I grabbed my coat before mama noticed my shadow and I lit from the house to the open night air and the sound of crickets and the smell of cedar and pine needles. That's what our town smelled like in the fall, that's what a logger town should smell like.

Nights were the time for Kimmy and I to be alone. We'd head to the football field, lie in the very center and look at the stars and smell the sweet earth.

"Tonight it smells like lavender from France," she said on one particularly cold October night.

"No," I said, "it smells like honey from the sweetest boy bee you could find."

Something happens after you bleed. Boys start treating you differently, as if they can tell.

One night two boys followed us to the field. We were night dreaming, wrapped in heavy coats, because it was November. We were lying on our backs staring up, when the angles of their bodies above us blocked out the moon.

"Well, if it isn't Emma and little Kimmy," said Monty, he wore his hair slicked back, a bandana around his forehead. He was Jenny Lasater's boyfriend. I knew that and Kimmy knew that.

"What are you girls doing out here alone in the dark?" asked Loopi. His real name was George, but everyone called him Loopi. He was Native American, a Snoqualmie.

"We're not alone, we're together and we are stargazing if you hadn't noticed," said Kimmy, sitting up. "Star…gazing," she said real slowly. Her beautiful blond hair hung to her waist and glowed in the moonlight.

"I see a star." Monty stared hard at Kimmy. She smiled. He sat down on the blanket beside her. "Besides you, I see the Big Dipper and Pegasus and…" He named constellation after constellation and I grew dizzy trying to keep up with his pointing.

Loopi sat down beside me. "I only see two pretty girls," he said.

I stared at Loopi, at his hair, black as the night and his angular jaw and cheekbones.

"Hey starlets," said Monty, standing up and brushing off his Levis. "We'll meet you here tomorrow night, okay?"

We didn't have to answer, because it was already decided for us. It was embedded in nature and the cycles of the wind and the water and the trees. It became Emma and Kimmy and the two older boys and the winter of innocence.

I noticed this about boys in the dark; they grew extra hands. Their hands went everywhere, up your shirt, over your face, around your back, down your pants; it was amazing how fast those hands could go. Kimmy and Monty hooked up. They panted and whispered on the grass. Loopi and I hooked up and we kissed a lot. I loved his jaw and his neck and the way his hair cascaded over mine when he was over me, kissing me. I thought of nothing but Loopi day and night. Kimmy and I brought the blankets and we would meet them Wednesday and Thursday nights. Those were the nights Kimmy's dad went to his A.A. meetings so we were sure she wouldn't get caught. Mama didn't know what I was doing, so it didn't matter. Sometimes we smoked a joint first, sometimes not, but every time it ended in a frenzy of hands and sweat.

"You know what you're doing, don't you?" I asked her one afternoon on the back porch of my house. We sat bundled up in coats, waiting for a snowstorm. The sky was a blank slate.

"What do you mean, do I know what I'm doing? Do you know what you're doing?" She snapped her gum.

"Loopi doesn't have a girlfriend. Jenny Lasater will kick your ass if she finds out you are messing with her boyfriend."

"You think I don't know that?" She tossed her hair, "She won't find out, that's for sure."

"Then maybe you should put some make-up on that hickey." Her hand flew to her neck.

"Yea, I guess you're right."

One night in December we got caught. Her father came back early from the A.A. meeting and was waiting on the porch when we came back from the field giggly and heady with our blankets under our arms.

"Where?" was all he asked.

"Oh!" Kimmy was startled, her eyes grew wide; she looked at me.

"We were just looking at the sky Mr. Franklin," I said, "We went to the park and laid in the grass and looked at the stars."

"I don't want you girls out at night by yourselves, do you understand. If you have some stargazing to do, you can do it from your own backyard."

"I was crying Mr. Franklin, I was very upset. I was the one that asked Kimmy to take a walk with me," I said.

"What's wrong with you Emma? Is there something wrong with your mom?"

"No sir," I said, "I'm on my period."

"Oh."

That always shut them up.

I'd never known anyone who was pregnant before, not a kid anyway, until I saw Jenny Lasater puking in the toilet in the locker room before gym class. Another girl held Jenny's long dark hair up. Jenny wrapped her hands around the edges of the toilet bowl. I stared and tried not to stare at the same time. She puked for twelve days in a row. I counted. Everyone knew she was pregnant. Everyone knew she was Monty's girlfriend. And everyone knew he was kissing on Kimmy.

Jenny cornered Kimmy by her locker one morning. She pushed her against the grey metal. "You fucking bitch!" She was two inches from Kimmy's face and her spit flew in Kimmy's wide blue eyes. "Do you know I'm pregnant? How does that make you feel? He's using you! He loves me!" Kimmy looked down at her shoes, her chest heaving.

"Jenny, leave her alone." I put my hand on Jenny's arm, tried to pull her off.

She whipped her head around, "Shut the fuck up! Just shut up." She grabbed Kimmy's chin with one hand. "He loves me! He loves me!" Tears streamed down Jenny's face. Kimmy stood motionless, and looked Jenny square in the eye.

"I'm…sorry," Kimmy whispered.

"Isn't everybody? Isn't fucking everybody?" She gave Kimmy one last push and walked away, her head bent. A strange sound came from Jenny, a mewing sound, like a wounded kitten.

Kimmy collapsed to the ground and covered her face with her hands.

"Aren't you glad you didn't go all the way with him?" I asked. "Then you'd be the one pregnant and puking instead of her."

"Yea, but he'd marry me." She looked up at me. Her eyes were as blue as ice.

Jenny dropped out of school before the spring daffodils showed their heads. She stopped coming to class. Monty and Loopi stopped coming to the field and it was harder and harder for me to get Kimmy to come out at night. I threw pebbles at her window until she couldn't ignore me any longer. She climbed out her window and I showed her the blankets I had brought and the two bananas, and she began to giggle. We laid under the stars in the far field by the cemetery. We could not stand to go to the football field.

"He didn't marry her after all," I said.

"I heard she went to live with her aunt." She was quiet for a moment. "You know, I really thought he loved me. I thought the way we kissed and the way, you know, the way we felt about each other was just for me and him. You know what I mean. I never thought about him with her, for me she just didn't exist, so I thought she didn't exist for him either."

A star fell from the sky. A cloud passed over the white moon. Soon the flowers would begin to bloom and they could stop wearing the ridiculously heavy coats of winter and the nights would begin to stretch to an imagined infinity.

"If there's one thing I've learned from my mama, it's that nothing's permanent. You can love someone forever, you can love someone more than you love yourself, but it doesn't mean they're going to stay."

Kimmy cried beside me. "I miss my mom. I can't play the flute at home. It makes Carl cry."

"I know. I love you Kimmy, forever."

"I can't sneak out anymore," she said. "I don't want to leave my dad."

That February I felt a snowstorm coming. I smelled it in the air and watched it in the wildlife, like Ned had taught me. "If you notice a particularly heavy bird nest in a tree, you know it's going to be a hard winter," he told me. He'd sent me six postcards. I kept them taped on my wall above my mattress. They were pictures of nature, two of Mount Rainier, the other wildlife photos; deer with heads cocked, baby squirrels and birds of every color. "Studying to be a reforestation manager. Miss you like the wind," he wrote on the back of one of the mountain cards. There was a stick figure of him holding a bird in his stick hand. I wrote him back and told him I knew a storm was coming.

When the snowstorm hit I noticed loggers in town at all hours of the day. That was good for mama, a lot of men around with a lot of time on their hands. She started hanging out at the 2x4 a lot, drinking coffee and reading the paper.

"Come to see your mama, Emma Jean?" Mazzie, the owner of the 2x4 asked me. Mazzie was a redhead, her hair was as red as the brightest carrot and her cherubic face crinkled up when she smiled. She was tiny, like a gnome.

"No. And it's just plain Emma," I lied. "I don't have a middle name." I spied mama in the corner booth rubbing her hand up and down a logger's arm. His name was Rob. He was young, one of my schoolmate's older brothers. I headed toward her. I wanted to ask for money. I wanted new mascara at the drugstore and they had flip-flops on sale and winter or summer I never had enough flip-flops. Mazzie put her hand on my arm and stopped me.

"Your mama said you need a job."

"I do?"

"That's what she said. And listen," her voice lowered, "I would do anything for your mama, anything. Marsha said you are an okay kid and I need a dishwasher. Do you want to work here?"

I looked around the inside of the café. I loved the sound of clinking glasses and the way the voices intermingled with the scent of coffee and bacon. I loved the booths. The red naugahyde wrapped around me like a second skin. From the window booths I stared at the passing traffic and dreamt I was somewhere else, in some other small town, any town U.S.A., anywhere. I could do that and get paid for it. "Yeah, I guess so. Yeah. Okay."

She smiled, "Come in tomorrow after school and I'll get you set up."

"Okay. I do play baseball in the spring though."

"Oh honey, I know that. Everybody in this town knows what a good ball player you are. We'll work that out."

I headed to the back booth. Mama looked up at me. Rob stared at mama. "I need three dollars," I said.

"Uh..."

"Here," Rob took three crumpled one dollar bills from his pocket and threw them on the table. He kept his eyes on mama.

"Thanks." Why not, I thought. He was getting my inside mama all to himself. He owed me, him and every other guy in town.

I worked three afternoons a week, sometimes until ten at night. Marsha walked me home when I worked late. She came inside, drank wine with mama, got her cards read or rolled a joint at the table, sometimes both.

One night mama pushed the local paper towards her. "Look," she said, "didn't I tell you? Didn't I tell you last summer? It's coming. Everything is changing." Mama cupped her chin in her hand, and looked out the kitchen window, her eyes soft and light.

Marsha read slowly. I looked over her shoulder at the headlines. "Listen to this, 'VALLEY MILL CLOSING TWO PLANTS! 165 JOBS LOST!' I heard about this. Everyone talked about it at the café today. This is bad. You were right, Rosalene."

"What good does it do to know something is about to happen if you can't do anything about it?" I asked.

"Who says you can't?" Mama stared at me. That was one thing about mama; she looked right at you, like she was seeing you for the first time.

"This is bad isn't it?" I was thinking of Carl, Kimmy's dad. What if I lost her? What if she moved?

"Kimmy's dad will be alright. I know that's what you're worried about. They are not moving anytime soon and he will get another means of work. I pulled his cards this morning. I knew you would be worried Emma."

"You can't tell from those cards. How the hell do you know?"

She turned away and took a very deep breath. Sometimes I couldn't believe the things that spilled from my mouth. It was like water running from a tap that never turned off tight.

"Sorry," I said. "Sorry."

Marsha looked back and forth between us. “Listen to the wind Emma, change is in the wind, your mama feels it.”

“She doesn’t know shit about nature. Have you ever seen her walk in the woods?” Mama didn’t hear me. All the sarcasm and the hatred of her magic spewed forth from me with no effect on her whatsoever.

"Emma, tell Kimmy to talk to her dad. Tell her to send him to me. I know he hardly knows me. He probably thinks I am a kook, well, and so do you, but I could give him some piece of mind. His cards were quite favorable. That is, of course after this rough period. If he will listen, I can help him." Mama got up from the table, folded her cards in their silk and disappeared into the bedroom.

"Emma, you should talk nicer to your mama.” She lit the joint she had been rolling. “Why don’t you take advantage of her gift?” She took a big hit, held her breath and let the smoke out slowly. It circled the table, and swirled between us.

“It's not a gift. You like her too much. Maybe you’re like your mom.” The words poured from my mouth like black tar, hot and ugly.

“I think you’re jealous.”

I felt a knot inside of me tighten.

“I know what that feels like. It doesn’t do you any good, jealousy. It's poison. God, you could take advantage of all that your mama knows.” She paused. “I wish I was you. I just can’t get enough of her. I understand you though. I can get in your head.”

“What color is it inside my head?” I reached for her joint, took a hit.

“Black and sky blue, the yin and the yang. You’re nasty and nice all rolled into one, like this big joint.” She laughed and the sound hit the kitchen window and fell to the ground.

Kimmy called the next night. "My dad won't get out of bed. I know he still has to work another six weeks, but I don't think he's going to get up. He didn’t get up all day." Her voice got real quiet. "Em, I heard him crying."

"Yea, men do that. How about I come over and we'll fix your dad his favorite cheese and pepper omelet. Maybe that will cheer him up."

"Okay, but you have to bring the food. He hasn't shopped for days. There's nothing to eat in the house."

I scavenged eggs and cheese and bought a pepper at the market. At the last minute I grabbed a small carton of milk. Kimmy's house was quiet and still when I got there. I rang the bell good and long so I didn't have to stand around on the dark porch.

"Shit," she said flinging open the door, "that was a little loud wasn't it?"

"The boogey man is out here. Let's do it!"

We cooked and we made a huge mess and we ate chocolate left over from Halloween and we laughed and the kitchen began to smell good. When the omelet was done we tiptoed to her dad's room. He was lying on the bed with a reading light on, but he wasn't reading, he was staring up at the ceiling.

"Daddy, me and Emma made your favorite omelet," Kimmy whispered, tiptoeing into the room.

"We didn't even burn it Mr. Franklin," I said.

"You girls made me dinner?" He looked soft in the face and old.

"Yea daddy, it's on the table."

We had decorated the table with a Halloween candle, the only candle we could find, and one crocus in a vase. We were lucky to find it in the dark beside the walkway. When he saw the table and the steaming omelet, he cried. He stood in the entrance to the kitchen, right by the "welcome all sailors" sign and cried. Fat tears rolled down his cheeks one by one and he didn't wipe them away or try to hide them. Kimmy looked nervous. I'd seen Ned cry and I had never forgotten. A man can be just as sad as a girl any day.

"Thanks girls," he said. He sat down at the table and he ate the omelet and soon the tears stopped falling out. "What's for dessert?" We laughed.

Kimmy and I didn't have the guts to talk her dad into seeing mama. We never brought it up, and he never did either so I forgot all about it, but not mama. She showed up on her own wearing a long purple cape and smelling like patchouli.

I was at Kimmy's house when she showed up. I saw her coming from the living room window. Her hair was tousled and curled and she wore a black beret. She really dressed the part. She carried her cedar box and on top, folded very carefully was her purple silk cloth. Mr. Franklin was in trouble.

"Kimmy! Look!" I said pointing at the crazy woman.

"Yea, I see her. I better get my dad."

Mama knocked. I didn't let her in; I waited until Mr. Franklin shuffled out of his room to the front door. He opened the door.

"Rosalene, what brings you over? Are you looking for Emma, because you know she's always here..."

Mama laughed. "No Carl. I'm looking for you. Since our daughters are such good friends I wanted to offer you a free tarot card reading. Just for fun." She smiled sweetly.

"I've never had a tarot card reading Rosalene. I don't really believe in that sort of stuff."

"It'll be just for fun Carl. Let's just see what the cards have to say." She sashayed past him to the kitchen before he could say another word. She pushed the clutter from the kitchen table and carefully smoothed out her purple silk, opened her cedar box and took out the deck of cards. They were wrapped in the white silk cloth.

"Do you have a candle Carl?" The way she said Carl was very sweet so of course he fetched her the Halloween candle that we had used the week before. "Let's turn out some of these lights shall we Carl?" And of course he did, because men always did what mama asked. "Why don't you sit and get comfortable Carl and tell me your birthdate." And of course he did.

The room grew still. Mama closed her eyes and breathed, slow and even. We heard her breathing in and out, in and out. She opened her eyes. Mr. Franklin was staring at her, his eyebrows crossed.

She unwrapped the cards from their white cloth and laid them out in a particular pattern, very slowly. Kimmy and I backed out of the room. We went to her room and shut the door and cracked up.

"That is too weird!" Kimmy said in between laughs. "I can't...I can't," she couldn't stop laughing. "I can't believe she got him to do all that stuff, and to tell her his birthday...and to sit down. Now Carl..." She mocked mama and we laughed all over again.

We stayed in her room for a long time. We watched a movie. We painted our nails. We laid on the floor and read Cosmopolitan. We played the Doors "Break on Through" over and over. Kimmy told me Jim Berry felt her up again in the basement. "He couldn't get my bra undone and I laughed at him. He got mad at me, but I didn't care," she flipped her hair. At midnight I told Kimmy I had to be getting home. We tiptoed out. Her house was dark. The hall had only a tiny night-light. I grabbed my coat from the kitchen chair and noticed that mama had left her tarot box and purple silk cloth on the table, two things she would never leave behind. Her cape was draped over one of the chairs and her shoes were on the floor.

"Oh my god!" I whispered to Kimmy, pointing at all the artifacts faster than I could talk.

"What does that mean?" she asked.

"Oh my god! Kimmy, I think this means we're sisters!" We covered our mouths and tried not to laugh out loud. "I don't want to go home if there's no one there. Shit, I can not believe it!"

"You better believe it Emma," she said, "because there's a light on in my dad's room. I think they're in there."

We tiptoed down the hall and put our ears to the door. Sure enough we could hear whispers, murmurs, a little giggle from Mr. Franklin. We tiptoed back. We were in shock. "What now?" I asked her.

"Come on, just stay in my room and in the morning we'll act like we don't know anything," she grabbed my hand and led me to her room. Her yellow and pink light shade cast a warm glow to the room. I grabbed a quilt from her closet and curled up beside her on her twin bed. She put an arm around me. Something inside of me felt really good. The black inside of me wasn't so black and I felt warm somewhere behind my ribs. Maybe tomorrow I wouldn't be so mean to everyone. If only the black stayed away, maybe I would feel the sky blue for a while. I pulled the quilt up and dreamed about sea turtles, crispy green against a pure white beach.

It was spring break, for some reason I woke up early, six a.m. to be exact. Kimmy was on a cushion next to my mattress; she was fast asleep. I tiptoed around Kimmy's feet. In the living room I found mama on the couch. Mama never slept on the couch. I shook her shoulder. Her soft red hair lightly laid across her cheek. Her mouth was open slightly and her hands were curled up around her face.

"Mama," I shook her gently. "Mama, is something wrong? Why are you on the couch?"

Her green eyes opened slowly, she looked at me like I didn't belong in the picture. She was dreaming of some far away place.

"Baby," she said deeply, "what are you doing up so early? You don't have any school today do you?"

"No. Why are you on the couch?"

"Carl had a rough night. He was crying and when he did finally fall asleep, he was tossing so violently he almost knocked me out of the bed. I just needed to give him some room, that's all."

It was like that; Carl called, asked if he could come over and see mama. She said, "Of course Carl, come on over and bring Kimmy so she won't have to stay alone." He came and brought Kimmy and she crashed out with me, and mama and Carl would end up going to bed with each other. We were the Brady Bunch.

By the time Carl got up, mama had already made tea for me. She made a pot of coffee for her and Carl, and a pot of oatmeal for everyone. Carl stretched and showed off his belly, which had a soft row of curly hair around the belly button. I turned away.

"What do you want to do for spring break?" he asked me. He drank his coffee. He had both hands wrapped around the mug. That's how mama held her cup.

"I can't think of much. What does Kimmy want to do?" I asked him.

"I hope not much, seeing as how I don't have a job. Your mama here seems to think it's only temporary, but a man's gotta wonder. She's amazing isn't she?" His eyes glazed over.

"Excuse me?" I asked.

"Your mama, she's amazing isn't she?"

"Yea, to you and every other man that's walked into this room," I said and then wished I could take it back.

In history class we learned about the roaring 20's. It got me to wondering, did they know in the roaring 20's that the great depression was coming, that they would be losing their jobs, their homes, the very core of their existence? Did any of them have "the sight" and see the rise of Hitler? Did they know that their sons or brothers or cousins or fathers were going to war? Did they know who would come back and who wouldn't? If they could see what was ahead, could they enjoy the moment that they were in? Could they enjoy the jazz age if they knew the fate before them? Were any of them like mama and foretelling of future events? All these things I wondered while the sun streamed through the window illuminating the dust specks on the desks. The room smelled of disinfectant and rubber erasers.

Kimmy was in class with me. We were starting to bicker because we were seeing too much of each other now. Part of me liked it and part of me wished Carl and mama had never hooked up. He came every night and Kimmy would come with him and she would sleep on a foldout foam pad next to me. We watched TV in my room until we couldn't hold our eyes open anymore. We smoked cigarettes on the back porch, stealing them from mama's pack after she and Carl went off to bed together.

"Carl won't be staying here much longer," mama said while she washed the dishes. "He and Kimmy will go back to their own house pretty soon, by the end of the spring season you will be seeing her less and less."

"How the hell do you know that?" I asked her.

"The way I know a lot of things; you know that Emma. Why do you constantly deny my gift?"

The air was heavy. I ignored her question. She ignored my lack of an answer.

"Carl will get a job and feel settled and then everything will return to normal. He won't need me anymore." She said it like it was common knowledge to the world.

"How do you know that for sure?"

"Nothing is ever for sure and that is the only thing that you can be sure of." She paused and looked out the small kitchen window, it was raining lightly. "I know what I know."

"I don't want to know shit about what's going to happen in the future. It's too depressing," I said and stomped off to the bedroom.

She was right. About the time I started softball that spring, Carl got a job managing the City's park department. He was happy and relaxed and hugged mama a lot. He took her out to dinner three nights in a row. Then he stopped coming over every night. Once in a while on a Friday or Saturday he came for dinner, he'd bring Kimmy and mama would make a chicken or something. Then he and mama disappeared into the bedroom and we heard whispers and low laughter and lots of silence. Kimmy and I walked to the market and bought ice cream and junior mints.

A lot of boys hung out at the market on late night weekends. They leaned into their cars and smoked or cracked jokes to each other. It was here, at the market, in the parking lot that we met Danny. Danny wasn't from our school; he was from the other valley high school, closer to the mountain pass. He had steel-toed boots and eyes the color of the bluest river. His hair was blond and his jaw square and he leaned into his car in a way that made my body heat up. He talked to Kimmy first.

He asked her if she had a cigarette when we came out of the market. It was a warm night in May. Mama was home with Carl.

"I don't smoke," she said, "but if I did, I'd give you a cigarette."

"What do you do?" he asked.

I melted right then and there on the sidewalk in front of the Super Eight market.

"We do a lot of things," she said, she hooked an arm through mine.

"Come on over here and show me."

She did. She walked across the parking lot to his car in the angled slot and she flexed her bicep muscle and you could see a little mound under her sweatshirt.

"See that," she said, "that's just one of the things I can do."

I didn't say a word. I could not stop staring at him. He was everything every boy in America should be.

He and Kimmy flirted. They talked. They teased. I stood, crossed and re-crossed my feet and stared at him. I was in love.

"Shit, he is cute," Kimmy said as we walked back to my house.

"Yea."

"Don't you think he was cute?" she asked.

"Yea."

"You just stood there. You didn't even say a word. He must think you're an idiot. I know you're not shy, are you? Why didn't you talk? You made me do all the talking. I got his phone number. Shit he was cute."

"Oh."

I laid on the mattress long after I heard Kimmy snoring and thought about Danny. I remembered his name. I remembered the shape of his hands. I remembered the smooth curves of his shoulders. I remembered his long legs crossed at the top of his boots and the shape of his back as he leaned into the automobile. His white t-shirt curved around the outline of his ribs and his smile was as big as the summer sun. I didn't sleep until the light began to creep into the room.

This is what you do when you're in love. Nothing. You don't eat, you don't concentrate, you don't sleep, and you don't talk. I had trouble playing softball.

"What's up with you?" asked mama one Saturday morning. Carl hadn't come over the night before so we were alone in the kitchen. She wrapped her arms around me from behind, rested her chin on my shoulder. For a moment she was the inside mama.

"I've got a game today."

"Are you nervous?" she asked.

I was never nervous. "No."

She broke away, "I just happened to pull your cards last night. The moon was just right so I pulled my cards, then I said what the heck and pulled yours too." The inside mama was gone.

“Why don't you just pry into my personal life?”

She sipped her coffee, wrapped her red fingernails around the chipped cup. "You have a man coming into your life and it is going to be serious, but he will break your heart. I'm telling you this so you can be prepared."

"Why do you tell me these things? Don't you think I can figure things out for myself? I hate boys! And I hate you too! And I hate this stinking fucking town!" I stomped out of the room, into my bedroom and kicked my beat up dresser with the missing handles. I couldn’t stop shaking. I was on fire. I pulled on my baseball clothes, grabbed my cleats and mitt and I left the house without putting my cleats on.

In my game socks I walked the two miles to the field. I was early, but my body got me there without any navigation from my mind.

That was the day I broke my leg. I slid into third, the baseman's leg tangled with mine and I felt an unusual twist, a pain shot up my thigh and into my hipbone. I turned my body over; my lower leg was limp. It didn't look right. I turned my head and threw up on the base line. The coach wrapped a blanket around me; he wiped my face with a Kleenex and said words that I couldn't comprehend. I heard sirens in the distance and laid my head back in the dirt. I closed my eyes and all I saw was mama and her scarred table and the cards with their gross images and symbols and I knew she had done this to me.

I was in the hospital. I had a cast on. I had pain medication and water from a straw and cool rags on my head. Mama came in the room. She ran her hands over the cool plaster.

Mama looked at me, smoothed my hair back, "I knew this was going to happen. I saw it years ago. This is why I couldn't come to watch you play, do you understand now?"

My leg hurt, my brain hurt. “I want you to stop predicting my future. You made this come true.” I didn’t look at her. I wanted her to hold me and make the pain go away. I wanted her to leave me alone. I wanted to be three years old. The hospital sounds and smells created a void between us.

Having a broken leg gave me notoriety at school, more time to spend with Kimmy, and a pair of crutches. The kids at school wrote stuff all over my cast and it spilled out onto my skin in permanent ink, a permanent tattoo.

Kimmy and I spent our days after school at the river or at her house on her deck. She played the flute for me when Carl was gone. I begged her to. When she put that flute to her mouth I closed my eyes and floated a thousand miles away. I avoided my house, avoided mama and the whole mess she had going of her life. When the sun began to set Kimmy and I went to the market and hung out in the parking lot. Someone always had a stereo going in an open car and a pipe of dope was passed, sometimes a bottle of beer. One particularly clear night the parking lot was void of music. We heard the frogs croaking, the air smelled sweet of buttercups and the moon was full.

Danny pulled up in his green Camaro and Kimmy shot me a look. I acted nonchalant, which was impossible with a broken leg. He parked next to Tom's pickup. We were sitting on the tailgate of Tom's truck and were in the middle of passing a cigarette.

"Hey Danny Boy, how you doing tonight?" asked Tom.

Danny opened his car door, swinging his legs wide. I saw his work boots and his Levi's and thought about the chest hairs beneath his white t-shirt. They were soft and blonde. He caught me looking and smiled at me sideways. The frogs were singing in the swamp behind the parking lot.

"What happened to you? I heard you were some kind of super athlete?" he asked.

"I took a slide and got this broken leg." It was a stupid thing to say.

He smiled, shook his head a little, "You guys got any?"

Tom passed him a loaded pipe and Danny lit it ceremoniously, dragging deep. For a while no one spoke. Kimmy was high, I was high, Tom was high, and Danny was on his way. We watched people coming in and out of the market. A cop cruised the main road. Danny tucked the pipe in his boot. He turned on his stereo. Aerosmith played and drowned out the crickets, the moon seemed to rise higher.

I watched Kimmy work her body. She raised a shoulder and lowered a hip and posed, making Danny and Tom sigh. She tucked her hair slowly behind one ear and cocked her chin to one side. I could not get my body to work like that. Her body was magic, power. Kimmy laughed with Danny, poked him in the ribs. She turned her head toward Tom and appraised him, up and down. Tom was handsome; he had an athletic build with sharp features and brown eyes dusted with long baby lashes. I liked him. He was nice. He played football and baseball. Kimmy made Tom flex his bicep. She ran her hand over the muscle and smiled her beautiful smile. Tom was mesmerized.

"You don't mind if I go for Tom do you?" She leaned into me.

"Uh…no." My heart beat fast. "I kind of like Danny."

"He's too blonde for me, I like 'em with dark hair." She paused. "Who am I fooling, I like 'em any way," she said laughing. "Let's pair up."

"Do you think he likes me?"

"Does it matter? He'll make out with you."

"Kimmy!"

"Emma, look," she brought her voice down, "I worry about my dad all the time. I feel like I have to be the wife. It's fucked up I know, but I didn't want to have a boyfriend because I thought it would be like, you know, betraying him or something. But since he got laid by your mama, I feel like a whole new person. Look at me." She swept her hands up and down her body. "I've got this gift, I'm using it!" She laughed, a tinkling in the night sky. She sidled up to Tom, hooked an arm through his and stroked his chest with her free hand. Her fingernails were painted like red tulips.

Danny looked at me, "Wanna stretch your leg out in the back of my car? I bet you're tired of sitting on that cold tailgate."

I clumsily slid off the tailgate. The frogs croaked louder. I hobbled to Danny's car. There was a mirage of paper cups and flyers from school and a couple of wrenches on the floorboards.

"Sorry about the mess." He tucked me in the backseat and crawled in beside me. He smelled of ivory soap and pot. I had trouble catching my breath. Besides Loopi, I hadn't made out with any other boy; unless I counted the spin the bottle game we played on the playground in fifth grade. I had kissed Ray Messier twice on the lips. I closed my eyes and leaned my head back on the seat. I drank in the smell of him. He leaned into me and kissed me on the neck. "I've never kissed a girl with a cast before," he said into my neck. He kissed me on the jaw line, up and down, then moved his lips to cover mine. I felt his tongue and his perfect teeth and his breath was minty and warm. I melted and floated at the same time and felt an incredible amount of heat between my legs.

"Jesus," I said under my breath. His hands went up my shirt and the moon grew larger in the sky. The night opened up before me and everything changed in that very first kiss from the boy I knew I already loved.

"How was it?" Kimmy asked me when we walked home.

I was using my crutches and moved slow. I stopped, "It was like, like the best night of my life."

That spring was filled with the Camaro and Danny and the backseat upholstery and my damn broken leg that got in the way of everything. But somehow it didn't seem to matter.

"You guys sure spend a lot of time together," Kimmy said on the phone.

"I'm sorry. I really love him Kimmy. I can hardly think of anything else. Let's go to a movie this weekend."

"Yeah, I'll ask my dad if he'll drive us."

"Or I can ask Danny to drive us," I said.

"If you do that, tell him to bring a friend. I'm sick of the boys at our school."

"What about Tom?"

"I'm done with him. He's not a very good kisser."

Danny set Kimmy up with Travis, a friend of his from his school. He and Kimmy hit it off, but she liked all the guys.

"So you really like this boy, don't you?" mama asked one morning as I ate cereal at the breakfast table. She leaned against the stove smoking a cigarette.

"Yeah, I like him, why? And don't you tell me anything about him."

"He's going to break your heart, I saw it in the cards. Don't get too attached. I'm just telling you for your own good. You can alter that reality for yourself if you want to." She blew out a plume of smoke.

"If I want to what?" I asked.

"If you want to keep yourself from getting too attached."

"Why, so I can be like you? So I can go through a couple of dozen guys a year, so I can love 'em and get rid of 'em like you do? So I can sleep with a hundred different people instead of just one?" My voice rose higher and higher, the blackness welled up inside of me.

She stubbed out her cigarette in the orange juice can. "Are you sleeping with him? Because I didn't see that in the reading I did for you today. It's not that I mind, Em, it's just that you need to be on birth control." She touched my shoulder, stroked me with her blue painted fingernails.

"I am not sleeping with him and it's none of your business anyway!" I was yelling louder, "I am trying to have a boyfriend, that's all." I dropped my voice to a growl, "It's something you wouldn't know about, keeping a boyfriend. You can't seem to keep any man!" I pulled my arm away; I didn't want her touching me with those ugly nails.

"You can't keep a man. You can't possess another human being. Why would I ever want to do that?"

"So I could have a father! Have you ever thought of that?" I stood up, my only steady leg shaking.

"You had a father Emma, I loved your father very much."

"Yeah, you love them all. You make me sick." I threw my bowl in the sink. It broke, the crash echoed in the small kitchen. I left the broken bowl for her to clean up and stomped out the door, dragging my broken leg behind me.

That night I met Danny at the corner. We drove to the top of the mountain, the one that overlooked Tolt. He opened a thermos. I took a big drink. It was full of vodka and orange juice. The vodka burned my throat, but I was glad to feel it. It was wonderful and warm and I felt like I was sinking. That night we went all the way. Steam and sweat filled the Camaro. His chest above mine, skin on skin, was encompassing and forgiving. When he went inside of me it hurt down deep and blood trickled from between my legs. Afterward I opened the car door and threw up the vodka and orange juice. Danny laughed.

Danny and I sat in his car under a thousand stars next to the baseball field. We had made love in the back seat. Now we were in the front. We passed a cigarette back and forth. I didn't inhale much; I just liked the way it felt against my lips. I felt like a model or a movie star. I thought of Carlos and the painted ladies on the House of Mirrors awning.

"My mom goes for this carnival worker every year, well, every year he comes. He'll be here next month." I looked at the stars and tried to find the little dipper.

"That's cool. Isn't it?"

"I guess. I don't really like him," I said.

"Why? Doesn't she like him? Your mom is so nice and pretty it seems like she would pick a pretty cool guy."

"I don't know why I don't like him," I said. "I just don't."

"Are you jealous?" he grabbed my cigarette. "I used to get jealous of my dad's girlfriends. Now I'm happy for him. It keeps him busy and it's good that he gets to have sex with someone."

"Ha! My mama has sex with everyone. She doesn't have a problem with that!"

"You're making me horny. Let's do it again," he said. We crawled into the back seat, maneuvering around my cast.

My cast came off the same month the carnival arrived. I spotted Carlos first thing. They hadn't even set up yet and I saw him from across the field. He had on a white tank top and his hair was longer and in a braid that hung halfway down his back. He felt my eyes, because at that moment he looked up, then waved. He walked toward me. I took a step back, then another, slowly retreating. He began to run. He was wearing cowboy boots and Levis and he was trim and muscular.

"Emma!" he shouted, "it's me Carlos!"

When he got close he was out of breath, but he managed a smile, his gold tooth flashed in the sun.

"Wow, wow, wow! Only a year or two and look at you!" He touched my hair. "You are so beautiful! Just like your mama! Where is your mama Conchita? Does she know I'm in town? I wrote her a week or so ago. Did she get my letter?"

"I don't know. We don't talk much."

"What? You're her daughter and you don't talk much?" He shook his head in disbelief. He put his hands on my shoulders. "Emma, I lost my mama when I was just a young man and my daddy died when I was six years old. If I had them now I would talk to them every day. And every day I would tell them that I loved them. Do you know what it's like not to have a mama or a daddy?"

"Yeah, I do."

He paused, he looked sad. "But you got to treat your mamacita right. You got tell her you love her with your heart. All of it, you hear me? Now take me home, I've gotta see her."

We walked the four blocks to the house. When we got close I heard salsa music playing and I smelled smoke from the barbecue. Mama knew he was coming. I felt the energy in the air five houses away.

We were half way up the walk and the door flew open. Mama ran down the cracked walkway and jumped into Carlos' arms. He swung her around and around and her purple flowered sundress went up and down and up and down like the carousel pony I'd won so long ago. That was when I knew she loved him. Of all the men that had walked in and out of our door, she loved him the best. Carlos the carnival man with the pony tattoo and the gold tooth.

A month goes by slow when there is an extra person in the house. Carlos stayed every night and every minute he wasn't working the carnival. Mama wasn't working so she had all the time in the world. I didn't go to the carnival much.

One night Danny and I went and walked around, Carlos joked with Danny and punched him in the arm with that camaraderie thing. Most of the time I stayed away.

Kimmy hung around with one of the workers at the haunted house booth. He was blond with two earrings, which you don't see in a logging town. Kimmy thought he was exotic. I thought he was disgusting.

"I meet him every night after the carnival's shut down and we go inside the haunted house ride. His name is Nick; don't you love that? We do it in the cart! Can you believe it?" She grabbed my arm. "I sit on top of him and god, Emma, I can't even tell you how good it feels. He knows so much more than guys our age." She dipped her toes in and out of the river making a swish, swish sound.

"How old is he?"

"Twenty five."

"Shit Kimmy, if your dad finds out..."

"I know. Don't tell anyone. Not even Danny."

"Okay." I lied because I told Danny everything; I thought that's what lovers did.

By the time the carnival was due to leave Kimmy had started crying every day. "I'm going to miss him so much. He says he loves me and wants to marry me. What do you think?"

"Are you fucking crazy? You are going to marry him? What are you going to do, travel around with the carnival?"

"Well, they've been to Europe. He said he could get me a job with the group, I could run one of the rides or something."

"Get real, they don't even shower." In the sunlight I saw tears on the edge of her eyes.

From that moment of that day everything shifted. We were talking about marriage and life changing and it was all too much. I wanted to freeze-frame everything the way it was. Kimmy and me in our flip-flops in the sleepy logging town with the wild river and the soft undertones of our life, even if we didn't like it most of the time. But nothing can stay frozen forever, not if it's edges are touched with heat.

The day the carnival left the air smelled like alfalfa and rosemary.

"I'm pregnant." Kimmy was crying. Nick was gone. Carlos was gone. We were standing at the edge of the field and staring at the tire ruts and scattered hay they had left behind. "I just know it. I know it, I know it."

"God Kimmy, what were you thinking? Didn't he wear a condom?"

"He didn't believe in them, and I believed in him and well it just was so good and now he's gone and he says he'll come back and I told him I might be pregnant and well, he didn't believe me and shit, I don't know what to do."

"Let's just wait and see." I put my arm around her shaking shoulders. "If you're pregnant, mama will help us."

That night mama sat on the front stoop, smoked a cigarette and looked at the stars. She had her old green cardigan sweater wrapped around her and her feet were bare. I came out to the porch and sat next to her. "Mama will you give me a reading?"

"I thought you'd never ask."

"Not for me, for Kimmy."

"Oh." She got to her feet and stretched. It looked like she might have been crying, or maybe it was the way the stars shone on her face. "Let's go inside. Get my cards and light a white candle."

When she had the cards laid out, she closed her eyes and sighed. "Kimmy's in trouble," she said softly as she opened her eyes.

"Why?" I asked.

"Because I see two of her."

Mama took Kimmy to the abortion clinic. She borrowed four hundred dollars from the pharmacist at the drugstore. He grabbed her delicate wrist tight and said earnestly, "Anything for you Rosalene." He held so tight she had to forcefully pull her hand away.

"Thank you Jake," she said very quietly.

Kimmy did not cry the night before, we spent the night together, curled up on my small mattress. We rode the 1049 bus into the city and walked the five blocks to a nondescript brown building with tiny signs of the enclosed professionals. Inside, the office was quiet, just a hum of a fan and the click, click of the receptionist typing. She smiled in a sweet knowing manner. We waited on the brown tweed sofa. I saw one tear slide down Kimmy's cheek. "I love babies," she said. She grabbed my hand and rubbed her thumbnail up and down my index finger, over and over, until her name was called. Mama went down the hall with her. They walked very slowly, like two old women in a church holding each other up. I read the Women's Day Magazine, until the pictures and the words were a blur.

I heard a door open and mama walked into the waiting room. She shook her head "yes" and looked at me hard. She was done. It was done. Done. A nurse brought out Kimmy. Kimmy was crying, pale, holding her abdomen. Mama signed release papers at the front counter; the nurse spoke very quietly to Kimmy and held her hand. Kimmy nodded and nodded like her head was weighted with a thousand tears.

Kimmy was in terrible pain all the way back home. The next three nights and four days, she refused to leave her house. She told her dad she had the stomach flu. He asked mama if he should take her to the doctor.

"She'll be fine Carl, there's something going around. Give her some tea and soda crackers and leave her be. Do you want to come for dinner?" He came that night, the grandfather of the baby to be no more, and ate flank steak with new potatoes and broccoli. He and mama had whiskey and waters together on the back steps and he spent the night. Mama comforted and abetted both family members.

Kimmy came over the Friday after the clinic visit. She had a huge bag of pot, so we rolled joints at the kitchen table. We sat in stoned wonder and looked at the kitchen and the floor and the way the light crisscrossed the linoleum.

"I really did love him," she said. Neither of us spoke for a while, we cozily drifted in our own heads. "You know, you and I make a whole. You don't have a daddy and I don't have a mom, but between both of us we have it all, you know."

"Yeah I guess. I miss Ned." I thought about Ned and the way his t-shirts were always white and fresh and the way his long legs would swing from the truck when he got home. He sent me a journal to log animal tracks, "I miss you, Emma," he wrote in curvy letters on the inside of the cover. I kept it under my mattress.

The door opened and mama burst in smiling like a cat with a bird. She waved an envelope above her head. "Look at what I've got, look at what I've got!" She stopped when she saw the marijuana on the table, the rolling papers, the looks on our faces. "Put that away, are you crazy? I can't let people see that on my kitchen table."

I rolled up the baggie and curled the rolling papers in my fist.

"What have you got Mrs. J.?" Kimmy asked.

"I got a letter from Carlos, and in it...," she slowly pulled two bills from the envelope, "two hundred dollars from that snake in the grass Nick who got you pregnant."

Leave it to mama to just throw it all out there, like a bad pitch in a winning all star game. It hung in the air before dropping on the floor with a thud.

Kimmy was still stoned and her voice was small. "I don't understand."

"I wrote Carlos when I found out you were pregnant and Carlos shook Nick down for the money. He didn't get all of it, but he got two hundred dollars. I'm going to give it back to Jake. I think Carlos really laid into him."

"Did he ask about me?"

"Carlos always asks about you girls. He loves you both."

"No," she said, "did Nick ask Carlos about me?"

"I don't know darlin'."

A slow moving circle of silence went around the room and touched Kimmy, then me, then mama; breath on our shoulders.

"Let it go Kimmy. Let it all go to the wind. It has to be that way or you will get caught like a mermaid in a fisherman's net." Mama reached for her hand.

"But he loved me, he said he loved me!" Kimmy cried. Round tears landed on the wooden table.

"Honey, they'll say anything when they've got their pants down," said Mama.

"Mama, jesus, how can you say that!"

"Emma, that's the way the world works."

Kimmy stood up fast, bumping her hipbone on the edge of the table. She didn't even flinch. "Fuck it," she yelled. "Fuck it all, fuck everything, everything, do you hear me?" She faced us square on before she ran out the door.

That night I threw pebbles at Kimmy's window until she finally came out. We went to the river and stripped our clothes off. We waded into the cool rippling water. Kimmy was not supposed to take baths yet, but she said, "Fuck it!" and went right in, over her head swimming and swimming while the moon rose in the sky. When we were done, we laid on the shore. I think that water cleansed the dirt in her soul, because she cried and cried, right there on the rocks, with the earth and the night sky as her witness. I cried too, for her and for her baby and for not having a daddy and for her not having a mama.

Chapter Three: Kimmy; The Tower

I haven't had a mom since I was six years old. The day my mom died, I put all the things she had ever made for me in a box and put the box under my bed. This included a birds nest made from cardboard and twine, an ornament made of clay, a picture of a robin with real feathers glued to the paper and a jar of sand with shells inside that twirled around and around like a tossing wave. These things and more went into the box and I have not looked at them since that day. I can't. That door is closed forever and will never reopen. The only thing I kept out was her silver flute. She played the flute in the evenings, sitting on the back patio when the weather was warm with the sliding doors open so Carl could hear. Her blonde hair hung over one shoulder as she played notes so sweet I flew away.

My dad cried the day she died and again four days later at the funeral. His massive shoulders shook and strange gurgling noises rose from his chest. I thought he was choking. It scared me; I could not lose him too. We buried her in Yakima next to her mother and father, in a cemetery that overlooked the valley. Dried grass grew around her, up and over her grave. From the day my mom died I made a vow to look after my dad. I knew she would want me to. I cleaned the house for him, did the laundry, and tried to cook simple things. As I got older I got better and better at it. Sometimes I felt like the wife, a lot of times actually; and at home I called him Carl instead of dad. How to be a kid, I didn't know. All I knew was that I was alone with a grown man to take care of and a whole wide world to beat back from the doorstep. And that is why I loved Rosalene, Emma's mama.

At Emma's house I watched her mom, memorized the things she did. She swayed to music, flowed through the kitchen, cooked meals and smoked at the same time, all very gracefully. Emma said she didn't like her mama, but I loved her. I wanted her in a way that left a burning hole in the bottom of my stomach.

Emma and I became friends in second grade. I liked her because she was tough. When she fell down, she never cried. She bounced back to her feet like a kangaroo and shouted, "Want to try that again?" I could not do that. I hated my body being tossed about. The games the kids played on the playground hurt, and besides, I didn't like to sweat. Emma was poor, but it didn't matter because she was so tough. No one called her poor even though her clothes never fit right, she wore mismatched socks, and her shoes had holes in them. She still looked cool and I envied that. Her mama though, you would think by looking at her that she was the queen of Scotland. She dressed weird in a way that made her exotic and beautiful and when she walked through town, everyone stared. Emma hated that. That year, I began to put a lot of thought into my clothes. I wanted to be a fashion designer someday, if I could ever quit taking care of my dad.

"Friends forever," Emma cut my hand with the single razor blade I had stolen from Carl's medicine chest. I couldn't look. She squeezed the cut, a large drop of blood rose to the surface. She had already cut her hand and the blood was running down her wrist. "Put them together," she ordered. I put my hand against hers. "Blood to blood, sister to sister, never to be broken, never to be parted. Now close your eyes." My eyes were already closed, I felt faint. "I love you Kimmy."

"Is it over yet?"

"Yea, chicken," she said. We were ten years old standing in the field of the elementary school.

Emma and I liked different things, so we balanced each other out. I liked to buy fashion magazines and look at the pictures of the models. I studied the shapes of their bodies, how they stood, how they presented the clothing, how they accessorized. It fascinated me. Emma had little time for that. I showed her pictures; she rarely looked.

"Look at this girl's haircut, isn't that cute?" I held the magazine before her, the model looking at us with a smiling face from the glossy page; a perky impish haircut framed her face.

"Hmm…let's go to the river."

We shared a love for the river. It was the best part of the town. The river cut through the town three times, once at the beginning; hence a big beautiful bridge created the archway into town. It cut through again at the end of Entwistle, down the road where the old houses and farms were. If you rode your bike far enough, you could reach the crossing point and cross the rickety logging bridge that the mill had built so they could access the vast timber that stretched beyond. I knew this because my dad was a logger. It crossed again at the end of town, by the dairy farm whose smell overpowered the smell of the woods when the wind blew just right.

High school kids flocked to the river in the spring when the weather changed. They smoked and drank and made out in the sand above the rocks where the low bushes partially covered them. I listened to the sounds they made, the murmurs of their voices and the sound of skin against skin. It was compelling and mysterious. Emma watched people too, but she cared more about nature, looking for tracks and spotting birds or tracking how the flow of the river had changed. She was weird like that; sometimes I think she should have been born a boy.

That summer, the summer we were both eleven, the carnival came to town. It had come before, but this year it was a different company and there were more rides and more game vendors. There was a new excitement in the air. Emma and I watched the greasy men set up; it took forever. Carl gave me twenty dollars to spend. He left it on the table one morning before he left for work. He left the house at 4a.m. Monday through Friday and sometimes on Saturdays. His writing was hurriedly scrawled, "Kimmy, here is twenty bucks, have at it and stay clear of boys, Love D.!!!!"

I told Emma I had twenty bucks, her face fell. "Shit," she said, "I don't have anything. I guess I'll just watch."

"Ask your mama," I told her. "She'll give you something."

She stared ahead, not saying anything. Emma didn't have a daddy. Well, she did, she just didn't know who he was or where he was. At least he wasn't dead like my mom. You can never find a dead person.

Later that night I told Carl that Emma didn't have any money for the carnival. He told me to give her mama a ten-dollar bill. "Let her mom give it to her." Carl always gave me what I wanted, all I had to do was ask. I walked the ten-dollar bill over to Emma's house. Rosalene answered the door.

"You here to see Emma sweetheart?" she asked. She smelled like roses.

"No. Mrs. J., my daddy gave me extra money for the carnival and I wanted you to give it to Emma."

She looked at me for a moment and said nothing. She cocked her head. "Okay."

"It's not that I think you're poor..."

"We're all poor in some way Kimmy."

"Yea, umm...well, if you could give it to her and not tell her it's from me. I'd like that best."

"Okay, I understand. That's awful nice of you."

"Well, actually, it's my dad."

"Oh. Well, you tell Carl thank you and give him a kiss on the cheek for me."

"Yeah."

I walked home in the moonlight. Clouds came and went over its face and changed the hues of the sidewalk. I thought about what Rosalene said, "Everyone's poor in some way." I felt sad

That night I slept curled up in my comforter on the couch. I fell asleep staring at the picture of my mom that sat on the stereo console in the window. She was barefoot on a beach, holding her pants up above the sand. The wind blew her blonde hair up and away from her face and she was laughing. The ocean waves crested behind her.

That night I dreamed I was on a boat. I stood on the edge and looked into the gray water of the sea. A voice called to me from below the water. "Jump, jump," it said in whispers. I jumped into the ocean. I was afraid at first, but then I discovered the water was warm and I could float and swim easily. I saw other people around me and they were having trouble swimming, gasping and calling for help, but I felt free and strong. I knew I couldn't help them so I kept swimming; rotating in the water and diving like a porpoise. The voice spoke again, "We're all free in some way Kimmy. I love you. I love you. I love you. Do you hear me?" The voice was my mom's and I started searching for her, swimming and thrashing about as I called for her. I shouted, "Mom! Mom!" and with every shout it became harder and harder to swim. The seawater entered my lungs; I could not shout any longer, I was sinking. I woke up gasping for air, tears on my cheeks and pillow, my t-shirt soaked with sweat.

The next morning, the house was quiet. Carl had already left for work. The phone rang.

"Hello?"

"Kimmy?"

"Yea?" It sounded like Emma's mama.

"It's Rosalene." She took a deep breath. "Your mom came to me last night, I just want you to know."

"What?" A shiver ran up and down my spine.

"She was swimming. It was very beautiful. She gave me a message for you."

I couldn't say a word; it was hard for me to breathe. I gripped the phone and twirled the phone cord tight around my other hand, cutting off my circulation.

"Are you there? She said to tell you that she wants you to enjoy her, even now… and not be sad for her." She paused. I heard noises. She was putting dishes into the sink. "Kimmy, do you hear me?"

"Yes, I hear you." That's exactly what my mom said in my dream.

"Don't be afraid. This happens to me all the time."

"Mrs. J., can you give her a message for me?"

"Well, that's a little more complicated."

"Oh." My chest hurt.

"If I get a chance I will. Write it down, what you want to say that is, and I'll think on it. Don't tell me now on the phone, I'll never remember, my head is full."

"Okay."

"And Kimmy…thanks for the ten dollars." She hung up and I laid my head down on the kitchen counter and wept until my heart and my head were empty.

I couldn't write anything down. What do you tell a dead person? Why did I even ask for Rosalene to give her a message? What kind of message did I want to give her? Tell her I loved her, missed her, wished to god she would come back, wished she had never died of cancer? Tell her my life was over the day she took her last breath? Tell her my body was a shell, with nothing inside, just making the motions of breathing? Pretending to be a young girl when in reality I felt a hundred years old? Can you even talk to dead people? What do they hear with, a rotten decomposed ear? I didn't write down a message that day. I walked to the edge of the cemetery and played her silver flute sitting cross-legged on a flat wooden tree stump. I played with tears on my cheeks and holes in my heart. I felt her heart beat in my fingertips. She taught me to play when I was five years old and I practiced every day. She clapped after each song and blew me kisses, "Encore," she said, even from her sick bed. I couldn't play when Carl was home. He cried real tears when he heard the transparent melodies. I played simple songs at first; then began making up my own songs. I played full-length concertos of my own mind, sailing the notes into the ethereal so that she could hear me. If I played hard enough maybe the notes would stay suspended in time and I could follow them like Hansel and Gretel into the afterlife and find her. The stump became my stage and the cemetery my audience. I went back again and again and if it were night and I squinted my eyes just right, I saw the dead rise from their graves and dance like Isadora Duncan, floating and free.

Emma's mama went gaga over a carnival worker named Carlos that summer. He was good looking for an old guy. He was dark and smoky looking with long black hair. He reminded me of a crow or a raven, but when I told Emma that she said angrily, "He's not good enough to be a bird."

I liked the way he walked, his legs swung loose and easy and he had this great way of putting his hands on his hips when he was thinking about something or looking out over the carnival. Rosalene told me he was the boss. "Isn't he magnificent, such energy," she said, her eyes stared right at him. He let Emma and I win at the milk toss game. I liked that and he showed us his tattoo, which was fascinating. I'd seen a tattoo before, but it was a handmade one on the wrist of Gene, one of Carl's co-workers. It was a girl's name with a heart on it, the letters were crooked and the heart lopsided and it looked dirty on his hairy arm. Carlos' tattoo was a carousel pony with beautiful colors, red and blue and a burnt orange, as bright as the sun. He flexed his bicep and made it ride the pole up and down. Emma said it was ugly. Rosalene stroked it and said, "The colors are perfect," she purred like a kitten.

I loved the fact that Emma's mama loved men. She took men into her heart and just plain loved them. You could tell, because when they were with her they always looked healthier, pinker, and softer somehow. She was a gardener of wilted men, women too actually. She fed them and nourished them and when they left her they were straighter and taller and reaching for the sun. I wanted her to nourish me. She tried; I was just too wilted to grow.

"Kimmy, let me stay at your house," Emma said over the phone. "Carlos is here and it's making me sick."

"Yea, sure come over." I thought Emma was lucky to have love like that right under her nose.

That fall my body started to change. I stood naked in the mirror and saw that I was getting boobs. They poked out and when I turned sideways, they stuck out. I jumped up and down and made them jiggle. I told Carl the next weekend that I needed a bra. His face turned red. He took me to the supermall in the city.

"I'm not coming in. You go get what you need, here." He pulled four twenty-dollar bills out of his wallet. "Is eighty dollars enough for a bra and whatever else you want?"

"Uh...," I looked at the money in my hand. "Sure."

"I'll go get a coffee. I'll meet you in the front of the Frederick & Nelson in an hour."

I wandered the aisles looking for the sexiest bra I could find. Some had foam pads and shaped cups and I thought if I got one a little bigger that was already shaped it would make my boobs look even bigger. I could put a sock in there, or some tissue.

The saleslady walked up, clicked her gum, an amused smile on her face. "That's not your size honey." She looked around. "Where's your mom? She should help you."

I didn't like her, "My mom's dead."

"Oh..." She stopped clicking the gum. "Sorry." She looked around again, sighed. "Come over here, I'll help you."

I followed her to a rack with the prettiest bras I had ever seen. They didn't have the shaped cups, but they were soft and delicate. They were white with lace and stitched flowers along the edge. I couldn't fit socks in them, but maybe that would be just as well. Next year I was starting junior high and if a sock fell out in the gym locker room, it would be hard to explain. I tried the bra on, looked in the mirror and stared at my new self. My mom should've been there. Every girl had a mom to take her for her first bra, every girl except me. "Where are you?" I whispered. I dropped to my knees and covered my face and cried.

Emma got jealous when I got new things, but she acted tough and tried not to show it. "Big deal," she said when I showed her my bra. "What do you need that for?"

I felt bad, but the bra, the clothes that separated me from her, gave me a feeling of power. Emma might have a mom, but I could get anything I wanted from Carl and he always seemed to have money. All the loggers did. Emma and I hung out at the 2x4 café and drank hot chocolate, so we saw them. They came in the afternoons for coffee and a meal before they hit the bars. They smelled of wet wood and their boots tracked in mud and pine needles.

Marsha, the waitress yelled at them, "You think I'm your maid? Wipe those boots before you come in."

"They leave big tips," Marsha told us. She sat at our booth, her feet up, taking a break. "I love big burly men." She looked around the café and observed the customers. She picked at Emma's french fries. "You wouldn't believe what goes on here, especially in the bar." She leaned forward over the table. "Last weekend I walked in on a couple doing it in the ladies room."

"Doing what?" Emma asked.

"Jesus, you ought to know with the mama you got. She doesn't keep any secrets."

"Oh that." Emma looked down at her mug. I laughed.

"Well girls, I gotta get back to work." I watched her walk away. Her Levis were too short, they showed her red wool socks. She wore sandals and a t-shirt that read, "Drop out" with a picture of a monkey hanging from a tree. She dressed like a guy and wore patchouli oil, her hair stuck out of her ponytail every which way. She wore no makeup, but she was still pretty in a weird sort of way. I kept staring at her. I tried to figure it out. She went against every law in every fashion magazine I had ever read, but still she looked comfortable and happy.

I didn't get it. You have to use what you have to its fullest extent; that was my motto.

That year we had a winter flood. The streets swam with water and the electricity was shut off for two days, but no one's house flooded, only the incoming and outgoing roads and the outlying farms. It made the town smell weird, like the fur of a wet dog, and Carl didn't go to work. He paced the living room, looked out at the rain.

"I can't stay home any longer," he said.

We went to the 2x4 for breakfast. They reopened that morning when the power came back on. Carl spread his hands out on the table, waited for his breakfast. He watched Marsha walk back and forth from the kitchen. Her ponytail flipped from side to side, her hips swinging.

A tall, sandy haired man walked through the front door. He was tan in an outdoorsy way with legs as long as a soccer field. "Carl!" He walked over to our table, extended a hand to my dad.

Carl grabbed his hand, stood up and gave him a male bear hug. "Sit down, sit down. You back here for a while?"

"Yea," the man smiled wide, his eyes were light blue, like a soft summer sky.

"Ned, this is my daughter Kimmy. Kimmy, this is Ned. Ned and I go way back."

"Nice to meet you," he extended his hand and I shook it. "You certainly are better looking than Carl." He laughed and I smiled for the first time that morning. "How you doing without the wife Carl?"

Silence fell. I looked at my dad. He gazed out the window and watched the rain running down the pane. He clenched his hands together. "You up in the Maloney woods?" he asked Ned.

"I'm living with Rosalene right now," Ned said. I sat at attention.

"Oh, Emma's mom. Emma and Kimmy are best friends, aren't you honey?" Carl reached across the table and put his hand on mine.

"Yea," I said. Ned with Rosalene? It figured. If he were new to town, she would be the first to snatch him up. "She read your tarot cards?" I asked.

"No," he laughed, his laugh was deep and husky. "I don't believe in that stuff. I'm just a nature guy. Actually I have been hiking a lot with Emma. Do you want to come?"

"No thanks," I said. "I don't like to get dirty."

He laughed again. "You're honest. I like that."

Emma spent most of her spare time with Ned. I was jealous. "You like him?" I asked her. We were sitting on the big log at the river. It was cold, but Emma acted like it was the warmest day in spring. She peeled her coat off and laid it on the log.

"Who?" She looked at me. At that moment her eyes were deep green. There was an odd thing about Emma's eyes. They changed color. One moment her eyes were a light green, like a cat's eye marble and the next minute they turned dark, like the color of a seven up bottle or a winter holly leaf.

"Ned. Do you like him?"

"Yea. I do. I really do."

"Do you wish he was your daddy?"

"Maybe." She kicked her feet back and forth in the sand. "I try not to wish for stuff like that."

"Yeah. I know what you mean."

On Fridays after school I'd go to Emma's house and watch her mama play with the tarot cards. I watched her from the beat up plaid chair in the living room. Her hair rolled down her back like a glorious waterfall. Her lips moved, puckered, smiled, and then twisted as she turned the cards over one by one. Most Fridays Marsha was there, sitting beside her at the round kitchen table. That day she was alone, reading for herself.

"Mrs. J…would you read for me?"

She turned to me and gave me the most magnificent smile. "Always Kimmy, come sit," she said. Emma flashed angry eyes at me. Her mama lit a cigarette and poured herself a glass of bourbon. Carl had never smoked and he didn't drink anymore and he spent most evenings at AA meetings ever since my mom died.

I sat at the table and spread my hands out. Rosalene shuffled the deck of cards. I cut it three times.

"Ask yourself your burning question. Think of it in your mind. Focus on it."

I closed my eyes and only one question came to mind. "When would I feel like I was a real person?" I thought in my head.

Rosalene laid the cards out slowly. She stopped and looked at me seriously, then shook her head and laughed.

"What?"

"I know what you asked," she said. "I hate it when that happens."

Rosalene laid the cards out slowly, face down. One by one she turned them over. The cards were magical and spooky, full of wild colors and distorted people in fantastical clothing. "It's your body Kimmy. Look at this card." She pointed to an old odd-looking woman sitting on a stump. "Your physicality and your spirituality are at odds, look at these two cards." Her fingernails click clicked over two other cards.

"What?" I shook my head.

"Your spirit has no control over your body and your body has no control over your spirit, a modern dilemma. See?" she tapped on a card that looked like a lady in the wind on a chariot. "You are disjointed. That can be fun, but agonizing. Take control. Meditate, breathe, walk, play music…all those things that are important to you."

"Uhh…none of those things are important to me, except the music."

"They should become important to you. This comes from a past life Kimmy. You have brought this feeling into this lifetime with you. It is time to break free."

I felt disappointed. "When will it happen? When will I break free?"

"I don't know, but I see you have some hard lessons coming. Be strong and…"

"What?"

"Stay away from the boys."

I found Emma sitting on the back steps, smoking one of her mom's cigarettes.

"Well?" she asked.

"Well what?"

"Are you all healed?" She looked at me.

"I don't really get what she said. I didn't understand it."

"It's all a bunch of mumbo jumbo crap anyway."

I picked at my fingernail polish. "But a lot of stuff she says comes true. She knows stuff."

"Maybe. I don't think she knows her head from her ass, she just makes you think she does."

"Why do you hate her?" I asked.

Emma stubbed out her cigarette on the concrete. "I don't. I love her."

She stood and stretched, showing her belly button to the wind.

The next day I tried to meditate, but all I could think about was boys.

I turned thirteen. I got my period. I knew it was my period. It was red. It was gushy. I stuffed my pants with paper towels and called Emma.

"I started my period," I said.

"Really? Are you sure?"

"Yea. I'm sure. What do I use? Do I buy a tampax or what?"

"Uh...I'm not sure. We'll go ask Marsha."

"Why don't you ask your mama?"

"No. She'll do some ancient ritual or something on you. Forget it. I'll be over."

Emma knocked at the door a few minutes later. I tied a shirt around my waist so no one could tell I had paper towels in my pants and we walked to the 2x4 together. Marsha was out back smoking a cigarette with Joe the cook.

"Ah, the pretty girls. You come for some hot chocolate?" she asked.

"No," Emma said. "Can we talk to you in private?"

"Oh, you want Joe to get lost?" she laughed. "You hear that Joe, get lost!"

"I'm not used to being turned away by women, but okay." He chuckled, His big shoulders moved up and down. He walked back into the kitchen.

"What is it girls?" Marsha asked.

"It's Kimmy. She started her period."

"Oh."

"I don't know what I'm supposed to put up there, you know," I said.

Marsha laughed. "Well don't put anything weird up there. You need some Kotex. Wait here and I'll see what I can get you from the bathroom."

Marsha came back a few minutes later with a brown paper bag. Inside were two thick pads. They looked like dish sponges wrapped in cotton. "You put one of these in your pants. It's peel and stick, lucky for you no more belts." She turned it over. "See? Don't shove it up there okay? You could use tampax, ahh...but...you're a virgin right?"

"Yea," I said quietly.

"Of course she's a virgin. Shit," Emma said loudly.

"Shut up!" I looked at her hard.

"That makes it a little harder...anyway, just change it out when it gets messy. Buy some at the market and don't flush them down your toilet for god's sake." Marsha handed me the bag. "Good luck, now you're a woman. Welcome to the club." She patted me on the back.

My heart swelled and I smiled. "Thanks."

I was a woman. All I wanted to do was curl up on the couch and sleep. My stomach hurt, my back hurt. Emma and I walked back to my house. We smoked a joint in the backyard, she went home and I fell asleep.

That year I learned what my power was. My body. It was the temptation, the Eve, the all-powerful potion that could turn heads, win favors, and gain attention and praise from boys, even men if I was interested. I had boobs, I was a woman, and I was pretty. I knew that. I knew looking in the mirror that I could take a boy's breath away and if I stood very close to him I could make him lose his own mind. I liked that. I felt I had a purpose. I may not have had a mother, but I had a purpose and I was going to see how far it would take me. And besides, it felt good. Being kissed, being fondled, having the weight of a boy on top of me, it felt very close to happiness. Carl was not a physical father. He didn't like to touch or hug or even kiss for that matter. Some days he could hardly look at me. He was stoic, perhaps because he was hurting, perhaps because I looked like my mom.

Emma threw rocks at my window. We went out in the dark, in the night when all things were possible. We got high. We walked to the market and hung out in the parking lot. We laid down on our backs on the football field and stared at the sky. I told Emma a lot, but not everything. I didn't tell her that I went all the way with Monty on the campus of the elementary school. Monty asked me, "Will you do it with me, because I love you?"

"What about Jenny?"

"She won't go all the way with me, she's scared. You're...," he rubbed my cheek with the back of his hand, "you're different. I really dig you." He kissed me all over my face, my neck, down the front of my shirt. I wanted him to love me. It felt good to be held in his arms, I knew he loved me so I did it. I went all the way with him, right there at the elementary school where I used to be a kid. We laid on his sweatshirt on the walkway in front of room three. It hurt. I cried, but I didn't let Monty see.

"Jenny's pregnant you know." Emma was staring out at the river. The log we were sitting on was damp and my butt was getting wet. I hugged my sweatshirt tight around me. "Everybody has seen her throwing up in the locker room."

"Oh."

"You should probably stop seeing Monty, what do you think?"

"I think he really loves me."

She turned and stared at me. "Right. Did you guys...you know?"

"No," I lied.

"Well, it probably isn't good if Jenny finds out you guys were messing around."

"Are you going to stop seeing Loopi?"

"I guess. I'm kind of scared of him anyway."

"Why?"

"Because when he kisses me I really like it."

There was silence, broken by a birds cry. I started laughing and then Emma started laughing and then we laughed together. "Yuk, Boy germs!" I said.

I should have gone to Planned Parenthood that year. Jenny getting pregnant and me not getting pregnant was just a stroke of luck. I should have known. But I didn't. I knew Monty really loved me. Jenny tricked him and then blamed me when he turned against her. We were different; he and I. Monty loved me. It just didn't work out. I couldn't talk to Carl about it and besides he lost his job that year so the world unraveled at my feet. I was afraid I would lose him. He traveled to some faraway place in his mind, sitting hour after hour in the chair by the sliding glass window just staring out at the birds, his shoulders rounded and sagging. He stopped going to his AA meetings. When he wasn't in the chair, he was in his bedroom with the door shut and the lights turned off. I was scared and lost and there was only one person who came to mind who could help me save him. Rosalene. She came to the house in her cape with her purple and red and gold colors drifting about her like halos. She had sex with Carl and he changed overnight. His steps grew light; his gaze grew soft and day dreamy. I knew what sex could do for you, the power of the body and the animal magnetism of the soul. It was a healing elixir. Trying to heal, that's how I got into so much trouble for so long.

When the carnival came back into town I knew Rosalene would go back to Carlos. They had an attraction for each other that you could smell in the wind. It didn't matter though, she had healed my dad, he was going to his AA meetings again and I owed her my life for that. He was a changed man. He had gotten a new job in town. He started talking about vacations and college and all sorts of topics when before, I was lucky if we could talk about the grocery list.

"You've gotta go to college honey. We'll make it happen," he said munching away on his cereal.

Well, I would think about college later, but right then I was too busy fucking the gorgeous tow headed guy who ran the haunted house ride at the carnival. He was my drug.

The first time Emma and I rode the ride, he took our ticket. "What's your name?" I asked him.

"Nick," he said. He tucked us into our car, lowering the bar and locking it into place across our laps. "And you two gorgeous females? You have names?"

I raised my eyes to him slowly. "I'm Kimmy, and this is Emma."

"Mmm, Kimmy, Kimmy I like that." He sauntered off to the other cars, mostly filled with kids, and secured their bars. I watched him steadily.

"You like him?" Emma asked me.

"Oh yeah."

"What about Travis?"

"Who?"

Emma sighed. "Are you and Travis done?"

"Emma, Travis is a kid. Look at that guy. Shit, he is something."

"Yeah, he's a fucking carnival worker. He's just like Carlos."

"I like Carlos."

I rode the ride three times that day. Twice with Emma and the last time by myself.

"Come tonight after I close up and I'll give you a private tour of the haunted house. Would you like that, huh?" Nick asked. His breath smelled like peppermint. He had sideburns and stubble on his chin that shined golden in the sunlight.

"Uh…yeah. That would be great," I stammered. "Tonight then."

I told Emma I was staying home. Carl watched television after dinner and I told him I was going to bed. "I have cramps," I told him. I knew he wouldn't come in my room or bother me once I told him I was going to bed. He never intruded. I crawled out the bedroom window. I wore my white shorts and a peasant top and a sexy bra with some sling sandals. I walked slowly to the field. I felt wild anticipation and nerves jumbled together. My breath was fast. Nick was leaning against one of the cars smoking a cigarette.

"Hey," he said. "I wasn't sure if you would come."

"I don't usually lie."

"I got car number twenty two all ready for you lovely lady. Ready for your tour?" He held the bar up. I climbed in, the seat had a slight tear in the middle, and white stuffing poked out. Nick climbed in beside me. He smelled faintly like sweat and machine oil and cigarette smoke. "Do you smoke?" he asked.

"Yeah."

"I got some weed, we'll have us a personal haunted fantasy."

Nick pushed the button on the post beside us and the car lurched forward. "There's control stations inside as well, just in case there is an emergency so I can stop us when we get inside and we can let the haunting begin."

The car traveled forward. I saw the same things I had seen earlier that day. A giant mummy that lurched forward as the car came close. Screaming came from a witch head. White smoke billowed up from the rails ahead of us. We traveled into the darkness. Nick hopped out of the car and hit a button on a post next to a bloody mirror. Our cart stopped and we could see ourselves in the mirror. It had a crack running through it and drops of blood splattered upon it so that when you saw yourself in it you looked dissected and wounded. Nick climbed back into the cart. He reached inside of his pocket and pulled out a joint. He lit it with a silver lighter, took a toke and passed it to me; he let out his breath like a dragon.

"Have I told you how incredibly beautiful you are? I love your hair." He reached behind me and stroked my hair as I took a drag from the joint. "Mm, I love the way you smoke."

Two more tokes, another toke after that. I was high. I looked in the mirror and saw Nick put a hand up my shirt. He stroked my bra. I turned to him and kissed him and the marijuana scent filled me to the core. He kneaded my breast and I reached for him, reached for his crotch, and kneaded him through his pants. He moaned.

"This is what I call a haunting. Stand up." I stood up. He peeled down my shorts. I stepped out of them. He massaged me through my underwear and my mind flew away, past the mirror into another space entirely. It was only my body and Nick's delicious body and the sweetness of the marijuana. "Mm," he moaned as he pulled down my underwear. He stroked me while he lifted my shirt with the other hand and began licking my breastbone. "Sit for a minute. There's only room for one of us to stand." He stood and unbuttoned his Levis then pulled down his boxer shorts. I soaked in the shape of his hips, the glow of his skin in the darkness. He sat down in the cart. "Ride me," he said. "I love giving rides." I straddled him and slid up and down on him as he lifted my peasant blouse over my head and unhooked my bra. I did not think about birth control. I didn't think at all because my mind was a hundred miles away. I filled myself with him and felt a peace settle over me. It was the best carnival ride of my life.

"We didn't use birth control," I said afterward. We had put our clothes back on and were smoking the rest of the joint. I watched Nick in the bloody mirror as he inhaled and exhaled.

"I don't believe in birth control," he said. "I've never used it and I've never gotten a girl pregnant before."

"Do you bring a lot of girls on private carnival rides?"

"You're the first."

I looked at my reflection. The crack cut me in two.

I met Nick fifteen more times. Each time he would stop in front of the mirror. "I like seeing both sides of you," he said.

One night after we had made love we ran around the inside of the ride and played with the oversized figures. I knocked the witch's arm off. We were so high we could not get her arm back on. I waved at him with the amputated arm and fell down in a heap of laughter. Nick made me feel light and fun.

I didn't feel anything, I just knew. One morning I looked in the mirror at myself. I had just come out of the shower and I could see from my thighs up, my body wet and naked. I looked the same, but I wasn't. I knew I was pregnant. It was a deep knowing. I told Nick that night.

"Have you missed a period?"

"I had a period about three weeks ago."

"Then you are not pregnant." He laughed. "Get in," he said holding the bar up on the car with the torn seat. I couldn't help myself.

The carnival was getting ready to leave. Nick told me two more nights and they would pack up for the next town.

"Stay," I said.

"I can't babe, this is my job. I'll be back before you know though. Every summer. We can call it our summers of love. Let's not say goodbye then okay?"

We made love three more times in the haunted house. Three days later I woke up late. I had been sleeping a lot. I hurried and dressed and made my way to the field, but most of the rides were packed and gone. Carlos was loading up his truck.

"Kimmy? Hi."

"Is the haunted house ride gone?" I asked. My eyes searched the field.

"First thing this morning Conchita." He stopped what he was doing and looked at me carefully. "What are you looking for? Did you lose something?"

"No. Yes. I don't know." I turned and walked away slowly. The world was as watery and broken as the bloody mirror. I had to find Emma.

Chapter Four: Rosalene; The High Priestess

My mom died at 10:02 the morning of August 2nd. She was in the garden staking up sunflowers. It was already hot. She wore her ridiculous hat, the one with the orange plastic flowers around the band. It was straw and shielded her eyes from the sun. It could not shield her from the brain aneurysm that erupted inside of her at 10:02. I saw her drop, I ran to her as a crow landed on the fence and squawked out his warning. It was over. I was alone. The paramedics called social services.

The woman came; Isabel or something was her name. She made phone calls from the avocado green phone. Her voice was scratchy.

"We've found a place for you Rosalene, a family that will take you temporarily. I think you will be very happy there." She pursed her lips together.

"Sure," I said. I had no father, now no mother. Foster family, that's what she said.

I went to my bedroom and packed a satchel. I put in my favorite skirts, shirts, underwear, toothbrush and paste, lotions and make-up. All the money I could find, jewelry that I liked, and a great picture of my mother and father, taken in Salem on the capitol steps. My father had left us seven years ago on a rainy windy November night. He snuck out without a whisper and took our family car, the Ford Fairlane. I knew he was going; I had known for months. I had seen it. I could see all kinds of things, things I wanted to see, but mostly things I didn't want to see.

I went to my mother's room and took all the money and change that I could find and all her jewelry. I grabbed her drawing pad and pencils. The social worker lady was on the phone again. I walked out the back door through the garden and the patch of the fence that held a gap wide enough for a fourteen year old body to slide through. I never looked back. I caught the 250, a greyhound bus for Portland and missed my mother's funeral. I held my own private funeral for her on the bank of the Willamette River. I cried and cried for my mom and myself because I knew I was alone. I was a runaway.

I traveled a lot and the main thing I learned was, keep quiet, listen with your ears and watch with your eyes; carefully. Follow the insides of you when it comes to trusting or mistrusting certain individuals, and above all, never get attached because what you have today will fall out of the palm of your hand and crash to the ground, often while you are looking it in the eye.

I saw things when people touched me. A pastor in Astoria guided me to a church hostel. As he put a friendly hand on my shoulder I heard the screech of car brakes and a thud. I saw his body roll up and over the hood of a car and fall limp to the pavement.

"Be careful father," I said.

"Ah, those are the words I should have for you my girl." His large body cast a shadow upon me as we walked side by side.

"Father, please be careful when you are crossing streets and walking in traffic, will you?" I asked.

"Always my dear. Now here we are, you can stay up to five nights. We have a shower and fresh blankets and you get a hot breakfast every morning. There are all ages here though, so be careful yourself. Another pastor stays in room C3 down the hall past the kitchen if you need anything, or if you want to pray. We ask no questions here." He had silver eyes with small flecks of color. Rainbow trout eyes, I thought.

I left when my five days were up. A boy my age took me in in Newport. I was sitting on the beach when I met him, watching for a whale because the sign in the coffee shop uptown said it was whale season.

"You'll never see one this way," he told me. "You have to go out on a boat, get in their territory."

He seemed to like the idea that I was homeless. "That's far out!" he said, "I wish I was homeless."

I followed him to his house downtown, a small grey and white house with beaten paint from the salt air.

He made peanut butter sandwiches, and served them with milk and Oreo cookies. I had not eaten since the night before so I felt extremely grateful. When I told him I had no parents he said, "Ah, you'll find some." He took rolling papers and a small baggie of tobacco from his hip pocket. He rolled his own cigarette and lit it with a fancy lighter from the side table. "This lighter is worth two hundred and twenty five dollars. You should steal it, my mom would never know."

I took a nap in his room on sheets that smelled like little boys, a mix of sweat and sweet milk. The sound of his mother's voice woke me. She opened his door, took one look at me; my wrinkled clothes and shouted, "Out, out! Brandon, if I've told you once, I've told you six hundred times, do not bring street people home with you!" I had not been his first charity lunch. She touched me as I was walking past. She fingered my shirt and said, "You need a bath! Now get out!" In that small moment of contact I heard a baby's cry. I saw the woman lying with her face beaming, a hospital gown, and a small infant in a nurse's arm.

"You are going to get pregnant," I said.

She laughed, "Says the whore to the saint! Now get out of my house thank you very much, and Brandon, don't you dare follow her!" He watched me wistfully from the porch.

Moments like that have haunted me all my life. The question, the thing I always wondered was, if I saw something bad, something life threatening, something heinous, could I change it? Could I tell the person to stay out of an alley or to avoid walking under a ladder on a hot day? I saw my dad leaving. I knew it before he did. I saw him on a ferryboat with a beautiful blonde woman. They were smiling into the sun, their hair blowing in the sea air. I knew he was leaving, but I never told my mom. If I did, could I have changed any of the circumstances? And what if I did change the circumstances? Would that set off a current of events that would change hundreds of things minutely related to each other causing perhaps, a baby not to be born, or a savior to miss the flight connection needed to be at a given location at a given moment? What was my responsibility? Why was I given this curse? That is why I believed in impermanence. I loved and hated, but never for keeps because I knew nothing was a keeper.

I had sex in San Francisco. How I got there is still a mystery to me. I was heading north. It was in my mind that I would go to Alaska and find a job because I read that it was the last frontier, that jobs were endless because Alaska was full of extreme conditions, few people wanted to stay. Only true Alaskans wanted to stay. I felt like it was the right place for me. I had endured extreme conditions already and I was ready for the trees and the mountains and the feeling of anonymity that Alaska represented to me. I boarded a bus for the North, or so I thought. I fell asleep almost immediately as I had gotten very little sleep on the streets. You had to be ready at all times, ready to hear, ready to see, ready to feel the threats and opportunities that came close; that left very little time for sleeping. When I awoke I was in San Francisco. I had boarded the wrong bus in the wrong direction.

I ended up in Chinatown and there I got a job as a dishwasher. The manager spoke enough English to hire me. I think his dishwasher had walked out because he insisted that I start immediately, putting my pack on a lacquer bench in the back room and pulling an apron over my head. I loved the job. I loved the sounds of the foreign language swirling about me. I loved how the staff bowed the top half of their bodies in greeting as I passed them with a tub of clean steaming dishes. I loved the plates of food I was offered when I had finished my shift. Plates of dumplings and fish and pastries with light glazes and unpronounceable names. It was there that I learned my gift was not as unusual as I had imagined. I was not alone. There were many seers in Chinatown.

There was an old woman with glassy eyes that sat at the small red table at the back left corner of the restaurant. She laid sticks on the tabletop and people came and sat across from her. Often these people were young, well-dressed Chinese. They chose a stick and the old woman told them their future, all from their choice of stick, their draw. One day a young woman bowed her head and cried until her makeup began to run down her delicate cheeks. The old woman kept speaking in the sharp singsong tones of the Chinese language. The old woman was one of many fortunetellers. I saw men on blankets on the street corners and encased in the corners of crusty old bars. In Chinatown a seer was revered and respected and sometimes feared.

I slept in a vacant hotel room I had found across from the restaurant. The bottom floors of the hotel were still being used as apartments, but the top floors had not yet been cleaned and refurbished and they smelled like piss. Old mattresses were strewn on floors with dirty towels here and there. There were forgotten clothing articles, hats, t-shirts and an occasional pair of women's panties. With my first tips I bought a straw mat to sleep on from a street vendor and a beautiful blanket with a red dragon on it. The vendor had given it to me for a song, as it had a cigarette burn on the corner. "Me boy, me boy," he said, pointing to the burn mark. He handed me my change, brushing my palm and I saw him in a pasture tending a flock of geese, herding them with a stick, the sun shining upon him. Three weeks later he disappeared. I went into the storefront near his corner and asked the woman where he had gone.

"Oh," she said in her broken English, "he get job on farm, no more blanket." I knew he was happy; I had felt his happiness in my belly.

Ling, one of the waiters at the restaurant followed me to my crappy room. He began to leave gifts on my straw mat. One day I came home to find a ceramic dragon with flashing eyes of green glass. Another day I found a sweet chocolate in a delicate gold wrapper. And on the day that was my birthday, although he did not know it was my birthday, he left me a red dahlia, probably stolen from a neighborhood garden. I was now 15.

Ling began to sing to me in Chinese at work. On his breaks he stood next to the kitchen door that led to the alley. He smoked an exotic thin brown cigarette and sung. The songs were very pretty in a weird, choppy sort of way. He was very good looking and liked to roll his cigarettes up in the sleeve of his t-shirt when he wasn't working. It was his aunt and uncle's restaurant and he had come to Chinatown when he was 13 to work. He was 20. When he smiled his eyes became waves of joy. He called me Pea, which means "naughty" if you come from Taiwan; which he didn't.

One day La Lo, Ling's aunt, asked me if I would stay late and wash dishes for the dinner crowd, as Jackie, the other dishwasher, was sick. I told her I would. It was that night that Ling offered to walk me home. The restaurant had closed. We had all shared a large meal of leftovers and steamed rice at the big round table in the back of the restaurant. The red neon lights of the street lit up the sky.

"I will walk you," he said. "Chinatown is dangerous at night." Didn't he know I went out almost every night and prowled the streets on my own? It was easy to be invisible when you were a skinny fifteen year old.

"No, no, that is okay." I was afraid of the way he made me feel. When Ling was next to me, I felt like I had the flu. My stomach hurt and I could not breathe, and if I were near him long enough my forehead would sweat.

La Lo yelled at Ling in Chinese.

"I must walk you, La Lo insists."

We walked side by side, his shoulder brushing against mine.

"Do you want to go to town?" he asked.

"I thought we were in town."

He laughed and put his arm about my waist stopping me on the sidewalk. He leaned his forehead against mine. He smelled of sweet rice vinegar. "No I will take you around, to the wharf then uptown. That is where the hippies are. We'll look at the hippies. We'll go to golden gate park, although you must stay close, it can be very dangerous." I knew I could stay close.

We were out very late and what I remember the most were the colors of that city; the colors of the lights and the people and the view into the windows where exotic people were living exotic colorful lives, drinking colorful drinks and laughing, letting the color spill from their lips. The smells. The smells of the wharf and the fresh smell of Golden Gate park; the smell of the glorious flowers outside the Japanese garden, and of course, the smell of the salt water from the docks at the wharf and the lonely cries of the seagulls.

"I like you Rosalene, you are my rose of China." He leant near and kissed me. His tongue went into my mouth and traced the lines of my teeth. My first kiss, unless you counted the truth or dare game we played in sixth grade. I kissed lots of boys in that game, but never the way Ling kissed me. And then we just kept kissing and kissing and kissing. We could not stop.

We had sex two days later on my dragon blanket on my straw mat in my small smelly room with the cracked window that looked over Chinatown. I bled on the dragon and Ling looked afraid.

"How old are you my Rose?"

"Fifteen."

He was silent for some time. He got up and leaned against the windowsill, lit one of his skinny cigarettes. "Shit."

"It is okay," I said. "I have no family. You did not force me Ling. It felt good to be in your arms. I have no one." I began to cry and Ling kneeled on the dirty floor and held me, rocking me in his arms. He made love to me again and that time it didn't hurt as bad. I traced the outline of his clear brown face with my fingertip.

"Ling, Ling, the boy who could sing," I said.

After Ling had shown me around I began to explore the city on my own. I would ride the trolley or the bus and go to different neighborhoods. It seemed like they all had a slang name. I especially liked the Haight-Ashbury district where young kids, barely older than me, were giving speeches on sidewalks and lighting up marijuana cigarettes in the streets. I met a girl named Stone. She said she was a poet.

"Is that your real name?" I asked her.

"Nah. I named myself. We all do it. I am like a stone. The waters of life rush about me and I remain constant, you dig?" She dragged on her joint, ran her hands through her knotted blond hair.

"I dig." I leaned against the wall of a supermarket. There was graffiti all over the wall. "Go daddy-o" and "Ferlinghetti lives it" in giant magenta letters.

"You need a name," she said. "I will call you Raven."

"Why Raven?"

"Because a raven represents the dead ancestors of a loved one and it seems that all yours are dead, so you are the raven. You are the last representation of all that is lost, the last one to walk the earth."

"How do you know my ancestors are dead?"

"Honey, a girl your age wandering alone is either without family, or needs to be without family. You cut your ties, proclaim your family dead and make your own family. Capisce?"

"Okay. Raven it is." That made me sad.

"See ya around Raven!" She hopped away like a sparrow.

I loved fisherman's wharf. The sound of the seagull's cry and the moan of the foghorns expanded me. I could stand on the dock and close my eyes and know that I was a small part of a really big thing, a minuscule fragment of a giant circular breathing entity that washed around me and through me. It calmed me. I knew my mom was out there somewhere, swimming in the ocean, frolicking with the fish.

"Ling, I want to swim in that bay." I was holding his hand and we were walking near the Polar Bear Club, where women and men of all ages came to swim in the bay no matter what the temperature of the air or the sea. I loved it. They wore bathing caps and old-fashioned swimsuits and their faces were flush and alive when they emerged from the water.

"We will my princess."

Two nights later, after the restaurant closed, Ling and I walked the city blocks to the bay. We stripped our clothes off and naked we walked into the bay.

Hand in hand, fingers entwined, moon in the sky, we let the waves lap against our waists and then the buoyancy of the salt water came to our shoulders. Ling could walk farther than I and still touch the gorgeous sand. I let his hand go and screamed out loud. "Yes…I love it!" He laughed and laughed and the moon washed his face with yellow light. We swam as long as we dared and when my fingers started to become numb we walked out, leaning into one another. We ran to our clothes laughing, grabbed them quickly and ducked behind the park building. A cop cruiser drove by, but we were hidden from view. It's one thing to get busted, it's another to get busted naked.

I learned some very important things from Ling. One was, always use a condom so you don't get pregnant, the other was, never expect someone you love to stay around. I think I had already learned that one; he just ingrained it into me further, because in December, right before Christmas, he went back to China to take care of his father. I cried, his aunt cried, his uncle cried, he cried and held me all the night before. We promised we would write, but I didn't even have an address and he could only write in Chinese. I received one letter at the restaurant's address and never another after. His aunt translated it for me and I blushed as she read the sensual parts.

Christmas came and went and my little "hotel" room was getting very cold. It was time to move on. I had saved quite a bit of money. I gave plenty of notice and was replaced by a homeless looking guy of forty-six with a ponytail down to his butt. "Sedgwick's my name," he said, shaking my hand in a limp way. He would be perfect. I even told him about the "hotel" and offered him my room, but he said, "Nah, I've got an old lady and six kids on the hilltop. I just smoke too much dope to get a real job." You can never judge, I learned that too, living in San Francisco. Always have an open mind and expect people to drift in and out of your life as often as a tule fog. I caught the bus for Napa. Goodbye my Ling.

I ended up in Sonoma. It was warmer than San Francisco and there were a lot of people there who smiled at me and moved slowly. "Live on the land" the poster said across the top. The poster hung on the grimy bathroom door at the gas station outside of town. I wrote down the phone number and called from the pay phone on the corner.

"Megatross here," the voice said.

"Um, I saw your poster at the gas station and I am looking for a place to live…and some work too actually. I just wanted to get some more information from you."

"I'll have someone meet you there. Stay where you are."

An hour later a baby blue surfer van pulled up. I was sitting on the curb of the gas station, my backpack beside me, and my hair long and in two braids. I was wearing levis with the hem cut off, a pair of army combat boots that Ling had found for me and a thin pair of boys cotton socks, a white t-shirt with "Rice-a-Roni" on it and a thin, worn pea coat, that Ling had also given me. I think he shopped at the navy surplus.

The guy who jumped out of the van had the most beautiful hair I had ever seen. It was blond and strawberry and hung to his waist with tiny curls at the bottom. His eyes were a beautiful brown with flecks of green. He held out a dirty hand. "Name is Miguel." I looked at his hand. "Sorry, I've been farming, this is God's dirt," and he laughed.

"Rosalene." I shook his hand; it was warm. I got a jolt. It was Miguel and a woman and a baby and the woman was grabbing the baby hard by the arm. The baby was crying. Miguel was shouting. Flash and it was gone.

"Rosalene. Do you want to see the farm?"

"Sure." What else was there for me?

We drove and drove and drove and the roads became more and more beautiful with each passing mile. Rolling hills, green trees, oaks and eucalyptus.

Miguel rolled down his window. His hair blew towards me. It was all I could do not to reach out and grab it. He read my mind, looked at me. "I think you'll like the farm."

The farm was a paradise of vegetable gardens and plots of green plants with signs for all kinds of different herbs. My mother had been such a gardener that a lot of the plants I immediately recognized. Things sink in when you are young, even when you are not paying attention. I loved the smell, a combination of earth and fresh greenery and wood smoke from the surrounding cabins. "We built all these cabins ourselves," he said, sweeping his arm across the property. "If you decide you want to stay, we can assign you to a cabin. We all do a share of chores and when those are done, we turn on, if you know what I mean."

"Sure." I had no idea what he meant.

"We don't ask where you come from, that's up to you if you want to share that. No third degree here man. Now why don't you look around? I've gotta go get some dirt tilled. We're growing the winter veggies right now. We eat all our own food. See those chickens over there?" He shielded his eyes from the sun, pointed to the corner of the property. I followed his gaze and saw brown and white chickens running wild. "That's where we get our eggs. Some stuff we buy or trade for, lentils, rice, that kind of stuff. See what you think then come find me." He walked away, his hair cascading down his strong back.

I wasn't sure what to do so I walked closer to the cabins. I could hear babies crying and the sound of voices. A man with wild wiry hair came out of one of the cabins. He was shirtless, carrying a naked baby on one hip. "Hey," he said when he saw me. A woman followed him. She wore a long flowing skirt with a wool sweater and no shoes. When she saw me she stopped. She pushed her hair back, straightened her spine. "You new?"

"I guess."

"You stayin?"

"I think so."

"You eighteen?"

"Huh?"

"You have to be eighteen to stay here. We don't need no cops."

"Yea," I lied. "I'm eighteen."

"You look real young."

"Yea. Runs in the genes."

"Well I hope you stay, you could take some of the heat off me. There's only three women left you know. Three women and fifteen men, you know what that's like?"

"Uh."

"Well, it's like a fucking turnstile in an amusement park, that's what it's like. We need some more women. Five just took off to join a commune in Arizona. Imagine that. What could be better than here? This is God's country, you know?"

"So I hear. God's dirt."

"Right. Why don't you put your bag in here? You can have some tea and meet the kids."

I followed her inside. There were two more barefooted kids at the table eating peanut butter sandwiches and three more kids by the woodstove on a dirty braided rug. They were weaving something out of colorful threads.

"They're making bracelets over there. That's Luna, Marsh and Sunbeam. This here's Tuscany and Olive. The baby you saw walking out the door is Moon. She's mine actually, although we share all the kids. It's not good to put a claim on a human life. We're all free. Well, unless you're in Vietnam, then you're owned by Mr. Big, you know what I'm saying?"

I didn't. "Yes." It smelled strange in the cabin, like some kind of dirty spice.

"You cook?" she asked.

"I could."

"Good, help me make burritos. I am on dinner duty tonight. Us women all take turns. This is my night and I am tired, I just want to get high, you know what I mean?"

Again. "Sure."

I stayed. It was warm and there was food and although I had no idea what I was doing or how the rules went, I helped that woman make the burritos. She put the strange smelling spice in them, cumin, she said.

"My name is Window."

"That's your real name?"

"Now it is. I gave up my family, therefore, I gave up my family name."

"Oh." I was rolling the black beans in the tortillas, sprinkling them with cheese in the aluminum pan.

"We'll put them all together now and I'll warm them up on the stove later. I ain't cookin' all day."

"Where's the oven?"

Window laughed. "I cook on that!" She pointed to the woodstove. "See why I need a helper, between that and spreadin' my legs I am worn out!"

"Where are the other women?"

"There's one for three of the cabins now, we had more than that before the other gals left. You'll be with me. I like you. What's your name?"

"Rosalene."

"I will call you Flower."

"Actually, call me Raven."

"Oh, I like that! Raven it is."

As Raven I stayed for a year and a half. I never had babies at the farm. I worked and drove vegetables, herbs, and eggs around with Miguel. We sold them to local restaurants and hotels. They especially liked the eggs, and if a woman was working, she always bought extra eggs from Miguel because he was so gorgeous.

I helped take care of babies. I changed a lot of diapers and soaked a lot of diapers in hot steamy vinegar water. "No bleach," Window told me. "Bleach is toxic to their little bodies."

I met the other women. One was startling beautiful with black hair that shone almost purple and violet eyes. She was very quiet and stood tall, her posture stretched to the sky. Her name was River. The other woman was a small overweight blond with a cherubic face and dancing eyes of blue. I really liked her. Her name was Billy. The men were numerous; some tall, some short, some wiry, all with wild hair and wild names. It took me a long time to know all the men. The deal was, you could sleep with anyone, anytime and no man belonged to a woman and no woman belonged to a man. It was a smorgasbord of sex, and if you got pregnant, everybody took care of your child, because you didn't really know whom the father was, and the mothers seemed interchangeable. I liked living on the farm, but I always felt like a visitor, maybe it was because I didn't have any babies. I used up my supply of condoms from San Francisco and then bought more from town whenever I needed to. I slept with every man there and learned a lot of tricks. I had a few favorite men. Nobody forced you, it was always optional, but I rarely opted out. Some I really didn't like going to bed with. One was Julianno. He was short, very hairy and always smelled like olive oil. He was a fast, forceful lover. He pressed too hard and sweated too much. I loved going to bed with Peace. He was tall and pale with dark hair that curled around his ivory face. He was sweet and quiet and smelled like fresh cut rosemary. When Peace came to me at night I felt like a loved child. I was stroked and murmured to. Cradled and enfolded. I guess I was still a child; maybe that's why he was one of my favorites.

Megatross was all right. He was Asian, but larger than my Ling and when he wasn't working he would drop acid and do Tai Chi. He was fun as a lover, usually telling jokes or making up rhymes. He was nice to be with, but of all, Miguel was my favorite. I loved the way Miguel could wrap me in his hair. It would cover our bodies like water over a Grecian urn. We fit together, Miguel and I and we never had to say a word. We would just look at each other over the woodpile, or over our dinner and we would know that we would be together that night.

River grabbed my arm one day by the woodpile. I was stacking kindling for the stoves. "You are spending too much time with Miguel. It's not fair. We share and I used to be his favorite. I had one of his children, I am sure of it."

I looked in her violet eyes. She was still touching me and I saw her falling. She was on the side of a cliff and there was a dog beside her, a reddish dog with pointy ears, and she was saying something to the dog, bending near its ear and then I saw her falling, could feel her falling, saw her dark hair fanning out to the sky. Her scream filled the air, penetrating the clouds over and above the dogs cry.

"Do you hike?"
"Not anymore." She dropped my arm. "Why?"
"You shouldn't."
"Leave me alone. And give me some time with Miguel."

We prayed on Sundays. We met in the clearing by the potato patch, all of us; even the babies, and we would get on our knees. Usually it was Starfire, a large black man with biceps the size of New York; that would lead us in thought for the day. One morning he talked about family and the creation of a family to be there for you. "This is our family," he bellowed. "Kneel in the dirt and know that the Lord has brought us to each other to be a family, to propagate as a family, to care for each other as a family, to love each other as a family." Miguel was staring at me. "Give us this day to be reminded of our duty to each other, to the children, to our dream of peace and living united in the cause. Amen." We sang a song, "Peace Train," from Cat Stevens. It was out of tune, but it was loud.

There was no electricity at the cabins so all our activity was in the day, unless we were getting high, dropping acid, taking LSD or having sex. Those were our nighttime activities. I slept on the floor, but it was definitely warmer than the hotel and I never spent a dime of my money, unless I bought condoms. We were self sufficient, selling our vegetables and buying what we needed. People in town talked about us though, it was hard to stay clean, so no wonder.

One day a new gal came, she was about forty or so. She looked like my mother and I lost my breath looking at her. The ache inside of me was as fresh as the clearest stream.

"I'm Consuela," she extended her hand to me. Her nails were crisp and clean and her hands as soft as a baby's. "I left my husband, left my life." She started laughing, loudly, frantically. "I just looked around and thought, 'why?', so I walked out and here I am." She laughed again. "I like the preacher man, he picked me up downtown at the market. Do you like it here?"

I didn't know. Did I like it there? I just was. I was just existing, floating in space and time, a child with no parent, a child pretending to be a grown up. "Sure."

Sometimes we had conflict circles. We sat cross-legged in the main field and shared our feelings. One day when the sun was high in the sky, but the weather was crisp, River stood. "I have a problem."

"Yes River, let it be known to the group that you have a problem that you wish to share." Starfire was the leader.

"My problem is with Raven."

"Raven, please stand."

I stood, my legs strong beneath me. I really didn't like River. I tried, but I thought she was bitchy, bossy and needed a lot of male attention.

River looked at me, through me with her witchy violet eyes. "Raven is spending too much time on her back and not enough time doing chores. I know she's young so all you boys really like her, but it is unfair to us, to the mothers of your children. Why, she hasn't even gotten pregnant yet and it's been almost a year. We are supposed to propagate, aren't we Reverend Starfire? Aren't we supposed to propagate?"

"Uh," Starfire seemed nervous. "The law states 'propagate if you will', meaning it is your will to conceive or not conceive. You must remember River that some women are barren and this is also the will."

"She uses condoms. I've seen her!"

"You watch me?" I felt a flush in my neck.

"I have. I can."

"Uh, River, I think there are some issues here that are larger than what they appear. Do you feel something on the inside that you would like to share?" Starfire opened his hands to her.

"I feel old and tired. I'm tired of taking care of all these kids. This peace thing is not working out for me…I don't feel loving, especially not to that bitch!" She pointed at me, her long finger moving in the sunlight.

"Maybe I should go?"

"No!" Window stood, her hands on her hips. "Why she's just a baby. You are not turning her out into the world!"

"She's eighteen, nineteen by now, send her out!" River was yelling.

"Listen River, Raven is broken. When you're broken you need fixing. That's why she's here." Window paused. "That's why we're all here."

"Here! Here!" Consuela cheered.

"You, my dear, are not broken. You grew up a spoiled little rich girl!"

"I did not!" River proclaimed.

"You did so! You told me yourself. Now riches don't make your life special, but you don't always see the downtrodden, now do ya? You leave Raven alone and let time do for her what it should. She sleeps in my cabin, she works the farm, she chops wood, and she plays with the kids. Leave her alone!" With that Window sat back down, beaming at me.

"Turn on, Window, yeah!" Megatross cheered.

"Perhaps, River," Starfire cleared his throat, "the men could make a more conscious effort to spend time with you and appreciate you more."

"That would be nice."

Starfire went on. "And perhaps you need to take a meditation break. If you would like to turn on today and walk the pastures, I think the other women will support you in that, won't you all?"

"Yes," they agreed.

"Yes," I agreed. She made my stomach hurt.

"Let us pray. Lord Jesus of infinite wisdom let us come together to heal River's pain and suffering. Let her rest in your abided arms and when the men hold her, let them hold her in your love, Amen."

"Amen," we all repeated. River stared at me from the corner of her eye.

Six months later when spring was breaking, River cornered me on the path from the chicken's pen. I was carrying a basket of eggs. I had two-dozen eggs in the basket, ready to be washed and cleaned for the market. She stood solid in my path, her hands on her hips, her body stretched tall and angular.

"I know about you now," she said.

"And what might that be?" I was ready for a catfight. I could take care of myself on the streets of San Francisco; I could take care of myself on the farm. I was a little scared of her, though. She was the snow queen, the ice princess, and the wicked witch of the north.

"I know how old you are. I found your real name in your backpack. I called my daddy and had him look you up. You're a runaway."

"You're lying." My hands shook; the eggs shook in their basket.

"No, sweet little princess, you're lying and I'm going to turn you in. All I have to do is make a call to the county sheriff and he will bust your ass before you can say, 'Argentina'."

"You wouldn't do that. You wouldn't let the sheriff come out here and bust everyone for drugs and whatever else they find."

"Why wouldn't I? You think I like any of these people? I came to piss off my rich old daddy and it worked and I don't give a fuck about any of these people. They are little lost souls in their own little fucked up world. Don't you get it? There is no "Peace Train". The world is fucked. And you're a minor."

"I'm sixteen now."

She laughed, "Sixteen! You know what that gets these guys? You know what that gets Miguel? Statutory rape! That's what it gets him. Six to ten in the county jail, that's what it gets him."

I made a move to walk past her. She pushed into me with her body, knocking the basket out of my hands and to the ground. Eggs cracked and spilled and the yellow yolks ran onto the soft brown earth. She laughed again, tossing her long black hair to the side.

"I feel sorry for you," I said.

I packed my satchel while Window was outside. I didn't say goodbye to anyone. It was sad to be leaving and I didn't know where to go. I found Miguel and asked him if he would give me a ride to town. "I have to go," I said. "My mom's sick. I have to go take care of her."

"How do you know? Did you call her?" His brown eyes searched my face.

"I called her the last time we were in town, and I have been thinking about it ever since. I need to be with her."

"I understand." He cupped my chin in his hand. "I love you Raven. I will drive you, give me a minute to finish the chores."

He took me in the same van I came in, the one we used for our deliveries. Halfway there he pulled over to the side of the road. We had sex in the back of the van for the last time and his tall body encircled me, making me feel lost and found at the same time. Is it all right to be alone? I didn't know, but it seemed that was the way my life was going. No dad, no mom, no home, nothing. Impermanence, there it was again. Like the mist of the sea, now you see it now you don't. Don't ever try to hold it because it will evaporate in your palm.

"Do you have enough money for the bus?" he asked.

"I think so."

He pulled a hundred dollar bill out of his pocket and gave it to me. "You may not know this, but I sell a lot of dope when we come to market. It's our side business. You've earned it."

"Thanks." I kissed him for the last time and watched him drive away.

I took a bus back to San Francisco. Where I would sleep I didn't know, but across from the bus stop, a high school was just getting out. I crossed the street and sat on a bench and watched. Girls laughing, their skirts matching, long hair flying, some in braids, some in ponytails. They were my age, or the age I should have been, the age I was on the outside. The inside was a different story. A girl with wire rimmed glasses and two long black braids stopped in front of me. Some of her hair was sticking out of the braids, wildly framing her face. Her eyes were as brown as the earth and she cocked her head at me, "You new here?"

"No," I said, "not new, old."

"You don't have a uniform. I see you have a book bag," she gestured to my pack, "but no uniform, how come?"

"I don't go to school here."

"Where do you go?"

"I don't."

She snapped a braid behind her back, "Isn't that illegal? Aren't you supposed to go to school?"

"I'm traveling."

"Cool." She looked left and right. "Hey, do you have a cigarette?"

"No," I said, wishing I had something to offer her.

"Well, see ya around," she bounded off, her skirt bouncing with her energy.

That should be me. That should be my life, in school, young, bouncing braids, with someone to iron my skirt and my blouse, someone to skip home to. I felt incredibly sad and rounded my body into the bench, folding up my knees, hugging my pack tight. Now what?

I probably could have gone back to Chinatown, gotten my old job back, but I didn't think I could face it without Ling. I went back to the bus station. I had enough money to go almost anywhere. I closed my eyes and ran my finger down the list of destinations. I stopped when I felt it was right, opened my eyes. Seattle. Wasn't that Washington, by the coast? That sounded okay. It was getting me closer to Alaska anyway. I bought the ticket and four hours later I was on the bus, headed for Seattle, hours and hours away from anywhere.

The woman next to me on the bus shook my arm, "Sweetheart, sweetheart, wake up. You're in Seattle, isn't that where you said you were going?" She was plump and sweet and when she touched me I heard hospital noises, machines and voices. I saw her in a white uniform, starched with white soft shoes. She was trotting down a vast hallway, stethoscope around her neck.

I shook the sleep off, peeled my head from the cold window. "Are you a nurse?" I asked.

"Well, funny you should say, I just signed up for nursing school. I'm coming back from Portland visiting my aunt and I start school this week."

"You'll make it."

"I hope so, they say it is awfully hard and competitive."

"You'll make it."

"How do you know? How did you know I was going into nursing?"

"I see things. When people touch me, sometimes I see things." I don't know why I told her, I had never told anyone before, let alone a stranger on the bus.

She looked at me odd, her head tilted to one side and her lips pursed. "I think I know someone you should know. Where do you live?"

"Nowhere."

"Seriously?"

"Seriously."

"A girl your age, pardon my prying, is too young to be homeless."

"Things didn't work out for me the way they work out for normal people."

"Honey, I think I have a place you can crash out, if you want."

"Where?" I asked. Anything would beat the streets of a town I had never laid eyes on before, a rainy town at that. I could see rain and grey surrounding the bus, drowning the buildings on either side of the street.

"I left my husband a year ago. He used to beat the crap out of me, hard to imagine isn't it, looking at the size of me," she laughed. "There's a safe house I stayed in for awhile. They don't ask questions, it's all women, or girls, and there are counselors there if you need them. They don't feed you, but it's warm and dry and clean. You want me to take you there?"

"Okay," I said quietly.

"Well, first we've gotta get off this stinky bus."

I followed her home. We walked sixteen blocks to her apartment. She carried her overnight bag. I carried my satchel. We could have been mother and daughter. "I take the bus everywhere," she said. "I never learned how to drive."

Her apartment was small, overlooking a city street. I liked the sounds that rose up through the windows, street traffic, and horns, sounds of laughter and shouting, the screech of brakes. It reminded me of Ling and the old hotel room I had called my home.

"Are you a runaway?" she asked me.

"Uh..."

"Don't tell me, it's best if I don't know. Do you want to stay here tonight? You could crash on my couch and I could take you over to the safe house in the morning. I don't start school for a few days so it's no problem for me."

"I would like that, thank you."

She made us a dinner, ravioli out of a can and toast. She told me all about her old life, she had grown kids. She told me about the fear she lived through and the strength it took to leave her husband. She told me about the incredible women she met through counseling sessions. "No man will ever touch me like that again. I broke that cycle, and now I am going to be a nurse so that I can help other women like me. If I see someone come into the emergency room looking the way I used to look, I will say something, you bet I will. Look at this nose. Been broken five times. Do you know how much blood you can lose from your nose? A lot."

I fell asleep to the flashing neon lights from the sporting goods store across the street. It was very peaceful; clean blankets, a warm couch and a full belly. Her blankets smelled like lilacs. I dreamt of Peace. He was holding me in his arms and telling me to dogpaddle. "When it gets to be too much, dogpaddle," he said. We were lying on a beach and watching the waves crash to shore. Dogpaddle.

The safe house was five miles away. We caught the bus and Irene; that was her name, introduced me to the lady at the desk. She had a soft face and a soft handshake. She had me fill out a form. "Just for us, we don't share any information." I put down a fake last name and listed my first name as Raven, just in case I was on a cereal box or a milk carton somewhere. I put down no address or phone number.

"No previous address?" she asked me.

"Not that I can remember."

"Okay. The deal is you can stay four months. We try to rotate women through here because there are a lot of you that need help. As part of the stay you have to help with chores. We have a cleaning schedule that rotates. We have a kitchen, but we don't provide any meals. If you want to keep something in the refrigerator or cupboard, make sure it has your name on it otherwise it will be eaten. If you use drugs or alcohol while staying here, we ask you to leave. You will get fresh blankets and towels every week, just like a fancy hotel. We ask that you talk to our counselors once a week, more if you feel you need it. We have group sessions as well. This is a safe house, which means we tell no one outside of this house who the other tenants are or where they come from. Our location is secret as well. Only the women who are here, or who have been here and our personnel know what it is we do here. Some of our guests have very violent people looking for them, do you understand?"

"Yes." I stood stock still, like I was in the military.

"Welcome to Compassion House."

Irene hugged me; there were tears in her eyes. "I will come and visit you," she said, "and bring you some food. My little Raven." She held me away from her, looked me in the eyes. "Good luck. And don't forget, there's someone I want you to meet."

I took to wandering the streets by day, exploring the city. It was definitely grey, but very beautiful and when the sun came out it was stunning. I made it back to the safe house every night before dark and usually grabbed a novel or a textbook from the community library room to take to my room. I shared my room with another young girl. Her name was Amber; she looked to be about eighteen or so, hard to tell. She was really skinny, skinny to the bone and her body was scabbed up. She itched her skin night and day and hardly spoke. She was short and dainty with bobbed blonde hair that bounced when she walked. Amber slept a lot and snored when she was on her back. It was comforting in a way, because here was another girl who was like me. Alone.

Irene stayed true to her word and brought bags of food every week. Although I still had plenty of money from the hundred dollars Miguel gave me and the money I had saved in San Francisco, I welcomed the food and shared with Amber. I put both of our names on everything and told her to take what she wanted. She smiled at me for the first time; her teeth were beautifully straight and pearly white.

"Why are you named Raven?" she asked me one night. It was the second time she had spoken to me. "I mean, you're hair is red, ravens are black as the night."

"I am called Raven because I represent all my relatives who have died. I am the last one to walk the earth." It sounded very mythic.

"I'm sorry."

"It's okay. You know what it's like to be alone."

"Yes."

I started hanging out at an Irish restaurant on the east side of the city. I could ride the bus and be there in under twenty minutes and the waiters, well three of them had hair as red as mine. One had an Irish accent and sea blue eyes. He wore a jaunty Greek fishing cap when he was serving and he was there on Wednesdays and Thursdays, so I was always there on Wednesdays and Thursdays.

I sat at a table in the window so I could watch people walk by. I always brought a book so that I could look busy, but really I watched the waiter. His name was Michael, so close to Miguel. When I thought of Miguel I felt a pain in my chest on the right side of my heart. Everyone you love leaves a hole whether you like it or not. I think I did love Miguel, and Peace and my dear sweet Ling. I loved Window too, and of course Ling's aunt and uncle and most of all, my mother, whose face was getting harder and harder to picture every day. Before arriving at Irene's, I had not looked in a mirror since I had left San Francisco. It was shocking to see myself, to see how long my hair was and the tone of my skin, which looked tan and surprisingly healthy from the outdoor living. I was skinny, though, and my hair was as red as ever, my eyes were greener than I remembered. They were the color of the sea. I looked older than sixteen; thank god. I didn't want to be picked up now, but how many people had time to look for a pathetic girl who ran away over two years ago?

Michael stopped at my table. "You sure come in here a lot."

"Yea, yea, I do."

"Do you have a boyfriend?"

"No."

"Far out," he said walking away from the table. That was it; he didn't talk to me again for almost two weeks.

It was a Wednesday when Michael spoke again. He lingered at my table, slowly pouring my coffee. "Do you go to school around here?"

"No. I am out of school, graduated early, a prodigy."

He laughed. "Yea, a smart girl. I'm going nights to community college. I want to be a mathematician."

A mathematician? Perhaps he was too smart for me, for a lying prodigy.

"Are you looking for a job?" he asked.

"Do I look like it?"

"Well...all you ever order is coffee so I figured you are probably broke or a college student or both since they go together."

"I suppose a job would be good. Are you hiring here?"

He scratched his chin, bounced his blue eyes around the room. "I think they are hiring a dishwasher."

Bingo. That's all I knew how to do. "I washed dishes in Chinatown."

"On the other side of town?"

"No. In San Francisco."

His eyes grew wide and lighter. "I've always wanted to go to San Francisco, what's it like? I read about it in the paper. Isn't that where a lot of stuff happens? You know, I see they have marches there and stuff."

I laughed. "Yea, a lot happens there. It's beautiful."

"Well, if you think you want the dishwasher job, you have to come back tomorrow and talk to Joe and you have to go out with me tonight. I'll take you to the theater. How's that?"

"Okay."

"Where do I pick you up? I have a car."

"Uh…" Not at the safe house. "I'll meet you here because I'll be in this neighborhood anyway."

He shrugged. "Okay. See you at seven."

Six o'clock I was in my room at the safe house when Amber came in crying. Her nose was snotty, tears were on her cheeks, her mascara running, eyeliner smeared around her eyes.

"What is it?" I asked.

"I'm getting kicked out. I shot up last night and they knew. They fucking knew. How do they know? I needed it bad, I mean can't they give that to me?"

Amber and heroin. Scabs and skin and bones. "Where will you go?"

"Out on the street I guess. I just can't fucking believe it. I need this place." She started sobbing. I put my arms around her. She smelled like baby powder.

"Amber, take my sweater. It's going to get cold out there if it rains. And take some of the food from the kitchen."

"I can't eat. I just want to get high. I'll take the sweater though."

She threw her stuff in a grimy canvas bag, wrapped my sweater around her thin shoulders and was gone. Her hollow eyes stayed with me for weeks and every time I slept, I dreamt of her falling into a deep crevasse on a mountaintop covered in snow and ice.

I caught the bus and made it to the Irish restaurant by seven. Michael was waiting for me, laughing and talking to another waiter. When I walked in he searched me top to bottom, then smiled. "Let's go," he said.

The movie was good. It was getting to be late summer, August actually and the air was heavy and thick, and felt good draped about me. We went to see "Come September" and had yellow buttery popcorn and soda. Michael held my hand and his fingers were light and soft. He paid for everything and outside the movie theater I thanked him. He leaned down and kissed me, once then twice, harder, backing me up against the wall where the movie poster hung.

"Let's go to your place," he said. "Where do you live?"

"I don't really have a place. I crash on a friend's couch, so that's out."

"Oh, that's right, you're from San Francisco."

Right. Wrong.

"I live at home with my mom. Let's go eat then."

We walked back to the Irish restaurant because Michael said we could eat there for free. We shared a shepherds pie and salad and held hands in the candlelight.

"Next time we go somewhere in my car."

The television in the bar was on and I saw footage of Vietnam from where I was sitting. War. I didn't understand the conflict. I had to read the paper more, get educated. Michael was watching too. "Tell me about it," I said.

"Tell you about the war? Huh. It's, well it's senseless, but necessary I guess. It's about communism; if we don't fight the Viet Cong we all eat potato rations and get told what kind of job to hold. I hate it, but my brother's going. He wants to go before they call him up."

"Call him up?"

"Yea, his draft number, you know. He's signed up for the draft. He leaves in October if he passes the physical. I'm in school so maybe I won't get called up."

"Don't," I grabbed his hand, laced my fingers into his.

"Oh, okay then I won't."

He wanted to walk me home, but I convinced him to put me on the bus. He kissed me very sweetly at the bus stop and I waved to him out the grimy window. When I got back to the safe house, I found that I had a new roommate. She was a very large woman; sleeping on her side, bleach blonde hair sticking out of her blankets. I tried to be quiet. All night I dreamt of war and woke up crying to the sound of my mother's voice, only it wasn't my mother, it was Irene downstairs talking to the front desk attendant; Maureen or Marla depending on what day it was.

I wandered downstairs and Irene embraced me in a big bear hug.

"I don't have school today so I came by to make good on my promise."

"What promise?" I was still sleepy from the dreams.

"My promise to introduce you to someone…remember? Now go take a shower, I'll wait for you and we'll go out to the pancake house and have some breakfast first. My treat of course!"

Over bad comforting coffee at the pancake house Irene told me about her school, about one of the campus custodians whom she found to be "very sexy".

"Talk to him," I said.

"Not yet. I have to feel out his energy first. I never want a violent male again and I just can't trust my initial instincts yet."

"You trusted me."

"You don't have a penis," she laughed so loud the waitresses couldn't help but stop what they were doing. I laughed, too, and the pancakes were good and sweet.

She took me uptown. We rode the bus, and then walked the Queen Anne area until we came to an older apartment building. Not old and run down, but old and preserved and stylish. She rang a front bell and I heard a craggily voice. "Yeess?"

"It's me honey. I brought Raven." A buzzer sounded, we were in.

Up the stairs it smelled like old lady rose perfume. I liked it. It was comforting.

The door opened and there she was. She couldn't have been over five feet. She was tiny and grey, grey hair, grey pinkish skin with red rouge and red lips. She wore blue eye shadow over her sea green eyes, eyes that looked familiar somehow. She stared at me hard, looked me down, then up, then down, then up, then square in the eye. "Hmmpff," she said. She stepped back to let us enter, shuffling in bedroom slippers. "You're the one." "I know what you know." "Don't think I don't know." "I was young like that." These lines came out of her arbitrarily as she shuffled to the kitchen, filled a teapot with water and put it on the gas stove.

Was she senile? Irene looked at me, nodded. Yes, senile, that was it, a crazy old lady. Maybe Irene wanted me to meet her so that she could have some companionship. Maybe Irene was afraid to come alone, because of all the gibberish.

The teapot whistled. I could still hear her muttering, but the sentences were indiscernible. She shuffled back into the sitting room holding a golden tray with a beautiful teapot and three Japanese teacups. I was sure it was merely a matter of seconds before she toppled over, but she made it, keeping the tray steady as a rock. She motioned for us to sit on an antique Victorian settee. She sat in a beautiful stuffed pink chair with carved wooden arms. She set the tea tray on a large emerald green ottoman between us.

"I am glad to meet you, Raven. Please pour the tea in a few minutes after it has steeped. We will be silent as we wait." Three minutes, five minutes. "Now please, Miss Raven, although I don't suppose that is your real name, but so be it."

I poured the tea, I felt sweat on my forehead, behind my neck. Why had Irene brought me to this crazy lady?

"Thank you my dear," she accepted the cup. "Irene told me you may be extraordinary and she was right. I know you see. It is no secret from me."

"What?" I looked at her, looked at Irene.

"I told her," Irene said. "I told her what you told me. You know, about the visions when you touch people. Miss Alexandria is a clairvoyant and a tarot reader among other things."

Miss Alexandria nodded to me, acknowledging this fact. "You are afraid of your visions, aren't you Raven?"

"Yes."

"Pray, tell me your real name."

"Uh, Rosalene." I would not share my last name.

She closed her eyes and began to sway. When her eyes opened they were watering. "You have had much pain."

"Yes."

"You are lucky to have found Irene. Irene is a jewel. I shall teach you the tarot. This will help you with the visions. You see, you cannot control the visions and you can do very little about them because they are not of those nearest and dearest to you. When one sees the future of strangers, there is not much you can do to intervene. You are seeing their life lesson and that is the way it should be for them, hard to break. But with the tarot, you can see things in those closest to you, things they manifest for themselves. These things they can change, they can change the cause and effect if you will."

"Okay."

"Look in my eyes." I did, they had changed to electric green. "When you look in the mirror, you will find your eyes look the same as mine. You are a seer. I am sorry for you, it is a difficult gift to posses."

"It doesn't seem to help me much. I am always alone."

"Seers are always alone, that is part of the curse. Now listen and watch. Hand me the cards Irene." Irene went to a dark bureau against the wall, opened the top drawer and drew out a wooden box; inside was a deck of cards wrapped in silk, white silk.

Miss Alexandria asked me to shuffle the cards and cut them into three decks. She restacked them and laid the top cards into a careful configuration. It reminded me of the Asian ladies at the back of Ling's aunt's café, they read sticks, but the light in their eyes was the same. She began to tell me things, so many things; my head was spinning. "Your destiny is comings and goings, never permanence. You are a tree trunk and those around you; the people you love are the wind. You will find one true love," she said, "that will be forever, the rest will be like vapors in the water. But that one true love you will fail to recognize because you will be too lofty to see. Perhaps this love will return to you, it is not showing me that. But, my girl, you must hone your gift now or it will gain momentum and it will kill you, that I know."

What was she talking about? She was scaring me with her intensity and I was anxious to get out of the apartment, out into the air so I could breathe.

"Be this my gift to you. You come seven times to me. Each time we will read the cards and I will teach you the patterns to lie out. The cards are our guides. Then you will read for me, you will perfect your powers so that you can see those in your life nearest and dearest and help them with their manifestations. Are you afraid of me?"

Yes. "No."

"You are, I see, but it is only because you are afraid of yourself. Oh!" She looked startled. "You're mother is here." She closed her eyes. "She says to tell you that she is sorry. She sees you are a beautiful woman and she cannot stay in this realm, she says she must go. She loves you, she must pass, and people are waiting for her. She says that it is you who brought her back. She is afraid of your power."

I started to cry. Irene brought me at tissue. The tears came and came and I could not stop. I started shaking, sobbing. Irene rubbed my shoulders. Miss Alexandria picked up her cards and wrapped them back in their silk.

"Now dears, I must rest. That was difficult. It is always difficult to lift the veil." Miss Alexandria shuffled to the door and held it open for us. Irene gathered me up and I managed to stop crying. "Next week, same time," she said.

Irene kissed her on the cheek, thanked her.

"Thank you," I said.

On the bus back Irene held my hand. "I am sorry your mother is dead Rosalene, or I mean Raven."

"Thank you Irene." I loved the feel of her hands. They were soft and puffy and big enough to cover my own.

"I will help take care of you as best I can."

"How did you meet Miss Alexandria?"

She laughed. "One night I stumbled out of the safe house and wandered the streets. I missed my husband so bad, you see you can miss someone even if they are terrible to you, and I did. I thought about catching a bus and going back to him, back to the fists and the slaps and the insults, I thought it might be worth it because I missed him so bad. The funniest thing though, I ended up wandering until I got tired thinking about it and I sat down right on Miss Alexandria's apartment steps and "poof" there she was, walking up with a small bag of groceries, her hair fixed up proper, her tiny little boots. I felt I had stepped back in time. She saw me, her green eyes looked me over and up and she held out her hand and brought me inside. She made me tea and read my cards, I didn't even know what a tarot was, I thought it was some kind of a snail. She said she saw a strength in me and she told me I was a beautiful new spirit and she gave me hope, hope in a night of despair and we have been friends ever since. She saved my life. If I would have gone back to Kyle, I would surely be dead by now, inside and out. Now, that's enough of me, it's time to put you back together again."

I squeezed her hand tighter and thought about my mother. Did Miss Alexandria see her? I wished on a far away cloud; I wished I could see her.

I had forgotten I had told Michael that I would check on the dishwashing job so I got off at a stop near the Irish restaurant. I walked in and the restaurant was packed tight, sounds and noise everywhere. Michael was working, waving at me as he bustled by. "Is Joe in?" I asked the small girl at the front desk.

"Yea, but he is really busy. Do you want a table?"

"No. I'm looking for a job."

"Here's an application. You can sit over there and fill it out."

She dismissed me with a wave of her hand to a corner chair that sat next to a small table with a plastic gnome on top and littered newspapers. The application was one page, but the questions were more than I could handle. Name. Address. Phone. Previous experience. I didn't know what to do. I crumpled it up, pushing it to the bottom of my bag and for the second time that day my eyes swelled with tears as I pushed open the heavy door. Shit. I didn't have an address and what the hell would I use for a reference? I knew nobody except the girls at the halfway house. All us half way people with fake names and no past that could be spoken of.

Michael caught up with me part way down the block; he was out of breath, still wearing his apron. "I've got to get back to work, but I'll see you tonight okay? Meet me here at eight o'clock."

"Sure," I said. I got the wave when he grabbed my elbow. It was a river, a weird dark river and he was on a strange shaped boat and there were jungle noises, gunfire. He stood in the boat, at the bow. He was sweaty, his red hair wild and disheveled, his camouflage shirt dirty and torn. He had a rifle in one hand, and the other shielded his eyes. He leaned and spit in the water. A trail of spit left his mouth in slow motion and then I heard a loud popping noise, and where he should have been, I saw only red, everywhere red, a red flash in my head, fast and explosive. I gasped and doubled over with nausea. I caught my stomach with one hand and a pole beside me with the other. It took all my strength not to vomit on the pebbled sidewalk.

"Are you okay," Michael looked at me sweet and soft and his eyes glinted so blue in the sunlight, his gorgeous red hair and his soft lips. I hated my sight.

"Michael, do not go to war."

"I'm not. Do you need to go to the hospital?"

"I mean it Michael, stay away from that war, and just keep doing math."

"Jesus Raven, I'm not going to war, not as long as I can help it. I've gotta get back. I told Joe about you, so fill out the application." He kissed me. "See you baby."

I could not catch the bus for over an hour, I could only manage sitting. I sat on a bench and watched pedestrian traffic and waited for the shock of the vision to subside. Why did I have to see something so horrific about someone so close? But we weren't that close, I had very few feelings for him. I was wildly attracted to him, but I had not given my heart, not like my Ling or Miguel. This was different. I could keep my distance from Michael, of that I was sure. I could have sex with him and leave him in the same day.

That night we went out in his Dodge Dart. We drove around, drank a bottle of cheap strawberry wine and ended up on the waterfront, walking and talking, holding hands, touching hips and torsos. He smelled good, like salt and smoky bacon. We chased seagulls, our voices mixing with the night air as we ran. We drove around some more and Michael drove us to an elementary school parking lot, surrounded by trees and greenery. We started kissing and steaming the windows and Michael undressed me quickly. He slid his pants off and we crawled over the front seat, into the back. I remembered my condoms were in the room at the safe house. "I have nothing," I said.

"I'll pull out," his voice was quick and desperate, "I'll pull out and then I'll look for something. I probably have something…I just really want you right now."

The kisses on the neck, on the breastbone, on the breast, on my thighs, I couldn't breathe and the heat from my body could have fed a hundred fires. His body was molded above me and around me and then under me and back on top and then he was in me, moving fast. Slow, then faster still until he screamed and pulled out. He was laughing, "I'm too late, god that was good. I'm too late, damn!"

It took me a minute to realize why he stopped and what he was saying and then I felt it, the sticky hot wetness leaking between my legs. I held his naked body above me. I looked out the window at the streaky reflection of the parking lot lights and I knew at that moment that I was pregnant, and that finally someone in this world wouldn't leave me, someone would stay.

Two days later I got a call from the Irish restaurant. I had uncrumpled the application and lied all over it and had left it with the snotty girl at the front the night before. I lied about my age, my last name, made up references, wrote down a fake address and phone. I put down Ling's aunt's restaurant under previous employment and listed the farm where I had lived and worked. That seemed like a lifetime ago, but if I closed my eyes I could still smell the woods and the wood smoke. Joe interviewed me in a tiny backroom decorated with shamrocks and truck magazines. "You've got the job," he said.

"Thanks, Michael said this is a great place to work."

"Actually, Michael didn't show up for work today."

Three weeks at the restaurant. Three weeks of no Michael. The front hostess said he better not come back. "He's fired," she said, popping her gum.

Three weeks and the nausea had begun. I felt weak and hot and sweaty all the time. My time was almost up at the safe house. The more I thought about it, the more twisted up and nauseous I became, so I tried not to think. Not to think at all. Pretend you're not pregnant. Maybe get rid of the baby, but that thought made me feel even more alone. I found Michael's phone number in Joe's employment files and one night after work I called him from the house phone at Compassion House. A very pert voice answered the phone, "Hello?"

"Is Michael there?"

"Who is this may I ask?"

"Just a friend."

"Well, friend, Michael moved to the coast."

"The coast?" What the hell did that mean?

"Yes, to Oak Harbor. I'll tell him you called." She hung up.

The line went dead. "Yes, tell him I'm pregnant." Open your palm and out he drops. Love in the night and gone in the day. I was due to see Miss Alexandria soon.

"You're aura has changed." She shuffled ahead of Irene and I in her bedroom slippers. She had just let us in; Irene had brought her a bundle of sunflowers from the corner market. "I do love yellow," she said as she arranged them in a clear glass vase. "Now the tea."

Once the tea ritual had been satisfied she turned her piercing green eyes upon me. "Tell me what you carry inside of you."

"Uh...I..." My mouth flopped open and shut like a fish. I could not speak coherently. How could she tell?

Irene turned her eyes upon me and her soft hand grabbed mine. I hung my head, very embarrassed. "What is it Raven?" Irene asked.

"I had sex with this boy at the Irish restaurant and now I think, well I think..."

"You know!" Miss Alexandria pointed a bony accusing finger at me. "Don't lie to yourself. This complicates everything."

Yes. Sixteen. Pregnant. Homeless. Alone.

"This means we have to move faster. You must learn to manage your gift before this baby is born."

"I saw something terrible about the baby's father. What can I do? I saw him being killed; being shot and I don't know what to do with that. Do I try to find him and tell him? Can I change that?"

"What do you mean find him? Did he take off?" Irene asked.

"He moved to the coast."

"So he gets you pregnant and then he moves to the coast?"

Miss Alexandria cleared her tiny throat. "Rosalene, do you believe that we manifest our own destinies or are our destinies mapped out for us from the beginning?"

"Miss Alexandria, if we manifest our own destinies then I have done a terrible job of creating mine. I don't think I can believe that I am responsible for all that has happened to me."

"Then that is your answer. If you see destiny as prewritten you are incapable of changing your visions."

"What do you believe?" I asked her.

"I believe that knowledge unlocks the key to every door, even the ethereal doors. Now let's get started."

Irene and I spent three hours learning the tarot, the meanings of the cards, the relationship in the layout. The colors and the magic of the cards enveloped me and I felt excited and safe in Miss Alexandria's lair. "Next time we go deeper, you learn to see visions whenever you desire. Come next week." She shuffled us out the door into the apartment stairwell.

On the bus back Irene started crying. "I am sorry Rosalene. I am sorry for you."

"Irene, I have to leave the safe house in one week. I don't know where to go."

"Let me talk to Marla. There is a home for pregnant teens on Queen Anne hill, I'll see about getting you in there. We may have to fudge some documents. Do you want this baby, Rosalene?"

"The baby wants me Irene and that is amazing to me."

I called Irene several times as the end of my week grew near, but all I got was ringing and ringing. I knew she had school; she wouldn't disappear too, would she? I had placed more faith in her and Miss Alexandria than I had in all of mankind. "Tomorrow you need to vacate," Maureen told me as I walked by her desk to my room. My roommate was sleeping, that was all she did. She snored, she slept, and she smelled.

I packed my satchel, I would not be able to come back tomorrow after work. Should I go to Irene's and sit on her steps and wait for her to rescue me once again? I was afraid of losing her and if I expected too much from her, "Poof", she would be gone. Better to just figure it out. Don't count on anyone; that was the mantra.

After work I ate my employee meal and almost threw up. I spent ten minutes catching my breath at the employee table before I could even stand and make my way out the door. I had my pack, all my worldly possessions in one overstuffed worn satchel.

"Movin' out?" Joe asked me.

"Something like that."

"Well…," he looked at me intently, "see you tomorrow." His big hands fidgeted at his sides. He was sweet, dark hair, soft brown eyes, and a nose too big for his face. I felt a pang of jealousy for his wife. I bet he was nice to her, bought her flowers, built fires in the fireplace and curled up with her under soft blankets on the couch in front of the television. Or perhaps he twirled her in the kitchen to the beat of Latin music.

I slept outside that night. It was just September so it wasn't that cold out, but I had given away my sweater and left my pea coat on the farm so I felt the dampness deep in my bones. I walked the city looking for the perfect spot and ended up prowling neighborhoods above the Irish restaurant. I felt like the "Little Match Girl" gazing into window fronts, spying on people's lives, and wishing I lived in their houses, lived somewhere, anywhere. I curled up under a rhododendron plant in the corner of someone's yard. It was even a little cozy under there and it smelled like clean earth. I woke to a dog barking and a feeling like I could be peed on at any moment. I headed to the YMCA. I had gotten my first paycheck and still had some money left so I could afford the minimal usage fee to use the showers and gain access to the gymnasium. I took advantage of this and after my shower, curled up on one of the bleachers and slept some more. This became my routine for four days and three nights, until Irene found me at the restaurant and enveloped me in one of her big bear hugs.

"I made arrangements for you to stay in the home for unwed mothers. It is a very nice old home with thirteen rooms, three meals a day if you need them and people to talk to, but…"

"But what?" I had just finished my shift so Irene and I went outside to the sidewalk. I stood stock-still and her feet kicked pebbles, litter, anything she could find. "But what Irene?"

"It's very Christian."

"I don't care about that. I'm not afraid of God, he doesn't even know my name."

"Well, they don't believe in young women getting pregnant you know. It goes against their views, so..."

"So why would they want to help then?"

"Well, they expect...they expect...they expect you to give the baby up after it is born. They are willing to take care of the unwed mother knowing that after the baby's born the baby will be placed with a good, religious family. It's their way of righting a wrong."

The street changed shape, cars swam in and out of lanes, street signs waving and bouncing. I could taste bile in the back of my throat. "I need to sit down, Irene, I'm going to be sick."

"Oh honey, yes, yes, over here." She guided me to the same bench I recovered on after I had seen Michael explode in my vision.

"I can't do that Irene." I barely heard my own voice. "I've lost everything I've ever had, I can't lose my baby, too, not on purpose."

"I know."

"I'll be fine where I'm at."

"Where is that?" The soft afternoon light bathed her hair in gold. Street sounds, people sounds, a bus going by. "You don't have anywhere, do you?"

"No."

"Well, listen, I have a plan..."

So I moved in the next day and it was sheer luxury. Clean sheets that smelled like roses, fluffy white towels, soft blankets and puffy chairs and downstairs, a pool; a real pool for big fat pregnant mothers to float in. The only draw back was the checkups with the doctors, the probing of their fingers and the periodic blood tests. That and the creepy janitor that looked right through you to your panties and bra.

I had a room to myself and made a few friends with the other mothers. I was able to work for the first six months; then I was required to rest. They wanted the healthiest, plumpest baby they could get. They wanted to get their money's worth, I suppose. I saved my money in a sock inside my satchel, which I kept packed at all times. I planned on taking one of the fluffy towels when the time came.

Joe at the restaurant called me in his office one slow afternoon and sat me down in the brown office chair beside his desk. "Can I help you with anything Raven? Because my wife and I, I was telling her about your, hmm…situation, we would like to help you if you need it."

"That's really nice of you, Joe, but I have a place to live right now."

"Yes, you are at the Protestant Home for Unwed Mothers aren't you?"

"How did you know?"

"They called to check on your…umm…fitness. See if you were okay at work. You know, not under too much stress or anything."

"Oh."

"Well, just keep in mind that if you need anything…"

"I will, thanks." I stood up, one hand supporting the small of my back. "Oh, Joe," I paused. "Did you ever hear from Michael again?"

"Oh, you haven't heard? He joined the army. Right there in Oak Harbor; got himself signed up."

"Oh." I felt a wave of dizziness. I steadied myself on the brown chair.

"You were real good friends weren't you?"

"Yes, you could say that."

"Maybe you should track him down."

"Maybe."

So that was it. I knew what would become of my baby's father. If you see something does it automatically come to pass? I had asked Miss Alexandria that and she said if circumstances remained the same, yes, it came to pass. I swore on that day that I would never tell my baby the truth about its father. I could never let on that I saw a horrible thing and was unable to change that horrible thing. It was as if I sent him to die.

Miss Alexandria taught me to control the visions. After six lessons with her I was able to control the sight to a certain extent. If a wave came over me and it was a complete stranger, sometimes I was able to turn it off, to disconnect. And when I wanted to see something, I was slowly gaining the power to go to the spot where the visions came. I was born a witch I guess.

Irene was true to her word, she had helped me falsify all the documents and we mapped out our plan very carefully. I was to call her the moment the contractions came, from a pay phone down the street, never from the house. There was to be no trace of her involvement. It was like living a spy novel. But what was a contraction? I hoped I would know it when it hit. I tried hard to see my future, but I couldn't. I was too close, too scared, working too hard to survive. My body was growing bigger and bigger and I had to give up working. My only outings were wandering around the city and visiting Miss Alexandria.

"I don't feel your baby having the gift," she said one afternoon, her gnarled fingers stretched tight across my belly.

"Good."

"You may be able to teach her, but, I don't know, without the inherent gift it is difficult, to say the least. The connection is hard."

"I don't want my baby to have the gift, the gift is a curse!"

"Nonsense," she shook her white hair wildly. "The gift is an honor and you are chosen, Rosalene. Now I have a gift for you."

"Why do you keep calling it her?"

"Because she is a girl. Hush! No more talking, I need to present something to you." She handed me a cedar box, very plain and simple. I opened it and it revealed a white silk cloth. Inside the cloth was a stack of tarot cards, very colorful and wild. I could feel the energy resonating from the deck.

"That was my first set of cards," Miss Alexandria looked teary eyed. "I want you to have them. They will guide you along your difficult path. Just remember, perceive everything with lightness and grace. You will be leaving soon and I need you to have these."

"I don't think I'll be leaving soon, I mean I have nowhere to go. Miss Alexandria, I don't know what to say, these cards are magical."

"Yes."

"Thank you."

"Yes."

The contractions came a few months later and it was impossible not to know what they were. I was doubled over with pain coming out of the pool, but I could let no one know. I tried to stand straight and tall, wait calmly, staring at the wall. Breathe, in and out and in and out. It passed. I quickly made my way to my room; dressed, left my wet, stretched out swimsuit on the floor, grabbed one of the fluffy white towels and stuffed it in my satchel. "Goodbye," I said softly to the air, "thanks for everything."

I padded softly through the kitchen and out the back door in to the garden, through the yard and out the side gate to the alley between the properties. No one had seen me; the house was usually quiet in the afternoons. All the helpers and the priests were praying I guess. Sneaking away with my life and my pack felt familiar and my throat caught thinking of the day I had left my home. How many years ago was that? It seemed like three lifetimes had passed. I walked to the phone booth Irene and I had agreed on and called the number Irene had given me. One ring, two rings…intense pain. I gripped the edge of the phone booth. Breathe. Breathe. "Hello," finally.

"Irene, it's happening."

"Okay, I'll meet you at the spot."

We had agreed on a location that was hidden from foot and car traffic; a small bench behind a garden shop in an alley. The bench was wooden, carved with cupids and water lilies. I liked it. I waited and waited and the pain was very intense. I thought about the farm and how good it smelled in the crisp mornings of winter and spring. I closed my eyes, tried to go back there, smell the wood smoke; see Miguel's smiling face. I couldn't. All I could see was Michael's face, so young and fresh and I could feel his hands caressing my back. "Damn it," I said aloud. I started to weep, slow at first and then faster until I found myself sucking in air, holding my hands over my face, gripping my forehead with my fingers, trying to hold on. I was alone again, alone, alone, alone. The baby moved inside me. I stopped, still as a hunted bird. I was not alone.

Irene came in a car driven by another woman. She smiled and held her arms as wide as the ocean. I cried when I fell against her. "Don't be scared," she said. "You're not alone."

We drove to Irene's apartment and she wrapped a big coat around me before we went inside. She wanted to hide the pregnancy. The woman with her was tall and thin, her black hair piled high into a bun, brown smiling eyes. Her name was Josephine and she smelled like the swimming pool towels.

Irene and Josephine went to work straightening, moving things, laying out towels, sheets. Josephine was a midwife. "I practiced in

Canada for years," she said, "but they don't want midwives here. I want to go back, but I stay for my husband. He is a native here; he likes it. So I am a baby deliverer with no babies to deliver, until today." She laughed and her laugh was like fairy bells tinkling in the wind.

Having that baby on a foam pad on the floor of Irene's apartment was the hardest and the most beautiful thing I had ever done. The earth contracted and swelled, and then when her head crowned, the earth cracked. Small visceral cracks and when her shoulders passed through and she slipped into Josephine's arms, the earth exploded into a million beautiful pieces of silver and light. She cried. I had been in labor fifteen hours. Josephine patted me and told me I did great. The baby was swaddled and put into my arms and when I looked into her eyes, I knew that she would have a hard life, but I would be with her always. She was a person, a lovely breathing person who wouldn't walk away from me. I named her Emma. Emma Jean. She took my last name. Josephine filled out the paperwork and I used my real name. I was seventeen now so if anyone came looking for me, at least I was close to being eighteen and on my own. The home for unwed mothers never knew my real name; still I had to be careful I wasn't spotted on the streets. I had signed the baby away in Raven's name, not my own.

Irene let me stay for a while, but the baby would cry. Irene would pace. "I don't want the neighbors thinking something's up. I told them you were my niece, visiting." She looked out the blinds. "You were reported as missing. I saw it in the paper. They had a tiny picture of you and your other name and well…I'm just nervous. We have to get you out of here pretty soon." She had risked her life for me, her potential career, and Josephine had done the same. I would never forget that.

"I must leave." I held sleeping Emma tight, her dark head lolled to the side.

"Yes. Let's put our heads together. Don't go out of this apartment until we've figured it out."

The next day Irene came home late. She looked tired and haggard. She dropped her book bag on the floor and sat down heavy on the couch. "I brought you some books on baby care. I want you to keep them, take them with you, because it gets complicated."

"Complicated?" I think I knew what she meant because Emma Jean had cried off and on all day and I could not figure out what was wrong with her. I tried to feed her, but my nipples were killing me. I changed her, rocked her, everything, and she still cried.

"Yes, complicated. At least you don't have anyone hitting on you. Every time the baby cried he whacked me one, as if it were my fault. 'Make her shut up!' he'd scream at me."

"I'm sorry Irene." And I was. Irene was the nicest, most generous, full of love person I had known, even more so than my memories of my own mother. And here some guy used her to punch on.

"It's over now Rosalene." She looked at me; her eyes brimmed with tears of exhaustion. "I'm good now."

She held the baby while I made pasta. We shared dinner and some wine. Well, she had wine; I had grape juice on ice. The baby slept, finally.

"I bet you're tired of sleeping on the couch," she said.

"No Irene. I'm more grateful to you than you could ever know. I love you," I said. And I did.

Silence passed while she took it in. I knew she had kids, but she never talked about them much. Once over a donut and coffee she had told me a little. She gazed out the window at the sheeting rain when she spoke. "They never wanted to face up to the beatings, even though they were my star witnesses. It was hard on them. They had to block it out. They see me as a victim, a screw-up that somehow deserved to be hit. Much as I saw myself, I must say. No, I'm waiting to get my life completely together and then I will contact them. They don't know my exact whereabouts yet, I have to be safe." The rain poured down, grey light shining in on the tears on her cheeks. I already knew life was hard, I didn't know it could keep getting harder.

"Oh!" She jumped up, almost spilling her wine. "I forgot to tell you!"

"What? What?"

"My friend from school, we got to talking. I told her I had a friend who was looking for a place to live outside the city and she said that her brother had a friend with a mobile home on the river. She said that it was empty and he was looking for someone to live in it, you know, just to keep an eye on the place, make sure no one trespassed or anything. It sounds like it would be cheap or maybe even free. And it would be far enough out it would be a good hideaway for you until things blew over at the unwed mother home." She scrunched up her face. "We should dye your hair though, that red is a dead give away. How about black?"

"Uh…" I knew I could live in the woods. I had done that before, but not with a baby. And black? Well, I was Raven for so long, I guess I might as well look like a big black bird. "Okay. Do you think I can make it?"

"I know you can make it. It won't be easy honey. But nothing ever is. Let's toast." She held up her wine glass, clinked it against my glass of grape juice, her face as wide open as a clear June sky.

I moved two weeks later. Irene borrowed a car and drove me out to the country. "Where are we?" I asked her as the sky grew darker and the mountains grew taller.

"I think it's called North Bend, but it seems like the end of the earth, doesn't it?" She concentrated on the road. She had never driven. I looked at my new black hair in the rearview mirror. The baby slept in the back in a used car seat Irene found at the Goodwill. She had brought home bags of clothes, and diapers and plastic pants, little socks and blankets and a car seat. "I couldn't find a high chair, or cart it on the bus, so this will have to do, " she said. I cried with joy.

AT THE TABLE

Circles, everywhere circles; the circular table, the cards in a circle, the circle of hands joined by the circle of women. Three. A trio; a circle.

"I feel her." Rosalene swayed back and forth, her chair tipping. Her grip tightened on Kimmy and Emma. Kimmy's eyes were wide; Emma's slanted in disbelief. "She's coming…here I go."

Kimmy said timidly, "Mom?"

"I'm here my love…I didn't want to go, but I did…do you hear me?" Rosalene's lips moved, but the voice coming from inside her was different, lightened.

Kimmy said louder, "Mom?"

"Yes, yes, it's me." Rosalene's eyes were closed; her head thrown back, spittle came from her slightly broken lips.

"Mom, I can't do it. I can't do it without you. I tried. I want to come, I want to come with you." Old tears spilled from Kimmy's blue eyes.

"No! Find your way, I will wait for you. Someone will deliver you and see you with my eyes, I promise, just wait, just…" the voice faded. Rosalene opened her eyes and lifted her body upright.

"What happened?" Rosalene asked.

"This is such bullshit," Emma said.

Chapter Five: Kimmy; Justice

I loved college. It was an incredible place. I shared a room with a girl from Indiana. She had a twang in her voice and said "Wershington." She wore braces and chewed gum and tobacco. She spit in pop cans and left them around the room. That's the only thing that bothered me.

I signed up for a History of Jazz class. It was in the theater and the professor set up his stereo on the edge of the stage and we lounged about in the soft theater seats. He played Miles Davis and Thelonious Monk and closed his eyes and swayed when he listened. Occasionally he tapped a stick, hitting the edge of the stage in perfect rhythm. I was in love, not only with college and jazz, but also with him, Mr. Jeranos, the professor of History of Jazz. I started sitting in the front row, and when he closed his eyes I closed mine. When his body swayed, I swayed. When he tapped his stick, I tapped my foot. He was all I could think about. I wrote to Emma. "Don't you think he's a little old for you?" she asked in the letter she wrote back. "Oh well, fuck it," she went on to say, "and him!"

It was late September and the trees on campus were lit with pink and white blossoms. I wrote Emma and told her how pretty they were. “You, the nature freak, would love it,” I wrote, “and the birds sing to me when I walk through campus.”

I spent the next month and a half meeting people, socializing, and doing my homework in the library that smelled like old intelligent dust. I met college guys at parties, but I didn’t hook up with anyone. I kept thinking about Mr. Jeranos. One October day when I was leaving the library a guy sitting one table across from me picked up his books to leave at the same time I did. He caught up with me on the grassy slope leading toward the dorms.

“I was watching you,” he said. “I couldn’t study because I was watching you the whole time.” His eyes were deep brown and his hair shone black and red in the afternoon light. He had a dark beard and sideburns and pink cheeks. He was handsome and childlike at the same time. “You are the prettiest girl I’ve ever seen.”

"Thank you." I said. I stood still, my book bag heavy on my right shoulder.

"My name's Tom. Will you go to dinner with me?" he asked. His teeth were as white as sea foam and when he smiled I could see a dimple above his beard.

"Sure," I said.

We went to a restaurant in town. He told me to order whatever I wanted. He said he was twenty-three and trying to make his way out of school. "I want to be a teacher," he said. He ordered two drinks from the waitress, gin and tonics for both of us. She called Tom by his first name and said, "Sure thing," never asking once to see my ID.

During the dinner I got up and used the bathroom, checked my make-up, put on fresh lipstick. Tom was nice, but there was something I didn't like about him. He looked at me like I was dessert.

When I got back to the table there was a fresh drink for me, and Tom had ordered a crème brulee. "Eat that," he said pointing to the caramel colored dessert. "I want to watch you."

I ate slow and drank fast. Tom kept talking, but I could barely make out what he was saying. His lips moved faster than his voice. The room shifted. I was wasted. Emma and I could down a bottle and a half of wine between the two of us and smoke a few joints and still be able to function and I hadn't even finished two drinks. Maybe the bartender gave me a triple shot. Being drunk and stoned at the same time was a comfortable feeling for me. This wasn't.

I don't remember much else, except Tom undressing me. I was standing, I think, or leaning against something in his basement apartment and he stripped me. The next thing I remember was lying on my back, motionless while he rocked and pushed my naked body into the mattress. I wanted to say something, but my lips wouldn't work. I wanted to think something, but my mind could not wrap around any one thought long enough. My thoughts were visions on a far horizon and I sank into a deep quicksand.

I awoke the next morning with him on top of me again and me still naked. My head pounded. He stood up and looked down at my naked body.

"Splendid," he said. "Get dressed I'll drive you home."

I forgot about it. I pushed it to the far recesses of my mind and I focused on Mr. Jeranos. He was older. He was safe. I wanted my dad.

"Dad?" he answered on the first ring.

"Yes Kimmy? Do you need something?"

"I just wanted to hear your voice."

"Are you having fun?" he asked cheerily.

"Yea, I am."

A pause filled the phone line. It stretched from Tolt to Ellensburg and back again. "Uh...anything else?"

"No dad. That's it. Everything is good."

"That's my girl. I'll send you some spending money. I love you."

I hung up and stared out the dormitory window. The trees were changing their colors, the sky a dark shade of grey. I needed Emma. I needed the flute I had left behind in the box beneath my bed.

One afternoon, after class, I finally got to talk to Mr. Jeranos, person to person. He called me up to the stage, said my first name, and said my last name and I was shaking as I stood before him. I tried to be casual, lean on the stage edge, lower my voice. I lowered my eyelids, and tried to look as though I just came out of a gallery in New York City.

"Kimmy," he said, "Kimmy Franklin. I've been watching you and well...well, I see you really appreciate jazz."

"I love it."

"In that case, would you be interested in accompanying me to a jazz club a ways east next Saturday night?"

My voice was the size of a mouse caught in an enormous trap. "I'd like that." His voice warmed my legs.

"Great. I will pick you up in front of your dorm at six thirty next Saturday. I know which dorm you're in; it's in your records. Oh and Kimmy...bring some extra clothes, you know in case it gets late."

Shit. That was my next thought. I didn't have ID. I wasn't twenty-one, didn't he know that? If he knew where I lived didn't he know I was only eighteen for god's sake? I couldn't go to a club even if I was the bouncer.

"No problemo," my roommate Vanessa said. "Y'all can use my sister's ID. That's what I use. I think you can pass for her."

And I did. The bartender never even asked. The club was dim, the candles on the tables were red and the drink he ordered for me was in a tall cool glass with purple straws and a plastic monkey hanging from the side. He told me to call him by his first name, Jeno. The music was good.

"Do you want some tapas?" he asked.

What the hell were tapas? "Sure, that sounds great."

They were appetizers on beautiful china plates with tiny knives for spreading and tiny forks for spearing. The drink was definitely going to my head, so, when the music ended and he asked me if it was okay to get a room, of course I said yes. And after he had checked us in; while I waited in the car of course; I grabbed my duffel bag and followed him up the stairs. And when he asked me if I wanted to smoke a little "grass", of course I said yes. He took off his clothes and peeled back the bedspread. He stood next to me and took off my clothes. He unpacked two tall white candles and placed them in the ashtrays. He lit them and turned off all the lights.

"That music really does something to me. So do you Kimmy." He began stroking me everywhere. The candles bounced light in a circular motion, like a soft hurricane above us. All of a sudden I missed Rosalene and wished I were back home.

We saw a lot of each other. I rode my bike over to his house after school on Fridays and usually stayed until Sunday afternoon or so. We had sex all over the house on Friday nights. We listened to jazz at home and rarely went out on Saturday. We screwed ourselves pink in the bedroom after smoking a couple of bowls and having croissants and coffee on Sunday mornings.

"This doesn't mean you are getting an A," he said. "I keep my private and professional lives separate."

Right.

One Friday night we decided to walk up to town and get a pizza, which was unusual as Jeno didn't like to be seen around town too much with me. We were rarely in public and when we were, he cooled off on the touching. That night though, we did go out and were sitting down waiting for our pizza and salads when Dustin from my chemistry 101 class came and sat beside us.

"Kimmy you are looking so good after that quiz we had today. How did you do?" His leg was touching mine with a lot of pressure.

"Okay I guess. I was tired so I might not have done so great," I said. Dustin rested his hand on my thigh. I smiled.

"Is this your dad?" He looked at Jeno and extended his other hand.

"No, I am one of her professors and a family confidant," Jeno said with narrow eyes. "And I'd adore it if you took your hand off her thigh."

Dustin beat it, the pizza came and all of the small talk might as well have been to the wall. When we got back to the house, Jeno went to the liquor cabinet and poured himself vodka straight up. He added three ice cubes. He swallowed it down like an apple juice or a glass of Gatorade. Then he had another. He turned to me and stared, "Don't you ever go out on me. Do you hear me?"

"What?" I could feel my legs. They felt soft. I thought they might not be able to hold me if I weighed another ounce.

Jeno walked over to where I was standing and grabbed my upper arm. "I said don't you ever go out on me. That's clear and precise English, don't you think?"

That night he fucked me hard and I was thinking over and over in my mind that I should run or walk or at least put on my clothes, but a part of me liked it. The next morning I had four bruises where his fingers had laid into my flesh.

"I am so sorry," he said. He kissed the spots. "You make me lose my head."

The next Sunday I called Rosalene and she started to cry. "Oh Kimmy, I want you to come home. I did your reading. I see something very bad. It comes in a nice pretty wrapper so you won't recognize it. I asked the cards the direction you should go and they told me you should flee." Her voice was breathy.

"I can't leave. I can't give up college. If I don't have college I have nothing. I am not leaving."

"Kimmy I will chant for you, but you're going to be hurt."

"Mrs. J, I'm fine. My roommate is nice. The kids in my class are nice. My professors are…nice and I…I like the classes so far. They do make us study a lot. Maybe that's what you're seeing. I get awfully tired," I said.

"No, it's not that good kind of pain. If you won't listen to me, there is nothing I can do for you." The line went dead.

Shit, why did she do that? I went back to my room. Vanessa was gone, so I smoked a joint and tried to study. I couldn't concentrate, was it the pot, or was it Rosalene's warning? Maybe she saw the incident with Tom. I shouldn't have finished those drinks and I had been too easy with him. I learned my lesson. I was only going to go for mature men. I put on my sweats and went downstairs and unlocked my bike. In the dark I rode to Jeno's. His lights were still on in the living room. I knocked on the red door of his house. He answered the door in flannel pajama bottoms and no shirt.

"Aw, my little Kimmy. Come in my little treasure pot. What brings you here on a college night?" he asked.

"I can't sleep. Make love to me Jeno."

That was the beginning of my moving in. I stayed with Jeno night after night after night, never missing.

A strange thing happens when you are sleeping with your college professor. You don't fit in anywhere. You don't mingle well with students your age and you certainly can't mingle with the other professors and their wives. What do you do? You become a recluse and stay night after night with the professor making love and sleeping between his Egyptian cotton sheets. Sheets that Emma would die for, sheets she could never hope to have. Sheets she could never find at the clothing bank.

One night after geology class Julie Webb, my lab partner, asked me to go with her to a party.

"Come on Kimmy, a bunch of us are going and the varsity baseball team will be there. There's going to be a great big roasted lamb and sangria. I need you to come. I hate walking into parties alone," she said.

"Okay, I'll go. I don't want to stay late though." I knew Jeno expected me home. He looked for me to come up the drive on my bike. He questioned me whenever I was late and scrutinized my answers for lies or slips of truths.

The party was in a five-bedroom white house. A two-story peeling paint house with music blaring from the windows and occasional roars of shouting and hilarious laughter. Julie hooked her arm in mine and we made our way straight to the sangria bucket where a good-looking blond guy ladled us up two drinks in plastic cups.

"Don't be shy girls."

People everywhere, small talk. There were baseball stories, sweaty baseball players, music, dancing, and lines of cocaine on the kitchen table, sangria after sangria. Mikey, the varsity pitcher was dancing on the coffee table in his striped boxer shorts. The other players clapped as he gyrated his hips in slow motion. I met them all, some I knew, some I got to know better. I felt my body filling with fresh air and sangria and I wanted to stay forever in the five-bedroom house. I danced with Vince the third baseman. I danced with him far away, then close, and then so close I could feel his heartbeat and smell the scent of him. He smelled like a red wine that had been left too long. Slightly fermented, slightly sweet. He licked my neck.

"You taste like salt. Mmm, I like that," he said.

Julie was gone. I looked in every room. I searched the yard, called for her.

"She left with big Mike," Frank said.

"I'll take you home," Vince said.

"Okay."

In the car I wondered with my alcohol head and my coked up nose, do I go to Jeno's or do I go to the dorm room? Did I admit to Vince that I'd been screwing my college professor for the last three months? I couldn't decide so I went to Vince's. He had an apartment downtown, blocks and blocks away from Jeno's. Three steps up to the door, Vince was holding on to me sweetly. Inside there was furniture, thrift store furniture and stacks of magazines and books and a fireplace that Vince lit. He took a sheepskin rug off of a chair and laid it on the floor in front of the fire. He lit three candles on the mantle. He laid me down gently on the sheepskin and said, "Is this alright?"

And it felt all right, in fact it felt great. I woke up in the morning in just my underwear, no bra and a wool blanket covering me. Vince was making coffee in the kitchen.

"Shit!" I said.

"What's the matter, you got a hangover?" he asked.

"Yea. Did we have...?"

"Sex? Yea, we had sex, really good sex. I thanked you, but you were out," he said.

"Fuck."

"Yea it was," Vince said. "Eat something and I'll take you home. I've got practice today."

Vince dropped me at the dorm after a very long kiss. My roommate was doing her laundry, carefully folding her underwear, but throwing her socks in a big pile. The room smelled like fresh cotton. I looked down at my wrinkled clothes and could smell the old wine on my breath.

"Hey," I said.

She started folding a t-shirt. "He called you."

"Who?"

"You know, the professor. He called about eighty two times last night and eighty five this morning." She popped a piece of gum in her mouth. "I heard y'all went home with Vince. I didn't tell the professor. Vince is a fucking dream."

"Yea, he is."

"Why do you go with professor Jeranos? I mean; I know he's kind of sexy, his dark skin and all, but isn't he old?"

"I guess I like them old."

She popped her gum. "He must be a good lay. Well Vince has him hands down. It's none of my business though. Tally ho." She walked out the door with her empty laundry basket.

Shit. Now I had to face Jeno. What was I afraid of? The night that he grabbed my arm and left bruises? He would never hit me. He didn't own me. I wasn't his or anybody's property. Why then was my heart beating so fast?

I changed clothes and washed up. I got my bike and set out to Jeno's. It was late afternoon on a Saturday. The campus was quiet. Students were studying or hanging over from the night before. I pedaled back, remembering my books. I had two tests and a midterm paper to write.

At Jeno's, the house was still. Leaves swirled from the maple tree in front of his house. I saw the kitchen light on through the living room window. I watched Jeno pass through my narrow vision of the hall.

He didn't look angry, in fact, I heard jazz playing from the stereo inside. I didn't knock. I never knocked anymore.

He stopped, stared, put down his wine glass. "Look what the wind dragged in today. Where has my little undergraduate been?"

"I went to a party," I said, dropping my backpack on the hall floor.

"So I heard. A baseball party...all the little leaguers playing off the field huh?"

"Something like that. What did you do last night?"

He hit the counter hard with his palm. "It doesn't matter what I did last night. What matters is that you were out whoring around. I don't put up with inconveniences like that!"

My knees buckled. "You don't own me, I can do whatever I please. I sleep with you, but I am a big, big girl. I can do whatever I want."

Within a second he had me by one arm, his other hand slapped me in the face. I raised my free fist to hit him back, but he pushed me hard against the wall, and pinned my arms at my side.

"Let's get one thing straight, if you're fucking me, then you're not whoring around with anyone else, do you understand that big, big girl?" His breath smelled like whiskey or vodka and he barred his teeth when he spoke.

"Well then I'm not fucking you!"

"We'll see about that."

I tried to black myself out, but these things I remember; the push that sent my feet out from under me, landing on the tile floor with a hard thud, the pain in the back of my head when it hit the tile, the tile that came all the way from Italy on a boat. The smell of alcohol that came from his skin and the spit that flew from his mouth. The flaring of his nostrils as he came over me, pinning my arms above my head with one hand. The sound of ripping fabric as he tore open my shirt, the popping of the buttons on my jeans. The scraping of my lower back against the tile as he worked the jeans and the underwear down, the feeling of his fingers digging into me down there, the scratching of his fingernails against my breastbone. The ceiling above him, white and pop corned with silver specks. I said his name over and over, but the sounds were strange, not my sounds at all, they were the sounds of a sad dog. His eyes darkened like thunder, his face moved back and forth above mine, the grout cut into the skin on my buttocks.

Afterwards he stood over me, his hands on his bare hips. I remember the sound of the stereo, Charles Mingus. I had been trained to hear.

"There," he said. "Get your stuff out of my house."

Somehow I got my sweatshirt over my torn shirt and my jeans back on even though the buttons were gone. My back was bleeding and my face hurt. I started to sob, involuntarily, snot running down my nose, salty tears on my lips. My hands were speckled red with blood. Jeno didn't look at me as I went out the front door. The tears came like water; the sad dog sounds coming faster and faster. I thought about the river back home. The sound it made after a heavy rain, when I could hear its fullness. I pedaled back to the dorm; it was starting to get dark. My roommate was out. I laid on my bed with my torn clothes and wrapped my blankets around me as tight as I could. The next morning I called Carl and told him I wanted to come home. I left my roommate, my dormitory, my books and Jeno the next day. I caught the 2pm bus and looked back a million times.

Carl picked me up at the bus station in Issaquah. We rode home in silence. He didn't ask me anything about school. He looked at my suitcases and said, "You're back."

"Yes. I'm back."

The town looked the same. I wanted to curl up in a circle and hide in one of its dark corners, disappear and never remember my name.

Emma came to see me. She opened her arms and held me and I could have hung on for a million years. I knew I looked like shit, but we went out anyway. We went to the river and it was the same. It changed, but never changed. I could always count on it to smell fresh and new and familiar at the same time. Emma made me swim with her in the freezing river and I knew she felt really free in that water, but I felt paralyzed. Nothing could wash my body clean. I told her about Jeno; she knew something was wrong. She got it I think, but nobody got it really. I hated the sight of my body and tried to keep it covered at all times. I didn't want anyone to see it and I didn't want to see it either. I took long showers and scrubbed my legs until they were red, scrubbed my back, my crotch, but it never came clean. The smell and the sight of myself made me sick. And I couldn't think, because if I started thinking I would remember things and I would want to find a butcher knife and plunge it into myself, just to see if I could feel it. It was that spring I started cutting myself because it felt so good. I took one of Carl's razorblades from the medicine chest in his bathroom and carefully drew a line on my forearm. It stung, but it didn't break the skin so I pressed harder. I thought it would hurt, but all it did was sting and the stinging felt really good. It felt powerful. I was in control. I could hurt or not hurt. The line turned red and drops of blood pooled from its sides. I felt sharpness, and the sharpness felt marvelous and it took away the pain in my gut. I hid the cuts with long sleeve shirts and sweaters. I was addicted.

I hardly went out. Unless I was with Emma, I was home hiding. Trying not to think. I watched television and watched the rain through the sliding glass doors.

If Carl noticed anything, he never said. Rosalene called me every day. When I heard her voice I hung up.

One day Emma came over and we sat in my backyard. Emma rolled a joint and lit it with a pearl blue lighter. She passed it to me. Her face looked fresh and healthy. She looked happy somehow.

"Mama says you hang up on her."

"Yea."

"God, I understand that. I'd hang up on her too if I could," she laughed.

"I just can't talk to anyone right now."

"It's the rape huh?"

"I guess you could say that." We sat in silence for a long time. I felt my head grow light.

"What do you want to do today?" she asked me.

"You don't work today? It seems like you're always there."

"I try to be. I don't want to be at the house watching mama and her sideshow."

The sun came out. I stretched my arms above my head. It felt good to be high, to forget for a moment. Emma was staring at me, staring at my arms, at my wrists, at my cuts. She stood up fast, grabbed one of my wrists.

"What the hell is this? Who did this to you?" She was yelling, standing over me, still holding my arm. She grabbed the other arm, yanked the sleeve of my shirt up. "Shit," she said. She dropped my arms and sat back down. She put her head in her hands, shaking it back and forth. She muttered something I couldn't hear.

"I gotta get back inside." I stood and headed toward the back door, back towards the house.

"Kimmy, did someone do that to you or," Emma's voice was very quiet, "did you do it to yourself?"

I wrapped my arms tight around my waist.

"Remember when we were in elementary school and we cut ourselves and we became blood sisters?"

"Yes."

"Kimmy," Emma's eyes were the darkest green I had ever seen. They were green like the leaves of a holly bush. "My blood is in your blood. When you bleed, I bleed."

"Look," I turned my back to Emma. I didn't want her looking at me with those green eyes. "I'm in a fucking well. I'm in a well and it's dark, darker than any dark I've ever seen. I am Tikki Tikki Tembo. You remember? You remember the fable boy who falls in the well and can't get out by himself? And I can't see in there and no one's bringing me a fucking ladder. I know I'm in the well because I've been here before and I know what it looks like. I know what it tastes like. I know what it smells like. I was there for a long time, but it's never been this dark before. You can't be in the well with me right now." I stopped. A flock of geese flew overhead. I watched them and wished I were riding on the back of one of them, high in the sky far away. "I was raped, okay. I don't know how to get that memory out of my body. Do you hear me? I don't know what to do…" Tears rolled from my eyes.

"Look, Kimmy, the river is all I know. It's the only power I've got. It's the one thing I go to time after time. You need to go down to that river and wash yourself clean everyday until that stink is gone. You go to that river every night from now until the first freeze. You don't stop swimming and scrubbing until you're done with it. You scrub your legs with sand so hard they bleed. The water from the hills is pure. The river never judges you or mocks you. It cleanses you. And you know what? If you do that, you'll get rid of it. You'll get rid of him and his horrible fingers and the way he rubbed you and the smell of him. You'll wash his shit right out of you and you'll get purified, you'll testify like fucking Jesus. Got it?" Emma paused.

I turned to her; watched the pulse in her neck. "Got it," I said quietly.

"I'll take you tonight after work. I'll even bring towels this time and then we'll lie on a blanket and look at the stars like we use to, we'll go to our field. You know where it all started?" She looked out at the fence, her eyes unfocused.

"Okay."

After work Emma came to the house and we walked to the river, each of us had a cigarette. Mine was thin and dark, hers a short Salem. I hadn't been away from the house for five days.

"I steal these French cigarettes from Carl. He doesn't even smoke. I think he keeps them for when your mama comes over," I told her.

We hiked the trail to the river. The moon was out even though the sun was setting in the sky. I heard the tumble of the water on the rocks and saw a blue heron alight upon a log as we came down to the shore.

"Look at that!" Emma said.

"Damn."

We stripped. We stood naked and Emma kissed the top of my head. "I now pronounce you free of injury and harm, anoint yourself with the pure water my fair maiden." She laughed.

We walked in the water, our bodies moving in unison, our gasps at the cold water simultaneous. "You have to testify. Tell the water what you want to be free of, shout it to the mountain over there and hurry up, because I'm freezing my ass off."

"I want to feel whole again. I want to be clean."

"Shout it," Emma said. "Shout it loud."

"Clean me… I want to be clean! I want to be rid of Jeno and I want out of this black fucking hole goddammit!" I yelled to the sky and myself and Emma and no one. "I hate you Jeno! Do you hear that? I hate you. I hate you and I hate me. I hate myself and I hate every fucking thing in this whole fucking goddamn lifetime!" My body went underwater, the current rushing against me. I bobbed up again taking big gulps of air. "Do you hear that Jeno? I hate you and your stupid jazz class and all your stupid crystal ashtrays and your stuck up fucking wine glasses! I fucking hate you!!!"

Emma laughed and dove under water, letting the current carry her downstream. I followed her and when I came out she was beside me.

"Say it again," she said.

"What?" I asked.

"Say you hate him."

"I hate you Jeno! You fucking professor dictator fascist Nazi!"

"Good one. Now say you love him."

"No," I said, "I'm not."

"Say it," she said. "Say it or I'm going to hold you under water."

"No!"

"Say it!"

"I love you!"

"Say who."

"Fuck," I said. "Okay…I love you Jeno! I love you Jeno. There. I love you Jeno." I started to cry. The moon watched me, the setting sun watched me, and Emma watched me, pushing her wet hair back.

"Now say you forgive him."

"I don't"

"So," she said, "say it any way."

I didn't.

"Say you forgive him!"

"I forgive you."

"Say who you forgive," she said.

"I forgive you Jeno."

"Say it again!"

"Okay, if it will shut you up, I'll yell it." I yelled it as loud as I could. "I forgive you Jeno!" I left her side, swam underwater to the big log and crawled on top. "Are you fucking happy now?"

"Oh yeah," she said, "are you?"

"Yes. And I'm fucking cold!"

We toweled off and walked to the football field. We laid on our sweaters and smoked a joint. We looked at the stars starting to appear. The sky was beginning to twinkle. Emma wished on a star. She said, "Your turn." I wished, and then wished a second time in case the first didn't come true. Emma grabbed my hand. We stayed that way for a long time, until the crickets got so loud we could hardly hear each other. We shook out our sweaters. We walked to Marsha's house. I felt my feet beneath me. They were hard and solid for the first time since I had come back. Finally I could feel the earth again.

I walked to the river by myself every day. I went down the shaded trail to the private area on the shore. I stripped off all my clothes and floated, letting the current carry me. I stroked my way back up the river, floated down again and so on, over and over. And when I looked at the sky, I saw Jeno's face over me. His skin was red, his eyes wild with anger. I felt his rage. I shut my eyes tight and begged for it to go away. I opened my eyes to a changing sky. I took big breaths of air and closed my eyes again and tried to think of nothing at all. I took a rock from its banks and slept with it in my bed.

Chapter Six: Emma; The Hierophant

"I think we should see other people," Danny said one night when we were necking hard in the front seat of his car. His hands were down the back of my shirt; my bra was undone, my shirt almost off. We had a fifth of Jack Daniels on the floorboards and had been taking turns taking swigs off the sweet tasting bottle. We were at a turnabout at the end of a dirt road, the windows were rolled halfway down and I heard the frogs chirping. His words didn't fit with the liquor or my body heat or the sounds of the night. He might as well have been coach saying, "You didn't make the team," or mama saying, "I'm going to marry Carlos." I felt my breath catch in my chest and the weight of the air was enormous. I felt the weight in my abdomen, in my womb, in my crotch, down one leg.

"What?"

He said again, "I think we should see other people."

"Who?" I asked. "Who are these other people?"

"No one specific, just people."

"People."

"I'm going away in a year or two Emma, you can't just sit around and wait for me. I love you, but you can't be left here in the dust."

"You'll come back...besides, I could work at a plant over the mountains or somewhere in Mt. Vernon and be near you. We could get an apartment or something." Danny was already out of high school and working full time at the milk plant with his dad and his uncle Robby, he was trying to get a job at his uncle's ranch in Eastern Washington or at his friend's dad's pea farm in Mt. Vernon. He rolled his window down and leaned his head against the door; he gazed out into the night.

"You know that's not going to happen Emma." He laughed. "Emma, it's not like we're breaking up. I'm just opening doors so new things can happen for both of us. I've gotta get out of here."

"Oh so you can get laid by some other girl, is that what you mean by opening doors?" I was shouting and the front window was beginning to steam and the dashboard was wavering and twisting in my teary eyes. "Take me home Danny, I love you, but I have to pee." I felt sick, sicker than I'd ever been.

Two weeks later I got pneumonia and Danny got Myra, a sober long legged clarinetist from our high school band. I told Kimmy about Danny and she said, "Fuck it." That's all she ever said anymore. Kimmy told me a week later that she was leaving for College.

"I'm moving to Ellensburg. Carl wants me to go to school and there is…well, there's nothing for me here, besides you of course. I'll miss you more than the river, more than my flute," she hung her head, her blonde hair hanging over her cheeks. "I'm leaving it behind. I can't conjure up anymore ghosts, it makes me cry," she added.

I lost a boyfriend, the only boyfriend I would ever love and my best friend was leaving within a few months. All I had left was my job and my last season of baseball. I wished I were a heron. A grey blue heron that could take flight and raise skyward with majestic wings stretched, spanning infinity.

Kimmy left in August. Our summer was fleeting. No Carlos, only "Vinsssent". The carnival that came that summer was small, a carnival company out of Marysville. I hated it, but loved the fact that Carlos wasn't taking over our house with his Spanish music and his empty whiskey bottles. When Kimmy left, I cried for three days straight. One August night I dug around in my drawers until I found Ned's phone number. I hadn't written him for a long time. I held the phone number in my hand and felt him, the warmth of his strong hands, the softness of his voice, the image of him pointing to a bird in flight, one arm around my shoulders. He loved me, I thought. He was the only one who ever loved me. I walked to the market loaded with change for the pay phone. I dropped quarters in one by one. The operator said, "Just a moment please." I heard shrill ringing, the pick up of a voice, Ned's voice. I started to cry.

"Ned," I said between sobs, "it's me, Emma."

Silence filled the line. "Emma? Well how are you…is everything okay? Is your mom alright?"

"Yes, yes, she's fine."

"Then what is it? You sound like you are crying."

"Ned, I am so lonely."

"Oh honey, I know, the world is lonely. I miss you. I am sorry I haven't written for a while, I've just been working a lot. I'm going to send you a book. It's a book on tree identification. I've been taking more classes and well, I'm almost done and then I can look for a job in my field."

"That's great," my voice cracked.

"And Emma…I'm getting, well…married. Married to a really nice woman. I would love for you to meet her."

"Oh."

"I had to move on Emma." I heard him sigh. "I couldn't wait for your mama forever. She didn't want me."

"I wanted you."

That night I curled up on my single mattress on the floor. I curled up as tightly as possible and wished I could become small enough to disappear like a ball of lint that is swept away by a broom without a care.

I had no more school. I was graduated. Summer was over. Coach asked me if I would help him with the high school team, but that wasn't until spring. In the meantime I had nothing to do and nowhere to be. Ned would never be my daddy. I didn't want to go to the river anymore. I was dried up. I had nothing left to give to nature and I didn't really feel like absorbing anything either. All I had was my job and if it weren't for that I could disappear. As it was I did disappear into the recesses of my own mind, which wasn't a very cool place to be. I spent all my time at the 2 x 4, either working or hanging out and listening. I loved the clang of the dishes, the shouts from the kitchen, the restaurant banter that went on all the time. I loved the smells, the bacon, the fryer, and the stale coffee. It made me feel a thousand miles away from my own self. The 2x4 made time move fast in a slow hazy sort of way.

At the end of one of her shifts, Marsha pulled me aside. She smelled of fresh air and wood smoke. Her hair was pulled back in a ponytail that couldn't contain the wildness. "You come by tonight. I'm having a gathering. You know with some food, a bit of wine, some coke, some grass. It'll be fun."

"Okay," I said.

"You know where I live? That's a crazy thing to ask isn't it, in this town? It's hard not to know where everybody lives." She tossed her wild ponytail and laughed out the door.

I walked to Marsha's. The light in the sky was softening to shades of pink and purple, coloring the edges of the rain clouds. I walked down the river road, not too far out of town. Marsha lived by herself in a tiny house covered in cedar shingles and ivy. Her steps were covered in elves, plastic, ceramic and wood gnomes that peered at you through laughing eyes. Elves were on either side, making it hard to pass.

Marsha opened the door and I heard a unanimous shout, "Hey!" Everyone greeted me. Some I knew, some I didn't, some I barely knew as customers of the 2x4 and some were customers of mama's.

A tall dark guy with pale green eyes walked up to me. "Get you a beer or some wine?" he asked.

"Wine," I said.

He bowed, "My lady, I shall return." And he did with a beautiful glass of red wine for me.

"Thanks," I said.

Marsha's place was incredible. It was decorated with imported cloths in oranges and greens. The walls were painted a suede color and everywhere were pillows of beautiful fabrics. I smelled incense burning and the buzz of talk and laughter wrapped about my shoulders like a warm coat.

"I'm so glad you came," said Marsha as I sat next to her on the couch. "I was afraid you wouldn't make it."

"No, this is great," I said looking around the room.

"Yea," she said. "It's not how much ya got, it's how much you do with what ya got. I told you my mom was an interior decorator back in the 50's when it wasn't cool to work as a woman. She even had a couple of her client's rooms featured in Sunset magazine. She was amazing."

"Where is she now?" I asked.

"She's dead." She paused. "Oh it's okay, she's been dead for years. I have sort of gotten used to it. That's why I love your mom so much;

she gives me a little piece of mothering you know. She reads my cards when I go over to your place. Sometimes she will come into the café and just look at me real serious, you know, and then she'll say, 'Marsha, don't go out tonight. I see something bad happening to you', and I don't. I always listen to your mom."

"Hmm," I was staring into my wine glass, swirling the red around the edge.

"Yea," she said dreamily, "she's really something. You are a lucky girl. Hey Mick," she yelled across the room. "Bring the white powder over here man."

Mick brought over a mirror, a red and white striped straw and a silk pouch. Marsha opened the pouch and took out the bag, shaking some of its white powder on the mirror. She pulled a razor blade from the pouch and began chopping rhythmically at the white powder. Chop. Chop. Chop. I had never done coke before, and I stared at that razor blade with the intensity of a cat. Marsha made perfect even lines, and then she leaned down with the straw in her nose and inhaled one of the white lines up her nose. She lifted her head up, sniffed hard, smiled at me and handed me the straw.

"Ah man! That makes it all worthwhile. Here," she said and handed me the straw.

I copied Marsha and sucked up one of the pretty white lines with the straw, set the straw on the mirror and leaned back on the couch. I felt a burn in my nostril.

"Thanks."

She put her hand on my knee. "I like you," she said. "You are a lot like me."

The room turned into colors and sounds mingling in the air with the smell of weed and patchouli incense. I was wired and tired at the same time and knew I couldn't walk home. I laid my head back and closed my eyes drinking in the night.

When I woke up I was lying on the couch, my head on Marsha's lap. She was fast asleep; her head tilted back, her dark hair splayed around her. She had a hand on my shoulder. Another girl was curled up on the other side of me, her reddish brown hair covering her face. Around the room was a dozen or so sleeping bodies. I sat up slowly, carefully taking Marsha's hand and laying it on her thigh, I lifted the other gal's head off my leg and she hardly stirred. I found my shoes in the middle of the room, tried to get my mouth to work. It was stuck together, could be the wine, it could have been the coke. I tiptoed past the elves. "Shh!" I said, raising a finger to my lips.

My moods became darker and darker.

Out back of the restaurant following the lunch shift one day, Marsha and I were having a smoke. I still washed dishes, but occasionally I would wait tables. The money was much better. The cook came out to join us, leaving no one in to watch the customers, which was typical.

Joe looked at us, "You girls grow up in this shithole?" He had a way of crossing his arms when he smoked. He rested them above his belly. He didn't wait for an answer. "I didn't. I come from Arcadia where bear make men nervous." He laughed a deep belly laugh.

Marsha stamped her cigarette out in the dirt. "Someone's gotta watch the restaurant," she went back inside with a grunt.

"How is it?" asked Joe.

"How is what?" My head was a million miles away.

"How it is to be in the black?"

"What?"

"I know you're there. I can smell it. I know because I was in the black for a long time." He dragged on his cigarette, tapped the ashes into the crisp air. "After my wife left me I couldn't see no light, not a speck, it was black in and out, it was all I could see. I used to sit on my deck and wish I could shrink, me shrink, can you imagine?" he laughed. "I wanted to shrink so small I could crawl down a hole and get under the roots of the apple tree in our backyard. I just wanted to burrow, you know? Just be safe and hide in the black of all them roots, be hugged by something." He took another drag and blew it out in a single line. "One morning I woke up and I must have been drinking, because there I was, curled up around the base of the apple tree. My fingernails were full of mud and beneath me was a little hole. I was trying to get under that tree! Huh! Yea, black is dark alright."

A customer cracked the door, "Joe. Order."

When the winter solstice came mama had a big party and so did Marsha. I went to Marsha's of course, even though I knew I could get just as messed up at mamas. I wasn't in the mood for tarot cards or fire pits or Vincent's "famous" dessert crepes or chanting to the moon goddess, although mama didn't need the excuse of a party to sing to the moon.

At Marsha's there was wine and a keg of beer and ashtrays full of half smoked joints. John Coltrane was playing on the stereo. Marsha came to me, put an arm across my shoulder and led me to the futon couch with the navy blue and emerald green throw on it.

"What is it Emma, what's wrong with you? I know you're suffering, because I watch you at work. How can life be that bad…what is it?" she asked.

"Nothing. Nothing at all, that is the problem."

"I know all about nothing. Nothing is sometimes bigger than your own mind." She sat quietly. She lit up a joint and smoked to herself contemplating the window and the sliver of starlight falling on the torn oriental carpet. "What do you love?" she asked me.

I had to think. I tried to clear my wine filled, pot buzzed mind and think. What did I love? I couldn't think of anything. "Nothing," I said.

"Everyone loves something, even a suicidal maniac loves something. Not someone, something. You must love something."

"I love the river I guess, or I did. I love baseball." There that was it.

"What do you love about it?"

"I love the feel of the bases when you hit them with the side of your foot. The feel of the bat cracking when you really hit the ball, you know, there is a great feeling to that. And the smell of the grass mixed with the dirt, I miss that. I really miss the sounds of the chatter and, god, I guess I just miss it, you know. It made me feel good about myself, because I was good at it."

"Okay then." She walked away from me and circulated around the room. I listened to the rise and fall of voices trailing her.

"Let's go then," I heard Marsha shout. There were a lot of shouts and shuffling of feet. Marsha looked down at me. "You have to get up now and get your shoes on."

"You want me to go home?" I asked.

"No, you fucking moron. We're going to play baseball. All of us."

We walked to the high school field. I saw dozens of people scattering ahead of us. Cars parked on either side of the field. Their lights came on, lighting up the ball field, and there was everyone, the whole party. There was a bat and some balls and a dozen or so mitts. People had gone home and rounded up their equipment. Martin Newly held up a couple of bottles of whiskey and gave a yahoo yelp. He set them on the bleacher steps. When I approached the field with Marsha I heard Colby, the red head who clerked at the feed store shout, "You're up Emma."

There it was, the moon shining on home plate, the lit field, and the wine in my blood, the bat and me. Jimmy Carlson, who I barely knew, pitched me a ball and I hit that ball like it was the last ball I would ever see. I hit that ball like the smack of the bat would send me to the other side of the moon. The bat cracked and I heard someone shout, "Jesus!" and I ran. As I neared first base, I grabbed Marsha's hand and made her run with me. We ran around the bases once, and after we hit home, we ran around again and I could hear a shout of, "Foul, you can't run twice," but the dirt felt so good beneath my feet and my breath going in and out was the finest air I had taken in for months. We hit home plate after the second run and collapsed, Marsha landing on top of me, and I laughed and other people laughed and then Marsha yelled, "Play ball." And we did, we played ball for hours. There was no great set of rules and we all ran amok and twice there was a pig pile on the pitcher's mound, but the whiskey kept the warmth in everyone's breath and we played until the moon grew pale in the sky.

"Shit, I gotta go," said Jake.

That was followed with a chorus of "yeahs" and a gathering of things and parting words. I saw Marsha on the pitcher's mound talking to a girl named Sasha and I ran up and hugged her. I hugged her so hard we hit the ground and rolled in the dirt and when we stopped rolling I said, "Thank you Marsha."

"I love you Em," she said, "and you are a bitch at baseball!"

I think that night Marsha saved my life. I started to crawl out of my hole and get a little glimpse of my soul. I started to scrape the muck off of it. I started to go back to the river.

And then mama told me Kimmy came back.

"She's back, but Carl said she isn't seeing anyone." She looked at me. "I know what happened."

"I'm sure you do."

"Do you want me to share? I haven't talked to her since she's been back, but I pulled her cards twice. It's a lot of heartache Emma."

I answered her with my loudest sigh and slammed the front door on my way out of the house.

Kimmy stood in her doorway, she looked the same, but her hair was longer, her blonde hair curling and spilling around the front of her shirt.

"Hey," I said. "Mama told me you were home."

She reached out and hugged me, holding me tight. She smelled like peppermint and ylang ylang, two of my favorite smells. "I missed you so much," she said in my ear.

"I missed you too." She wouldn't let go. "Why'd you come back? I thought you liked it there, being a college girl and all."

"I just did. I guess I missed this piece of shit town."

I laughed. "Get dressed, let's go out. I've got some great weed; we can walk around town. I'll tell you what you missed, ha!"

We smoked a joint behind my house. We were wrapped in our sweaters and our coats and walked the streets of Tolt, our breath making fire patterns in the air.

"I cannot even tell you how much I missed you. I kept busy and I worked and all, but I mean it wasn't the same. I almost became friends with Melissa Boyd. You remember her. God, I was getting desperate. There's nothing to do but work, hang out at the 2x4 and avoid mama. Boring!"

"You're still dishwashing at the 2 x 4? Don't you think the coffee smells like your father's closet?"

"No, I wouldn't know what my father's closet smelled like."

"Right," she said, lighting another joint.

"You're going to smoke right here in town?"

"I don't give a fuck. Carl said there are no cops around here anymore since they switched us to King County. All those bastards do is drive around and glare at you. You see them about once every three months." She blew a puff of weedy air out.

We walked through the streets, kicking pebbles out of the sidewalk cracks. We were very high.

"What happened with Danny? You never wrote me about him," Kimmy asked.

"He moved to Burlington to be with his sister. He broke up with that music girl, the skinny one. Want to go to the river?"

"Of course." And there it was, the running tumbling water, cold and crisp and new off the mountains. The gray and blue and occasionally red stones of the bank, looked inviting, tantalizing.

Kimmy had tears on her cheek and maybe it was the pot or maybe it was the sound of the geese overhead or the roaring water, but she started to cry uncontrollably. Her shoulders shook in her coat. She held her hands over her mouth, her blue eyes staring at the river and at nothing, all at the same time.

"What is it Kimmy, what is it?" I put an arm around her.

She said nothing, just stared, crying like a wounded bird.

"Come on," I said, jumping up. I took off my coat and pulled my sweater over my head. I stripped off my tank top and bra. I kicked off my shoes and peeled my socks off, shedding my jeans and my underwear. "Hurry," I said, "before I change my mind."

"Are you nuts?" she started laughing, through all her tears she laughed.

"Yea!" I ran over the rocks as fast as I could manage toward the breathing river not feeling the 45-degree air. "Get over here!"

Kimmy did the same, and when she turned to strip, I saw the scratches on her back, the bruises on her butt bone. She walked stone after stone to the edge and like a follower at a baptismal, waded into the river. "Oh my god!" she cried out.

"I know, we can only stay in for a minute or we'll get hypothermia, but Kimmy, quick, wash it away…shit whatever it is, get it off of you, here in the fucking freezing river. This is the only way you could get rid of the dead baby memory, remember?" I shouted. "Fuck this is cold!"

And it was cold and it hit me in the chest and I put my whole body in, like the Polar Bear Club swimmers I had read about in San Francisco. The women who dared themselves to swim in the coldest of temperatures, the women who gave in to the siren songs of the San

Francisco Bay to wash themselves anew. I understood what made a person do that, for in the frigidness of nature you could forgive yourself and everyone of sin and stupidity, because it just didn't matter, nothing mattered as much as mother nature.

We shivered uncontrollably when we got out. "Dry yourself with your tank top and then don't put it on, put the dry clothes on, then I'll take you to the 2x4 for some rank coffee." I talked to Kimmy as if she were a small child.

The booths at the 2x4 had a view of the kitchen over the serving bar. I could see Joe, sweating and hovering over the grill. Marsha smiled and waved when she saw us slide into the red booth. She had on her Birkenstock sandals, red wool socks, tight jeans, and a Ramones t- shirt.

"Hey Kimmy," she said, "you just checking out the scene or are you bored out of your fucking mind today. Aren't you supposed to be at college?"

"Nah."

She brought us two dusty glasses of water. "I got a reading this morning from your mom." She paused, looked at Kimmy, "I thought you were away at school? You on break?"

"Something like that," she said. "Can we have a couple of coffees?"

"Sure thing."

We wrapped our hands around the heavy mugs, our hair was still wet and it was beginning to curl on the ends.

"That was insane," she said smiling.

"Hey, I noticed the bruises and stuff. You got hurt didn't you?"

She looked out the window at the traffic, cars, station wagons, a log truck, a dump truck with hand done lettering on the side, spray painted letters, "A & B Trucking". This could be any town anywhere, USA. That's what I liked about it, non descript. A person could get lost here. I wanted to be lost here.

"It was some dude at a party wasn't it; a date rape sort of thing? I read about that in the paper you know. They slip something in your drink and it immobilizes you and you can't fight anyone off. That's a shitty thing. That's what it was wasn't it?"

"No," she said quietly. We both looked out the window. I could see our faces reflected in the glass.

"It was that professor dude wasn't it? The guy you wrote me about, the incredibly sexy Mediterranean guy. You did it with him and fell for him and he…you're not pregnant again are you? You don't have to tell me."

"No," she looked at me hard, her eyes as blue as a winters sky. "He raped me. He lost his temper and fucking raped me…"

"Oh." I wrapped my hands tighter around my mug. "God Kimmy, you can't be raped by someone you love. You loved him, you told me. People you love don't rape you, that's what strangers do, you know in the dark alleys and all that crap."

"Shit Emma, get it. You don't get bruises on your ass and big long scratches on your back from making love. Rape is when you don't want to fuck and they hold you down and stick it in you anyway. That's what gives you bruises on your ass, because they throw you like some slab of beef on some hard fucking surface and…. It doesn't matter whether they love you or not. You read about fathers raping their daughters every day Emma, and they love 'em in some fucked up way. Shit, get real." She lit a cigarette.

I stared at her. "You sure read a lot."

"Fuck. Just let it be. I gotta leave it down there at the river, like you said. It's done, "fini". How's that for Mediterranean? I deserved it okay? I went out on him and he went crazy over it." She looked elegant in her long hair, her cigarette poised in one hand, bright red nail polish on every finger except the thumbnail, which was painted black. "I know all about rape. I was date raped in October, before I started seeing Jeno, by a real "sweet" guy from Seattle." She took a drag, rolled her cigarette in her fingers. "I liked him. I met him at the library and he asked me to dinner. I don't know if I would have fucked him, but he sure was sweet and I sure was having a good time. I remember drinking gin and tonics. I was on my first and I was totally in control, you know. I wasn't drunk or anything, just relaxed and chatty." She got a dreamy look on her face. "Then I had to go to the bathroom and when I came back he had ordered me another drink. That was fine, right? Only this drink got me so messed up. I remember being led down the hall by him; we went to his apartment somewhere. It was in some basement somewhere. The next thing I knew I was on his bed and candles were lit all around me like I was some sort of fucking shrine. I was naked, nothing on, and he was fucking me. I could not move one part of my body, not even my fingertips. I could think of things to say, but they wouldn't come out. I just kept thinking, 'I don't think I want to fuck you'. But I couldn't say it. And then I don't remember anything until morning when he was on top of me again. By the time I could think he was done. He rolled off and said, 'That was spelndid'. Shit, I could barely walk, could barely get myself dressed. The only good thing was he used a rubber. There was a pile of used ones on the nightstand. Full. God only knows how many times he did it, I saw three, maybe four. I threw up outside on the walkway of his apartment. Yea. I know about rape." She paused. "At first I didn't admit it. I told myself I probably asked for it myself because he was so good looking and I can be easy you know. I'm kind of a slut, I know that. But then I saw an article on date rape and it was there right before my eyes." She stubbed out her cigarette. "I was at the campus clinic getting my birth control for Christ's sake and there it was in a Better Homes and Garden or something. I just started to cry. I couldn't get my pills. I had to leave. I told the gal I was sick or something, I don't know. It stank, it stank like old fucking dog shit on a fucking party shoe."

"God Kimmy, I'm sorry."

"You see now why I missed you? Who do you tell that to, your dad? Carl would hunt him and kill him like a rabid coyote. I did tell your mom though. She got it. She said she would do some prayers and chants for me."

"Jesus."

"Hey, in my state, I would have taken anything. Someone could have done a sheep sacrifice for me and that would have been all right. Anyway, I know all about rape. It's dirty. Jeno raped me too. I loved him."

"I didn't do so good without you either." She reached across the table and laced her fingers through mine. She held her other hand up.

"Show me your blood sister palm," she said.

I held up my other hand and we pressed our palms together across the littered table.

By the time we left, the moon was in the sky, the sun beginning to fade. It was the veil between night and day letting you know it was going to be a clear night with thousands of stars.

"Your mama and my dad still sleep together sometimes, your mama told me. I think it's kind of cool. She's dating the new librarian dude though. He's from Virginia. She said he has an accent and dresses nice. She said he's really good looking. Really young though."

"Yeah." I stayed away from home so much; I had no idea if Vincent was new or old.

"Your mama told me something bad was going to happen. I should have listened."

That night I laid on my mattress. Mama was out. The house was cold. I thought so hard about Kimmy that it began to feel like a dream. I closed my eyes and let the moon light wash over me through the naked window.

Mama woke me up early, a hot steaming mug of coffee in her hand as she stood in the doorway of my bedroom. The light from the window hit her left cheekbone. She looked tired and fragile.

"How about a reading honey pot?"

I wanted to say, "How about not. How about you just leave me the fuck alone and quit trying to tell my future?" but instead I said, "No thanks."

"Alright, but I was playing with the cards early this morning and thinking of you and the nine of swords came up. You know what that means." She let the words hang in a dramatic pause. I didn't care what it meant, but she was going to tell me regardless. "It means that you're future is uncertain. You are in a place of self-doubt. You should have let me tell you what I saw for you and that boy you were dating. Forget about him, there are a lot of other men in the ocean."

"Like a librarian maybe?" I put my hands over my eyes and rolled over on my mattress.

"Yes, actually. He's on my fishing line." She laughed. "Anyway, I've got to go. There's coffee in the pot and I left some milk. I'll see you later today."

"Where are you going?"

"To the library. I work today. Then I'm going out with Vincent tonight." She said it real slow, like Vin-sseent.

"See ya," I said, thankful that she was leaving. God I hated those fucking cards. I called Kimmy, but she didn't answer. I called Danny's old number just to hear an unfamiliar voice pick up. I rolled a joint and smoked at the kitchen table. I got dressed and headed down to the river. When I reached the riverbank I drew in a long breath and held it. "Clean me," I whispered. I took off my jeans and sweatshirt and swam in my tank top and underwear. I heard the call of a blue jay. It sounded optimistic, hopeful somehow. I swam as long as I could stand the cold, then stripped off the underwear and tank top and wore only my jeans and sweatshirt. I sat on a log for a while and closed my eyes. The rushing water became my blood, the sounds of the birds my heart and the tumbling of the rocks became my mind. It helped me think. I thought about Ned and how he deserved to be happy, even if it made me sad. My childhood fantasy of having him for a dad was dead and I needed to bury it. I thought of Joe and his sorrow and the apple tree that he so desperately tried to crawl under. I thought about mama and her need to be loved by so many men when I was right there in the same house and I would have loved her just fine, but she didn't want just me. And I thought about Kimmy and the way her gorgeous body had gotten her into so much trouble. I thought and I thought and time melted away with the current of the river.

I helped coach that spring. I spent hours planning the lineup and I could run the girls around the bases with a flick of my wrist. The great thing about being with the girls was the fact that I was someone important in their eyes. They thought I was incredible because I could hit the ball, place the ball and throw a runner out at home from center field. Never mind I wasn't going to college and I worked washing dishes and waiting tables at a tiny café in a tiny town. That didn't faze them at all.

"What's it like?" Gina, a sophomore starter asked me after practice one day.

"What's what like?"

"What's it like to be so good at something?"

"You should know," I told her, "you are a very good ball player. Don't ever let anyone tell you differently. I mean that."

She looked at me with pale blue eyes and she smiled.

Summer came, I waitressed all the time now. Mazzie hired a new dishwasher, John. He was very quiet and had a long grey ponytail that fell almost to his butt. He was one of the loggers who were pushed out of work when another section of the mill closed down. "I'll do anything," he said, "to feed my family."

"Emma, come here!" Kimmy came into the restaurant one hot afternoon. She dragged me away from the counter and out the door of the restaurant. She pulled me around the outside of the building and pointed. Sure enough, there it was, the poster for the fucking Carlos carnival.

"You're order is up! You think you're in the goddamned union or something?" Joe shouted as he stuck his head out the back door.

Mama cleaned the house and got rid of "Vinsssent". She caught me one morning drinking coffee at the kitchen table. I normally tried to escape before she awoke.

"I read you the other day," she said. "You are a lot clearer."

I didn't say anything, just drank my coffee.

"I know what goes on with you. You don't even need to talk to me you know. I can read you like you were my other soul."

"Shut up! I don't want to be read. Don't read me anymore. I hate it when you do that." My voice cracked with morning sleep.

"Well that's fine, but you can't tell me who I can read and who I can't. You like it fine when it serves your purpose. In fact you like everything when it serves your purpose. You are just like him you know." She turned to the sink.

"Are you talking about my father? I thought you said you only knew my father for three weeks? How do you know I'm just like him?"

"Three weeks is plenty of time to know someone and besides I did his chart. I know his personality traits and the past life baggage he was carrying with him and I'll tell you, he had a lot. He had some heavy stuff to haul around. So now I see you with your brooding and your angry personality and I know you are carrying some of the same stuff.

Don't tell me I don't know. I know things you would never dream about."

"Oh yeah?" I was shouting now. "Do you know how much I hate all the men you drag home?" There it was out. I had said it, another dirty piece of me waiting to be scrubbed.

"Yes," she said softly. "I see that." And she left the room, her robe tied about her. Her shoulders looked sad and narrow.

When Carlos came, I had to admit, the world lightened up. I saw him from the front window. He ran up the walk and yelled out, "Rosalene!" But she had just left for the market, to get wine probably and whatever alcohol she could get her hands on so she and Carlos could really party.

"Rosalene!" he yelled again. I opened the front door and it stopped him. His breath went in instead of out.

"You look just like your mama now, except your hair's darker." He swallowed hard, touched my hair. "Hi Emma." He reached out and grabbed me into a hug and I could smell the machinery oil and the tobacco on his shirt.

"I've missed you, you and your mama." He pulled away. His hair was longer and he had braided it into a single braid that ran down his back. He smiled in the July sun. He had on a white tank top, like he always wore. He was so much the same it felt like an old familiar smell. I wasn't sure if I could go on hating him.

Later it was take out pizza, mama and the cards, smoke in the kitchen, bottles of red wine in every room, some opened some not. Mama loved to have more than one bottle open at a time so she and Carlos could do taste tests. Her feet were in his lap. She smoked a cigarette, shuffled the cards over and over. Her cigarette dangled from her mouth like a tree limb.

"Tell me who I love," Carlos said.

"Why, me, my borracho, why, me." Mama put her head back and laughed. Her red hair fell back behind her, red curls everywhere. Carlos stroked her feet.

Carlos announced that he was going to stay on after the carnival left. "I'm taking a leave of absentia," he said, "a long siesta with my baby."

He wrapped his arms around mama's waist.

Mama looked at me, her red hair tangled about her, "Won't that be nice Emma?"

"Great." I grabbed a cigarette out of mama's pack on the table and sat on the back step. I heard the frogs singing. Spring and summer they sang, tonight it sounded especially sad. I heard the screen open. Carlos sat beside me. He let his breath out.

"You don't like me much do you Conchita?"

"What's not to like? You come to town, eat at our house, sleep at our house, smoke and drink at our house, have sex with my mama at our house. What's not to like?"

"I love your mama Emma. I have loved her since the day I laid my eyes upon her," he said.

"You and everybody else." I paused. "Do you know how many boyfriends she has while you're gone? Do you have any idea how many men she sleeps with? You are just one of a zillion."

He looked at me hard, his brown eyes soft. "I know, aren't I lucky?"

I shook my head. I couldn't believe it. He was content to be one of hundreds, just to take his time with her and be thankful. It was screwed up, it was. I tried to blow smoke rings.

"I love you too, Emma. I hope you know. I worry about you and I think about you when I am traveling." He kicked at the pebbles in front of his foot. "I never had a child, you know. Well, I did once, but the baby, she died. She was two months old and it ruined the love my wife had for me. I laid that baby in her basket one night and kissed her head at the top, kissed her where her black curl stood up. The next morning she was so still. My wife, Lucita, was still sleeping so I was very quiet. I let the baby sleep, but she was not asleep. All that time she was dead Emma. God had taken her in the night. He snuck right into the house and sucked the breath out of her. My wife never forgave me. She thought I let the baby die. She thought I killed Josephina."

I stared at the maple tree. Its twisted trunk was full of faces in the night shadows. I didn't know what to say to Carlos, but I felt like crying. "I'm sorry," I said.

"Thank you."

The frogs sang louder.

"That is why I am so happy to be with your mama, even if I am one of thousands, because I know what love is like to lose and I like to keep all the love I can get, you know Conchita?" Carlos stood and went back into the house. I could hear him rousing up mama, calling her for a whiskey drink. She was answering him and laughing.

I thought about Carlos having a baby. A baby girl and I thought I would like to be someone's baby girl, a father's baby girl. A baby girl who got kissed on the head and held in big strong arms that wouldn't let her fall to the floor. Josephina was lucky for two months of her life.

Carlos planned on calling his nephew to come and run the carnival. "I've got two more shows this summer and I know Jesus can handle it. If I can find him, he will come."

"That's his name?" I asked.

"That is his name and he is just like the divine protector, just you wait and see."

Jesus came. Two weeks later he arrived from California on the Greyhound. "I'm going to pick him up today," Carlos announced early one morning. The heat was beginning to settle into the ground, a slight breeze above it. "You want to come Emma? I am taking the truck to Seattle. I knew I could find him. I ask the saint of lost things to help and *voila*! There he comes!"

"Where was he?" I asked.

"He was in Anaheim working for Disneyland. Those Mickey Mouse people, they are hard on their help, I tell you, too many sticky children. Hmmpf, much worse than the carnival, I tell him. Better to be your own boss." He lit a cigarette and watched its smoke float. "What do you say Emma, you want to ride with me to the city? I will take you to Chinatown."

"I guess. I don't have to work so, all right. You have to buy me an egg roll though."

"Yes, deal." He fingered the gold Saint Christopher that hung against his dark chest.

I changed into a sundress and dark sandals and that is the day I fell in love again.

The bus stop was in the heart of a downtown block. There was graffiti on every inch of the cinderblock walls of the station. As we walked down the sidewalk I could smell the piss. Two guys asked me for change. Carlos gave them each a dollar and they gave him the peace sign. "I have begged for money. As a boy in Cuba I begged for money to feed my aunt and my sisters. I would have died for one dollar. There is no pride in begging and nothing to shame oneself for either. Oh God of Cuba, I do love money!"

We came around the corner into the din of the terminal and I saw the most beautiful man I had ever seen in my life. Tall, legs like a race horse, dark long hair in a pony tail, two gold hoops in one ear and eyes as black as the tar on the street. He wore Levis and a black shirt with a red dragon crawling down the front. His upper arms were strong with tattoos on every inch. He yelled in Spanish when he saw Carlos and Carlos hugged him tightly, spinning him without lifting him. He was heavier than mama; he wouldn't come off the ground.

Carlos introduced me and I held out my hand to shake his, but instead he embraced me and in those arms I felt six years old, tucked into my mattress bed with the moonlight spilling on my body and the smell of cut grass in my hair. "So beautiful," he whispered in my ear. Then he let me go.

"We are a very close family Emma. Always lots of body contact, huh, Jesus?" He clapped Jesus on the back. Jesus' gaze wrapped circles around me. I didn't know if I could walk.

We stopped at Chinatown and bought a dozen egg rolls to go and some Chinese pastries for mama. Jesus spoke fluent Chinese with the pastry woman. She was short and her whole face crinkled when she laughed. Jesus' laugh rang out like crickets on a summer's night.

"How did you learn to speak Chinese?" I asked. Our legs were touching in the truck and I could smell his skin. It smelled like honey.

"It was Mandarin and in L.A. you have to learn to speak all kinds of languages if you want to talk to people. My landlady spoke it. I taught her some Spanish, she taught me some Mandarin. I know how to say beautiful lady in four different languages."

"Enough," Carlos barked from the drivers side. "You are not Don Juan. Emma is like my daughter. Charm some other man's daughter."

I am like his daughter? I held that thought in the palm of my hand while I watched the sunlight skim the water as we crossed the bridge.

We brought Jesus to the house. Mama had made dinner and we all drank chianti and were still drinking chianti when Carlos and Jesus went out on the back porch to talk business. Mama got out her cards. She laid the silk on the table, shuffled the deck. Cut the cards three times. Laid out a circle of cards, face up. She slowly lit a cigarette, took a sip of wine, looked at the cards. She looked up at me and smiled. "I won't tell you what I see. I know how you hate it, I understand that now."

I wanted to ask. For once I felt like knowing. "What do they say?" I ventured.

She lifted one eyebrow. "They say that you will be entwined with another's heart and this heart will be magic for you. But the destiny is uncertain. You must live it for every minute and not another minute past at any given time."

"What the hell does that mean?"

"Be in the present with this heart at all times Emma." She blew a smoke ring, tapped her red fingernail on her glass. She was drinking out of a beer mug that said, "Drink it! Love it!" on the side.

I wished I wouldn't have asked.

"A twin heart does not necessarily mean a man Emma. It means a soul mate and that can be found in friends too," she said. She put the cards in a pile and set them to the side. "Carlos wants me to read for Jesus. He is a good looking young man, isn't he?"

"How old is he?" I asked.

"Twenty eight. Young enough to be my son."

Jesus worked every day with Carols at the carnival and every night he slept on the couch. He and Carlos usually came home late. They ate leftovers at the round battered table while mama poured glasses of whiskey for everyone. I usually had wine if anything and I would sit on the periphery and watch. Watch Jesus' big arms, stained with grease, flex and release, flex and release. Listen to his deep laugh and watch his white teeth flash in the candlelight. "How about another read Rosa?" He called mama Rosa and she seemed to think this was the prettiest name she had ever heard.

"You hear the nickname he has for me?" she asked me one morning. "I adore it. He has the nicest voice."

Sometimes Jesus would cook and the spices would sail down the sidewalk clear to the next block. Marsha noticed one night when she was picking me up for a party. She came to the door, her car was idling in the driveway and the first words I heard her say were, "Christ almighty what is that glorious smell?" She took one look at Jesus and said, "Jesus, who is this glorious man?"

"Marsha, this is Jesus," I said. He extended one hand, holding a spatula with the other.

"Oh sorry," she said.

She turned her car off and stayed for dinner and later at the party, sitting on cushions and smoking a bowl she said, "What of that gorgeous man Emma?"

"He's like a brother. He is Carlos' nephew."

"Your mama told me that, that makes him fair game. No blood exchanged there. He is one beautiful looking human being."

"Yeah."

"A regular Michelangelo subject if you ask me. Pass me that pipe."

Sometimes Jesus would come to the 2 x 4 and eat lunch.

"How did you get away?" I asked him one afternoon.

"I am a shape shifter. One minute you see me, the next minute you don't. How do you think I plan to get into your room tonight Emma?"

"Right," I said, walking off with limp knees. I pictured him in my room, shirt off. I tripped.

One day he sat at my favorite front booth at the 2x4. I served him coffee and two grilled cheese sandwiches. "The carnival leaves in a week Emma. Tonight, show me somewhere special. I feel I hardly know this place. I want to know what you know."

After work I showered and waited. I could sense he and Carlos walking home from blocks away, laughing and talking fast in Spanish.

They came in and Jesus grabbed my hand, pulling me off the couch. "Let's go Emma." I waved my hand to Carlos and left him looking surprised in the kitchen.

We walked to the river, carefully down the rocks, as the moonlight was not as strong as usual. All over we could hear the frogs burping. The rush of the water grew louder as we grew near. "Ah that sound is magic!" Jesus said. He held my hand as we stumbled along in the dark. We sat on a large rock, our thighs touching. We were silent for a very long time and then Jesus said, "This is just how I want it to be for me."

"What do you mean?" I asked.

"I mean silence. To be with someone I love and have silence."

"Love? What did you just say?"

"Sure, I love you. I love your mama and my uncle and many people. I love to love Emma."

"Oh good," I said, "you're just like mama. She loves everybody, especially if they're men."

We walked to the football field. It was still very warm; the moon was high now and filtering in and out of thin clouds.

"Lie down," I said. "This is me and Kimmy's secret spot. This is where we come and hold hands, smoke cigarettes on our backs and talk about everything that needs to be talked about. Before she moved away anyway."

We laid on the grass. Jesus grabbed my hand. "We have to hold hands, you said so," he said. He rolled on top of me and I could feel his heart pumping into my own. Vibrating my body.

"What are you doing?"

"Feeling you," he said, "feeling all of you." He started running his hands up and down the sides of me. He started singing to me, soft and sensuous, a Spanish lullaby and the rhythm went along with his searching hands.

"You are like a daughter to Carlos, and I, I am like a son. He tells me this everyday in the hope that I will leave you alone, but I cannot. I have been dreaming of this moment since I first saw you at the bus station. You are my one and only waitress, so sexy, so beautiful, so pure. The way you walk is like magic to my skin." He started to sing again and then he stopped because he was kissing me and I could feel his hands every where, fast and then slow and then fast again and I knew this was a lot like Danny when love was pure, before I was hurt. I felt like I'd recaptured something and it was good. I kissed him back and the night opened up like the river, tumbling and falling. I thought of mama and her cards and I think she was right.

A week is not that long, especially when you have to spend every moment you can find getting under someone's skin. It was the night before Jesus was to pack up and leave for the next town and the carnival was staying up late for its grand finale. I watched Jesus work and any chance we got we would slip into a vacant tent or the cab of a truck and search each other's bodies for all that we could find. I don't know if Carlos knew, and I wondered how he couldn't. Jesus walked me to the river after the lights finally faded and the last voices could be heard shouting over the rides.

"Come with me," he said. "Come with me to Spokane, that's the next stop for us. I want you night and day."

That night in my room I fell asleep watching the moon slip by a cloud. I woke up before 6 a.m. Jesus was still asleep on the couch, his back curled up facing the room. I could see the delicate bones of his spine through the blanket.

I went to the kitchen and called Marsha.

"What?" She yelled into the phone, "It's six o'clock and this better be really fucking good!"

"Marsha?" I asked.

"What?"

"Wanna cover my shifts for the next couple of weeks?"

"For what?" she asked.

"So I can go on a road trip with Jesus?"

"Are you getting laid finally?"

"Yea."

"Then of course I'll do it. Thank god you're not going to be a fucking nun. I'll check the calendar and what I can't cover I'll get the new girl to do it. She's been kissing my ass anyway, I hate that."

"Thanks Marsha," I said. "I love you."

"Damn right you do, and why wouldn't you?" She hung up.

Jesus rolled over and looked at me through his long dark eyelashes. "Does that mean you're going with me?"

"Yea, three weeks tops and don't put me in any freaky sideshow. Oh, and I want to be paid if I do any work because I'm losing my hours at the 2x4."

"Fair enough my beautiful maiden. Don't you have to ask your mama?"

"I could ask mama if I should join up with Patty Hearst and she would say, 'If you need to honey, but let me do a reading on you first.' So, no I don't think I need to ask my mama."

We left in the morning in the pickup truck with the lion and the circus hoops painted on the sides. Mama hugged me goodbye and said she would see me in three weeks. Carlos kissed me seven times on the cheek. "For good luck," he said.

We drove to Spokane with our hands entwined, windows open, knees touching. Jesus thumped out tunes on the steering wheel and I sang along. We stopped for lunch in Cle Elum and had burger dips with limpid fries, but I loved it. I loved every second of being out of Tolt, away from the sameness and the sturdiness that had begun to wrap around me like a tree trunk. It was not good to be a tree trunk in a logging town.

"We're are almost there Emma. Carlos brought me here years ago, when I ran one of the rides for him, when he was short handed on a summer. I love the river here, it is wide and deep and not so fast as your river, unless you get near the falls that is. I love the falls. It feels very much like the heart spirit there. We'll try to go to the falls." He smiled at me, his teeth white as the freshest snow. I loved to listen to him talk.

We pulled into Spokane and into a large empty lot in a downtown block. Jesus parked the truck and helped me out. Spokane felt hot, a dry kind of heat that went right into your bones. I stretched. He held my arms above my head, helping me. He kissed me long and hard and whispered, "I am so glad you came."

We walked the blocks around us, wandering, seeing a record store, a five and dime, a used car lot, a gas station, a used furniture store and a couple of empty dusty storefronts with for lease signs in the window. We got back to the lot and more trucks began to pull in. The Tilt a Whirl truck, with its massive bright colored apparatus tucked in tight. The History of Doom truck with its looming trailer depicting creatures of another planet and time, the Zipper truck with the cages rocking and rolling on the back; truck after truck after truck. The trucks parked in a circle like a wagon train and the drivers listened to Jesus describe the layout.

"Donny and Danny, you guys settle in west over there and around you I want the Tilt a Whirl and the Zipper. I want the little people rides all together like always on the east and in between we'll have the food and games so they have to walk by them every time they want to go from one area of rides to the next. Comprende?" I heard a lot of yes' and grunts of agreement. "Tents go over there, and my tent will be over here," he pointed to a corner of the lot by the only visible tree. "If you're sleeping in an r.v., keep it around the perimeter. The sani-cans will be here in an hour so hold it until then or hide it when you go. I don't want to scare off the neighbors yet." Nobody paid much attention to me and I was grateful, it gave me a chance to watch Jesus, watch his biceps flex and relax beneath his white shirt, watch his face light up when he heard a funny remark, watch his dark braid swirl in the light of the sun. Was this what it was like to be enraptured?

It took the rest of the day, but by dusk it was beginning to look like a carnival. The empty lot had been transformed into a feast of color, sounds, smells and energy. Jesus had gotten straw to lie down between the rows of games and rides. "It makes people feel more at home," he said, "better than looking at brown dirt and it feels soft beneath their shoes." He had thought of everything.

Our tent was near the back; behind the "Seeing Eye" trailer that was full of freakish things "the eyes could hardly believe". We threw down a foam pad and zipped two blue sleeping bags together to form our bed. It was better than my mattress on the floor at home. Jesus had a couple of battery operated lights and a big jug of water for washing up and a small table where he put a few books and a jar with some flowers he had picked at the back of the lot. They were black-eyed susans, their petals yellow and wispy against the gray of the tent. I felt like a whole new person.

"We'll shower at the city park when we need to Emma. I hope this will be enough for you. I forgot to tell you that it was not like a home, more like a camp of the simplest kind."

"It's good Jesus. I like it. I like you." I wrapped my arms around his waist, pulled him down atop the blue sleeping bags and kissed his neck, then his chest where the hairs parted his shirt. I lifted his shirt and kissed between his ribs, getting down to his waist.

"Jesus, the bottle blower up the ass needs you." A guy with two long red ponytails stuck his head into the tent. He looked me over then said, "He can't get his fucking bottles to stack, the fucking imbecile, I told him to give it a fucking rest and he said…well, sorry to bother you, but he said I was a fucking useless twat. I take offense at that."

"I will come."

I laid on the foam pad and listened to the sounds of the evening, listened to the rise and fall of Jesus' voice above it all.

In the morning coffee was brewing everywhere on any makeshift fire that could be found. Bunsen burners were going and tiny hot plates and a couple of bonfires behind some of the trailers. Jesus walked around with his cowboy boots and Levis, a tight white t-shirt. He passed the bonfires. "Put it out," he said as he passed them by.

The carnival was set to open at noon and it was my job to go into town as far as I could walk and hand out flyers. The flyers had a tight ropewalker and a swinging monkey, which had nothing whatever to do with the carnival, but looked dramatic on the handbills.

"You got circus girls in tight costumes?" one guy asked me.

"We've got it all," I lied.

When I got to a corner about five blocks away, I turned and headed down a narrow side street, an alley between two main streets. I thought I could cut over to the block that I hadn't covered yet. The sun was starting to get hot. I stripped down to my tank top, tying my shirt about my waist.

Two guys came from a doorway in front of me. They stopped still when they saw me. One started to whistle. Not a light and airy whistle. This was an animal down in the throat whistle. The kind of whistle that makes time slow down.

"What ya sellin' sister?" the non-whistler asked me. He had bloodshot brown eyes and I could smell the alcohol on his body.

"I'm buying!" said the whistler. He had muddy sideburns, muddy eyes, and a grin that hung down heavy in one corner. He reached a hand out and hooked the front of my tank top.

I started to walk backwards, he and his buddy moved forwards. I turned, jerking his finger out of my shirt and started to run. I was running back the way I had come, but I could hear them behind me. They were walking fast, and then running. "I think she wants to play," the whistler said. I ran faster, my heart pounding, my chest hurt. I heard their feet in the gravel getting closer. I rounded the corner looking at the ground and ran smack hard into the middle of a man's chest. He was dressed in a tan suit, his tie tucked into the buttons of his shirt. He was big and his face had a pinkness to it from the beating sun. At that moment it looked like the friendliest face I had ever seen. He grabbed my arms to steady me.

"Whoa," he said.

"Help me," I whispered. "They're chasing me."

He looked over my shoulder. "I've been looking all over for you Susie," he said much too loudly. "We've got to get over to the church for the bible study. Well hello boys, you need some help with something?" The whistler and his friend stopped. My new friend stared them down. They stared back for a moment then turned without a word and walked back down the alley. I felt my chest give way and a heaving sob took the place of the air I had been holding. The big guy held me close. He stroked my hair. "It's alright," he said sweetly. "Now tell me where you are supposed to be so I can be sure you get there."

"I'm with the carnival a few blocks back." I wiped my eyes, wiped my snotty nose.

"Oh!" he exclaimed, "I'm taking my little girls there tonight! I love the carnival. No cheating on the stakes of those games. I want to win my little girls a big stuffed animal tonight!" He held me at arms length. "Imagine, you working at the carnival! A damsel in distress and I get to rescue her! Let's get you back there little miss!"

When Jesus heard what had happened he made me go to the tent and lie down. He left and came back with a cool washcloth. It was very clean and smelled lightly of bleach. He stroked my face, washed my arms and wiped my breastbones. Then he laid beside me and held me close to him. He didn't say a word for a long time.

"Carlos was right. I can't take care of you. I cannot let anything like that happen again. If I ever see those guys I will cut them, I promise you Emma, I will cut them."

"Jesus, it's okay. It's over. I'm all right. Everything turned out alright."

"I love you Emma," he said. He buried his face in my hair and closed his eyes.

The carnival smells and sounds went on until eleven p.m that night. I had no real job to speak of, so I picked up trash and tried to meet some of the workers. There were a few familiar faces, but a lot of people I had never seen. Jesus passed me here and there, took a kiss, grabbed my ass, and winked at me. Each time my chest would fill like a red balloon and it was all I could do to keep from floating away. I saw the man who rescued me and sure enough, he had two large animals under his arms. One was a purple elephant and the other an enormous duck. He winked at me. "The girls are on a ride. You take care little missy!"

"Lock-down," Jesus yelled out at eleven. I could hear clanging and banging and shouts from up and down the carnival aisles. All of a sudden the air changed and everything felt lighter. The workers talked to me more and I tried to offer help to a few. I helped the dart and balloon game worker pull her stuffed animals from the edge of her awning and crank it closed.

"Your Jesus'girl ain't you?" she asked.

"I guess."

She popped her gum, looked at me sideways. "I'm Marla. Stay away from Danny and Donny, they like little girls," and with that she let out a cackling laugh. "I also read palms." She reached over and grabbed my hand. "You want your palm read cutie?"

"No thanks. I just got away from that," I said. I pulled my hand away.

"You don't never get away from that," she said, and she spit on the ground.

I heard music playing from a boom box and a lot of hollering at the end of the field. There were three barbeques going, the coals just started. A tall lanky guy set crates and stumps around the barbeques in a circle. I noticed a folding table being set up and on it a couple of ladies were stacking paper plates and bowls of chips. There were bottles of pop and paper cups and a large tin of ice. It had all appeared effortlessly. The smells were intoxicating and pretty soon a cooler opened full of small bloody steaks and I heard one of the guys from the demo derby ride yell, "Make it rare Stuey! You know I like my steaks like my chicks! Soft and bleedin'!" A lot of cheering followed that and then Jesus walked into the center of things and it got very quiet. He read off some numbers.

"Not bad for the first day. Let's eat!" he said. He came over to me, put his arm around my waist and said, "Things get a little crazy now. Let me know when you want to go to the tent."

When I looked over at the barbeques, they were loaded with steaks and someone had put five big jugs of tequila on the folding table.

The tequila flowed anywhere and everywhere and the boom box got louder. It was a rhythm and blues tune, and some of the guys jumped up and swirled their hips, running their hands up and down their thighs like strippers. Everyone cheered and laughed, letting the tequila flow through their veins. Jesus laughed and threw coins at them. The gal with the three golden braids who ran the cotton candy booth started putting dollar bills in the dancer's jeans and then she undulated with them, her braids swinging in circles around her head. I was getting warmer and warmer and the lights from the street lamps were moving in and out of the bodies, casting shadows and rainbows. I tried to focus, but everything moved too quickly. Jesus brought out some weed and rolled one joint after another and tiny Thomas, the mechanic lit them; he took the first toke off of each one before passing them. Two guys wrestled and then the crowd really started cheering. They both wore cowboy boots and they slipped and slid in the gravel and the straw, grabbing hold of each other's sweaty chests. Jesus put his arm around me and whispered in my ear, "My girl's getting fucked up. I need to take you home to our pretty little tent Conchita."

Sirens sounded in the distance and before I could turn my head, the tequila bottles were gone. The joints were out. The music kept playing, but everyone had sat down or dispersed into the shadows. A patrol car went by slowly, lights shining on the gravel and straw lot, casting yellow light on the aluminum sides of the trailers. A loud voice, "Noise ordinance boys, keep it down. Y'all go to bed now ya hear?"

The next morning there was not a trace of a party. No litter, no bottles, nothing, just a lonely barbeque with a bag of briquettes beside it. The daytime noise of the carnival began again.

On the third day, Jesus and I cut out in the middle of the afternoon. We walked eleven blocks to a park on the Spokane River. There was a merry go round inside a large steel building with big windows that overlooked the water. We went in and bought tickets. I rode the orange and pink giraffe and Jesus rode the blue elephant. We tried to hold hands, but we were too far apart, so on the next ride we broke the rules and sat on the same painted ostrich together.

We were lying on the grass outside the building. "I wish I had a camera," I said.

"We can go back to the carnival and use the photo booth," he said.

"But I want to capture this moment Jesus, this one right here. You and the sun and the merry go round in the background and the sound of the river and the children yelling behind us."

He looked at me and cocked his head. "You can't put sound in the picture."

"You can," I said, "because when you see it, even years from now you can close your eyes and you can smell and hear everything that happened when the picture was taken at that particular moment."

"Can you taste it too?"

"Taste what?"

"The moment."

"Oh yeah," I said.

"Then taste this," he said and he kissed me hard, sending me backward onto the grass. His tongue went everywhere in my mouth, brushing every tooth and feeling every hill and valley.

"I think I would remember that too," I said when it was over.

When we were walking back I asked him, "Have you had many girlfriends?"

"Dozens," he laughed.

"I'm sure. Do you remember them all?"

"Always," he said. "Especially the ones I've slept with."

"And how many is that?"

"Trillions," he laughed. "I am very desirable. Mucho desirable."

"Yeah, I know."

"And you?" he asked.

"Not many. You and another guy and a guy named Danny."

"Ah."

"What's the 'ah'?" I asked.

"It's an I know how you felt about Danny 'ah'."

"How do you know?"

He leaned into me and put his hot breath on my neck. "Every time you give it to a man he owns a piece of you. Forever."

"Is that so?"

He grabbed me around the waist and turned me to face him. "That's so."

Jesus gave the lock down call at eleven. "I need to call Carlos," Jesus said. We walked to a phone booth around the corner. Jesus lifted the receiver and started to dial, then stopped. "I do not know your phone number."

"Let me do that. You feed the quarters in."

She answered sleepily on the first ring. "Hello."

"Mama? It's me Emma."

"Emma." I could tell she had been drinking. I heard Carlos moan beside her, say something in a muffled voice. "It's Emma," mama said to him. "How's the carnival Emma? Are you a star yet?"

"No mama. I mostly pick up trash and run errands for the vendors. It's not real glamorous." Jesus frowned.

"Emma. Be careful around water. I saw something in your cards that was not good and it had to do with water. Don't swim baby."

"Mama, I didn't call you for a reading. How's Kimmy?"

"I think she is good. Do you want to talk to Carlos?"

"No, Jesus does," I said. "I want to talk to you. Do you want to talk?"

"Well, I was asleep, I think, and I am a little tired. I worked at the library today and tomorrow I have two readings. I have to meditate for that, you know. Yes…I think…well, I am sleepy."

"Is Carlos helping you?"

"Carlos is my Cuban dreamboat. Aren't you Carlos?" She giggled, "I have to go now Emma. I love you so much. You tell Jesus to take good care of my baby." She hung up.

I looked at the receiver. I looked at Jesus. "She hung up on me."

"Oh." He took the receiver out of my hand and hung it slowly back on its hook. He felt in the coin drop for money.

"I think she was drunk. I know she was drunk. We woke her up."

"Carlos will take care of her. Let's go." We walked back to the lot. The barbeque was going and I could see the red light of a joint and hear the clinking of ice cubes in a glass. It was whiskey and coke tonight and everyone was betting on a beetle race. Two beetles were side by side in the gravel, each heading for the same piece of biscuit in the lamplight.

"They look the same to me, I don't know how you would tell which one won if they ever crossed paths," I said aloud.

"Don't you know a beetle never changes course," said Donny.

"Yeah, just like a carni," said Danny. Everyone laughed and the moon rose in the sky.

Genevieve worked the curly fries and corn dog booth. She owned it actually, and hauled it behind her firebird from carnival spot to carnival spot. She was thirty-six years old and had ten tattoos. I'd seen them all, even the drunken monkey on her left butt cheek.

"I like it," I said. It was yellow and black with a ringed tail.

"It's a ring tailed lemur," she said. "I saw one at the Honolulu zoo, right before I did a surfer on the beach." She laughed and lit a cigarette.

"Should you be smoking around the fryers?" It was early and the fryers were just starting to heat up. Genevieve cooked all her food early then left it under the heat lamps to get good and soggy. That was how the kids liked it, she told me, "If you cook it fresh, they don't wait around."

"I smoke in here all the time." Ashes fell in the corn batter mixture. She stirred them in. I changed the station on the radio. "Give me some kinda rock and roll," she said. Her pink hair stood up straight, she had on eyeliner, thick and black and big blue swipes of shadow trimmed in gold. She looked beautiful. She turned toward the window and as she did her mouth fell open, "Fuck!" She was staring at something and as I got up to look out the door of the trailer to see what the "fuck" was for, an explosion happened in the fryer. Her cigarette had fallen sideways from her mouth when the "fuck" had erupted and it had landed in the fryer. Genevieve jumped and screamed. I grabbed a pitcher of water standing by the sink and threw it on the fryer fire when Genevieve screamed, "Don't! Oil and water don't..." but she didn't get all the words out before the flames leaped higher, catching the kitschy red and white striped curtains on fire and turning one whole side of the trailer into a sheet of white and orange light. I grabbed Genevieve and pulled her out the trailer door. The sleeve of her "I never go to bed alone" sweatshirt was on fire. I remembered the "drop and roll" speech we got in sixth grade and pushed her to the ground, rolling her arm in the gritty dirt and straw. Thank god the straw didn't catch on fire.

"Damn it, you're killing me!" she shouted. I fell on the ground beside her and heard the sirens of the fire truck in the distance. We watched the trailer glow from within. I heard footsteps behind us. Two of the floaty boat guys dragged us in the dirt until we were far from the trailer. They brought us paper cups of water and sat beside us in the grass.

"Jesus isn't going to like this," said the shorter one, Rikki. "He hates it when we cause a scene."

"Well, this is one fucking scene," said Genevieve. "There goes my life."

"Yep," the rest of us said, almost in unison.

Later that night, after the fire trucks had gone and the crowd had forgone corndogs and curly fries, we were sitting by the barbeque toasting marshmallows on pathetic sticks when I remembered Genevieve had seen something before the fire.

"What did you see out the window?" I asked Genevieve.

She was bundled in a red blanket sitting in a lawn chair next to Donny and Danny. The bumper car twins were going to put her up in their fifth wheeler.

"I thought I saw my ex. Strangest thing. I could have sworn it was him, walkin' down the road with a poodle. He hated poodles."

Later in the tent with my body curled around Jesus' strong back he said, "Your mama was right."

"What?"

"She told you to watch for the water, right? She was right. You should listen to her Emma. She knows, she always knows."

I shut my eyes tight and tried to shut out what he was saying. "It wasn't the water!"

"What the hell? It was the water. Why do you always have to not count her for what she says? She is a seer. If you listen with your insides you can hear her. You don't hear right Emma"

"Don't talk to me like that in your goddamn broken English, I hate that." I pushed the flap back on the tent and crawled out into the night. I pulled my sweat pants on in the dark and walked barefoot around the quiet carnival. I heard faint voices coming from inside trailers and tents and I heard laughing from the corner of the field. I walked in that direction, too mad to care about Jesus, too mad to crawl back in bed beside him. I saw Genevieve and Donny folded into each other on the grass, smoking a joint and their laughter was like breaking ice on a mountain stream, releasing all that you know is good and fresh in the world.

"Did you hear the one about the bearded lady?" Donny asked, passing the joint to Genevieve.

Genevieve shrieked with laughter, "Don't tell me. Don't tell me, I'm going to pee my pants." I thought about joining them, but instead I walked away into the shadows, quietly on my bare toes holding that perfect image in my non-perfect palm.

"In six more days Emma, we leave this carnival you know." Jesus talked to me while he cooked breakfast on the camp stove. He had eggs in a pan on one burner and toast lying across the other burner, searing in the center, still soft around the edges. It tasted good though, if you put enough butter on it. "I take you back to your mama and Carlos and I, we have to go to Bellingham next, then Canada. Do you want to come with us?"

"If I don't?"

"I will come back for you." He flipped the eggs. "I will always come for you Emma." He offered me a plate of eggs and half toasted toast, his arm out stretched. "You believe me?"

"Yes."

We sat on lawn chairs. The sun was soft in the sky, small white clouds danced around the edges. It was going to be hot again. It was always hot in Spokane. Even the rain was hot when it fell in big droplets from the sky. "Do you want to come?"

I could see myself following Jesus forever. Going without showers, eating on the fringes of time and space, sleeping in tents on the ground, smelling and hearing and tasting all the sights and sounds of the carnival. It was like living in a mirage or living inside a play that never seemed to end. It wasn't bad, but it wasn't great either. There were days I longed for coffee and a cigarette with Marsha or a swim in the cold current of the river with Kimmy, or the crickets I heard at night when the window was wide open.

"I don't know. Maybe I should try to find a way to go to school or something," I said. "I don't want to stand in the bread line with mama and I don't want my kids standing in the bread line either." The color rose in my cheeks.

"Yea, I know. You are really smart Emma. You should go and use your head and do something for your head. I love your head, it turns me on you know."

"Everything turns you on."

"Yea," he smiled shyly at me and took another bite of egg. "Don't be afraid to go to school you know."

How did he always know what I was feeling? And then the thought struck me, what would I do without him? I would not be able to live, I thought.

"I don't know," I said, "I just don't know. I'll have to think about it."

I worked that day on the Zipper ride, the ride that made people throw up. Six kids heaved out of the cars while it was running, throwing spew everywhere on the ground.

"Use a hose on it," Mitchell said. "Don't ever touch it, you never know what kind of parasite lives in barf."

We hosed the cars down too and sprayed them with some disinfectant that smelled as bad as the barf. I decided this was my least favorite ride.

"They don't all barf you know." Mitchell looked me straight in the eyes. "This can be a very fun ride. Do you want to try it? On the house?"

"No."

I left an hour later with a bikini on under my shorts and tank top and my soap and towel in a bag and headed down to the river where I bathed and washed my hair. As I was walking back I saw Jesus in the phone booth on the corner. I crossed the street to him and caught him as he was hanging up the black phone. His face was the palest of brown.

"We have to go home now."

"What? You can't leave."

"I will be back. You need to go home, I will need to drive you there."

"Why?"

"Your mama, she is sick."

"What do you mean sick?"

"Carlos said she won't get out of bed."

"What do you mean she won't get out of bed? She's probably hung over."

"No, Carlos said she hasn't been out of bed for seven days, that is not hung over."

"She's probably faking it. She wants attention. I can't stand that."

We walked the blocks back in silence. Jesus was kicking stones. "It doesn't matter if you think she fakes Emma, you still have to go. You are the daughter."

"I don't want to leave yet. I don't want to leave you. I don't want to go back there. We haven't even gone to the falls. I want to go to the falls," I was whining like a five year old. "I mean what could be wrong, does she have the flu or something; she have a virus? I mean if that's it, all Carlos has to do is…"

"Emma," he whirled about to face me, grabbed both my shoulders. "You have to go, Carlos said he can not handle her, he is lost to what to do. You have to go, you are the daughter; blood is blood."

"Blood is blood! Shit, you think this is some kind of a movie or something, that's so cryptic! I hate her. Her blood is not my blood!"

"I love your mama."

"Yea, well you can have her, all she does is ruin my life."

"Are you not even worried some?" he asked.

"No."

He packed up my things. Jesus gave directions to Danny and Donny and said he would be back in one day, which meant he was going to take me home, turn around and leave. I looked at the field, the tent, the crazy rides, the colorful booths that were starting to get grimy around the bottoms from the dust and the dirt. I took in a long smell, filling my lungs with the memory of Spokane and the carnival and the disjointed workers. I felt tears inside, inching their way up. I got in the truck and slammed the door. I couldn't say goodbye to anyone.

Jesus started chatting stupid antidotes. I wished he would shut up. He pulled off in Ellensburg.

"You want a bite to eat Conchita?" he asked

"No."

"Emma, you have to eat. You have to eat and let go of this bad feeling you have. You are acting like a little girl. Life is good Emma. I will take you to so many more carnivals it will make your head rotate."

"Spin."

"What?"

"It's spin, it will make your head spin. Get it?" It felt good to be mean to him.

"Uh…yea. We are getting something to eat. I am hungry as a herd of ponies."

"Pack. Pack of ponies. Herds are for sheep."

"Don't take it out on me Emma. I'm not your whipping board."

"Post."

"Fuck off. Fuck off and eat." He laughed.

He pulled into a campus pizzeria in Ellensburg, the same campus Kimmy had attended. When we walked in the sounds of the glasses and the young coed voices made me jealous. I wondered how these kids got there, who paid for them? How could I get there? What would it feel like? I felt the weight of books in my arms even though I was carrying nothing. I wanted to be a coed. I wanted to get out of Tolt, but not through the carnivals. We sat in the corner of a long table. I ordered a salad and Jesus ordered a small pizza with sausage, olive and mushroom. "Give us two drafts," he said to the young waitress, "your choice." She looked at him approvingly, even clicked her tongue as she was walking away.

"She likes you," I said.

"I know."

Jesus played with my fingers. He cooed in my ear. I started to feel lighter. Our food came and while I was twirling my garlic bread in the leftover dressing lakes on my plate I felt him, when I looked up, I saw him. A Mediterranean looking man, older than the young woman he was with. He had black curly hair, combed straight back, and wore a proper white shirt. He held one hand lightly on the girls back and she looked up at him earnestly and said, "Professor Jeranos, where should we sit?" She was blond, lithe, short skirt and heels, tight white t-shirt with Notre Dame on the back. He whispered in her ear, she tilted her head back and twinkled with laughter. He guided her to a table and motioned to the clicking waitress. "Bring a carafe," I heard his deep voice. He turned. He saw me, and for minutes he looked right at me, through me, past me to the wall behind me; the parking lot, the building next door. I was as transparent as the mist of a stream, and of course I would be. He didn't know me. I felt Kimmy in my blood; I felt her fear, her pain and humiliation.

"What is it?" Jesus looked hard at me.

"It's…it's the professor. It's… Jeno." My voice caught on itself.

"What?"

My voice was hoarse. "Jeno, you know, the professor."

"What? The one who hurt little Kimmy?" He searched the room. "Where? No let me see…there," he said pointing at Jeno's back. "The man with his hand on the back side of that girl with the white shirt? Am I right?"

"Yes. Yes."

And then Jesus was up. I reached for his arm, but he was already past me, pushing his chair hard into the wall, making a sound loud enough to turn the head of the waitress.

"Excuse me," he was standing beside Jeno tapping him on the shoulder. "Excuse me. Are you the professor who dates little girls?" Silence. Jeno turned slowly to look at Jesus, up, and then down, then up again until Jeno's brown eyes locked with Jesus' black ones. "Are you the man who is supposed to be teaching students instead of laying them? Could you please tell me what makes it okay for you to rape little girls? Is it because you are bigger than they are?" Jesus raised his voice; the sound of his voice rose and grew deep in his chest like a growl. I melted, melted into the chair, through the chair into the cold linoleum. The little blond stared straight ahead, her back rigid. Jeno rose to his feet, I felt the heat from Jeno's skin, it sailed across the room and washed over me. It made me nauseous.

"Jesus, don't," I said quietly to myself.

Jesus did not stop. "Is that it, or is it because you are their teacher, because where I grew up a man could lose his balls for touching another man's daughter, you know what I mean?" Jesus tapped Jeno square in the chest.

Jeno's face swelled, turned scarlet, the room grew hot. The restaurant was quiet. Not a dish, not a spoon or a glass, only breathing. I saw the veins in Jesus' neck, saw his tattoos rising and falling as his biceps flexed and unflexed. Jeno flew an arm straight out and caught Jesus square in the chest, sending him backward on to an empty table. "Are you talking to me you punk, you spic?" Jeno yelled. Spit flew from his mouth.

Jesus righted himself by pushing off the table. He put both fists into boxing position, flexed his brown arms, bent his knees, and lowered his body like an animal. He looked like the old raccoon with the half tail that roamed the garbage cans back home. When he saw you, he never ran, just crouched lower and deeper, meeting your eyes as if he were about to lunge. My chest tightened and I evaporated, disappeared into the green wall behind me.

"Yes, I'm talking," Jesus whispered and then he punched Jeno square in the jaw. The coed beside him screamed as Jeno fell into her, then past her to the ground. "You need to learn some manners," Jesus said. Jeno was still, and then slowly began to wipe himself as he sat upright. His neck was red with anger; he lifted one hand to his jaw, where the blood had run in droplets. Stained.

"Call the cops," he shouted to the waitress, the one who had clicked at Jesus.

"Come on Emma," Jesus was beside me, his hand on my elbow. The waitress ambled to the phone. We made for the door and as we passed her, she looked at Jesus and batted her made up blue eyes. Jesus threw a twenty-dollar bill on the counter.

"I haven't dialed yet." She popped her gum, showed us her finger on the hang up button. "I hate him."

"I hate injustice," Jesus said as we climbed into the truck.

Ten miles down the freeway I started to feel my legs again, my arms. I took small breaths and filled my parts with oxygen. I came back from my mandatory evaporation, reconfigured myself into a person, a being. I took a big breath of air, rolled the window down as far as I could and stuck half my torso out. I looked over my shoulder back at Jesus. He smiled at me. He had a little blood at the corner of his mouth. His smile grew bigger as he looked at me, then the road then me, then he burst out laughing.

"There," he said. "No man hurts a woman."

I smiled, then laughed and the laughter, well it wiped us clean. We didn't stop until we reached the next exit where we both had to get out because we were going to pee our pants. Jesus was right; blood is blood.

The driveway was bare when we pulled in. The lawn was brown with pits of dirt, the potted flowers on the front stoop tired and wilted.

"We have to water these," I pointed at the flowers as we walked up.

Jesus opened the front door. "Hola," he yelled. "Hola Carlos! Cómo estás, heh!"

"Ahh," Carlos came from the kitchen, his arms bare in a tank top. His skin was glossy, his tattoo illuminated by the sheen. The windows were open, there was a fan going, but the air was still stagnant and dry. Carlos gathered Jesus in a big hug and twirled him; Jesus smiled as big as the open sky. They talked in Spanish, fast and melodically, while Carlos hugged me. He smelled like cigarettes and coconut. He put a hand on each cheek and turned my face for one kiss and then another.

"Oh, Conchita, you look so good. Jesus he takes okay care of you…I see that he takes good care of my Emma."

"If you only knew," I said, thinking of Jeno and the pizza brawl. "He's my knight in shining brown armor."

Carlos looked at me and his eyes grew soft. "I though, I cannot take good care of your mama."

"What's wrong with her?" I asked.

"She won't get out of bed. I try and I try. I bring her flowers, I tell her people are here to see her, to get cards read you know, I cook for her, I tell her 'Quick come look at the blue jay,' I tell her all the things that used to make her jump and run, but she still does not move. She barely eats the food I bring her. She will drink the whiskey yes, but food, no. She misses appointments, you know people pay to come and see her, but she does not talk, she does not move. I am very scared."

I sighed. Jesus said he would get my bags from the truck. "Let me see her."

When I walked into the bedroom, there was a sheet hanging over the window so the room was as dark as the night. The smell of dirty scalp and laundry wrapped around me, permeated my clothing, and made me itch. I heard her breathing, saw her shape on the bed. She was wrapped in an old quilt, the one she had made out of my old baby clothes.

"Mama," I whispered. "Mama." I went to her bedside, sat on the edge beside her sleeping form. I shook her shoulder gently. "Mama, it's me, Emma. Wake up. Tell me what's wrong. Mama." I shook her, and then shook her again.

She rolled toward me, opened her eyes slowly. Her beautiful eyes were bloodshot and weepy, her face as pale as milk glass.

"Mama, talk to me."

"Baby, you're home. Did Carlos tell you?"

"He told me you were sick. He says you won't get out of bed mama. Tell me what's wrong. Did you see the doctor?"

"I'm dying Emma."

Chapter Seven: Rosalene; The Moon

Irene left me there, in the dark trailer in the outskirts of North Bend. I hit the light switch and the trailer was lit by a single light bulb, hanging over the worn kitchen sink. I had the baby, I had clothes for us, I had a pile of blankets and a pillow and I had a month's supply of food Irene had picked up at the market. It filled the rusty refrigerator. We spent our days outside when it wasn't raining. The trees were green and tall and dripped after heavy rain. The smell was fresh and new and filled my lungs with hope. We spent our nights on the blankets in the musty living room. My life became Emma's cycle; feeding her, holding her, watching her. We were alone, but not lonely. I read the cards and could see in my future a light. I wrote Irene letters and walked them down the lane to the dented metal mailbox. Irene wrote me long letters back and sometimes sent money.

The sun came out rarely, but one day it was luminous and inviting and the long grass smelled sweet. Emma and I explored the grounds. There were two large barns far down the path towards the river. They were padlocked and hidden with berry brambles so I had not noticed them before. While we were peeking through the brambles I heard the sounds of a truck approaching. A red pickup pulled up alongside one of the barns. The tires sank into the moist earth. I touched my hair; back to its red now, the black having long washed out; touched my face. I had seen no one for weeks. I had gone nowhere and had no idea what I looked like. The baby cried.

"Shh, hush a bye."

The truck door opened. A large man with a blonde ponytail lumbered from the cab. He hitched up his jeans, smiled and said, "Hey."

"Hey."

"That your baby?" he asked.

"Yes."

"Can I look?"

"Sure."

He lifted the corner of the blanket up and stared at the little baby in my arms. "Girl huh?"

"Yes."

"I'm Dave," he said, extending a hand. "I come here to work in the barns once in awhile."

I shook his hand, large and calloused. I saw him in a bar, playing music on stage, lights beaming down upon him, he was sweating. "You're a musician. Are you the owner of the property?"

He laughed. "No, but we're friends. I just use the barns. How do you know I'm a musician?"

"I just do. What's in the barns?" I asked.

"Stuff." He smiled again. His teeth were uneven and the right one in the front was brown. "What's your name?"

I hesitated.

"You can tell me. I ain't the cops." He winked. His brown eyes were flecked with green.

"My name is..." I looked around me, "Juniper."

"Bet not." He paused, studying me quietly. "You don't have to say. I know what it's like."

"What what's like?"

"Hiding. I've been hiding all my life from something or another." He laughed again. He had a dimple on his right cheek when he smiled. "What's the baby's name?"

"Emma."

"Mm, that's nice. Soft, pretty."

We stood in silence for a few minutes. I saw his aura, the color surrounding him. It had been happening to me the past few months. I could look at a person, squint a little and see their color. Dave's was pink, light and beautiful. He rubbed his hands on his jeans. "Well, I gotta get to work. I'll be done in a while."

"Could I ask you a favor?"

"What's that Juniper?"

"Do you think you could drive me to town? I'm almost out of food."

"I thought you'd never ask."

An hour later Dave knocked on the door of the trailer. I held Emma on my lap as the truck bumped to and fro. Dave pushed the cart at the market. I put one hand on his arm and saw him in a pasture surrounded by goats and geese. A fence on the right stretched for miles and Dave stood still, shielding his eyes from the sun. Next to him stood a young woman, her dishwater blonde hair was long, picking up the breeze.

"Oh," I said, "you're going to farm."

"I already do...sort of." He looked at me and smiled.

"Twenty one fifty," the checkout lady said.

I had twenty dollars in my pocket. My last twenty dollars, my only twenty dollars, twenty dollars Irene had sent me. "I need to put something back."

Dave looked at me and scrunched up his eyebrows. "What's wrong, you don't have enough money?"

"Something like that." I turned my attention to the checker. She snapped her gum. Her lips were painted orange. "Can I put back the bread and maybe...hmmm...the strawberries maybe, how much would that be?"

"No, don't put anything back," Dave said. He reached for his wallet. He handed the clerk a hundred dollar bill.

In the truck I said, "You didn't have to do that."

"I don't have to do anything."

"Thank you."

Dave stopped by every day. Some days he worked in the barns, some days he hung out and we talked. I read his cards on the floor of the living room and I saw conflict coming for him. "You have to run soon," I said.

"Where?" he asked.

"I don't know, but it won't be bad."

He brought me presents. One rainy day he brought furniture in the back of his red truck, an end table, a cute green side table and a golden colored coat rack. We hauled the pieces into the shabby trailer and wiped them down with towels. Then I turned to Dave and wiped him down. He shook himself like a puppy. He took the towel and wiped me down and we laughed. Another day he brought me a yellow formica dining table. It had two metal chairs with it, covered in sparkly red naugahyde. He brought an emerald green couch that folded out into a sleeper. And one day he brought me a box of the most beautiful tapestries and cloths, handmade in India. "My mother was a college professor," he said. "She traveled all over the world."

Dave brought groceries and baby food, which was good, because aside from the little monies Irene sent me, I had no income what so ever. One beautiful morning he came with two bags of groceries in one arm and a huge basket in the other.

"What's in the basket," I asked, trying to peek inside.

"Special delivery for baby Emma," he said, his face lit up in the early sun. The basket was low and wide and perfect for the baby to sleep in. I filled it with soft blankets and laid the baby in the basket and Dave sang her a lullaby.

After Emma was asleep, Dave and I drank wine. We smoked a bowl and toasted with our glasses of wine and he braided my long red hair.

"I love the color of your hair," he said as he worked it between his large palms.

Dave fetched his guitar from the red pick up. He sang me a beautiful love song. His voice was deep and restful. Dave and his melodic voice became my beautiful refuge.

I lived in the trailer a little over two years. Emma grew tall; she crawled, then walked and then ran. She walked the tall grass picking buttercups and wild lilies, throwing them in the air for the wind to take, always making her way toward the river at the edge of the property. She stood on the pebbled shore and stared motionless at the rippling water. If I let her, she would stay that way for hours. She was a beautiful girl. Her hair was dark and her eyes were as green as the wild river. I loved her with all my being and I think Dave did too.

One stormy morning a strange car drove up. Emma and I were alone that morning. Dave had gone into Seattle the night before to do business and wasn't coming back until the afternoon. I parted the dirty curtains and looked out the grimy kitchen window. It was a tan Impala. A man in a brown leisure suit got out of the car, pulling at his suit, adjusting his collar. I squinted. His aura was orange-red. I scooped up Emma and opened the door, balancing her on my hip.

"Yes?"

"Rosalene?" He fidgeted with his pockets, shifted his feet.

"Who are you?" My heart beat wildly in my chest. I was sure he was from the unwed mothers home, come to claim the baby I had signed away.

"Don't be scared. I am a friend of Irene's."

"Oh," I let out my breath.

"Can I come in...quickly?" He walked in the trailer, appraised the surroundings, the formica table with the half eaten baby food, the pulled out sleeper with the disheveled blankets. He brushed off a kitchen chair and sat down. Crossed, uncrossed his legs. "I've got to take you somewhere Rosalene. I promised Irene I would. So... I will take you somewhere where you will go."

"Am I in trouble?"

"No, but Dave is. Well, Dave and I are. You see...I'm sure I can tell you this, you being an unwed mother and all," he drummed his fingers on the table. "Dave is a grower, a professional grower. Those barns down there, well they are full of pot and I own this property."

"Oh, you're the brother of Irene's friend. Thank you so much for helping me."

"Oh no, you helped me. You kept the place looking halfway legitimate. Anyway, I got a tip that we're going to be raided this week, so Dave's cleaning out the barns right quick and I, well I gotta get you outta here because if they find anything...anything and you're here, they'll arrest you no questions asked. And then, well then, they'll find out about the baby, you know and...she's cute isn't she? We gotta go. Get your stuff together. Irene said. I promised her you know."

I packed what I could into the Impala. I left behind the furniture Dave had brought me, but grabbed the basket and the beautiful tapestries. "Will I see Dave again?"

"Maybe, maybe not. He's gotta make a run for it. I think he's taking off for Oregon," my driver said.

My heart broke and tiny pieces fell to the floor of the car, splintered and unrecognizable in the dust.

"Do you have somewhere to go?" he asked me as the car careened down the windy road, the windshield wipers flapping violently.

"No."

"I'll set you up. I have a friend in Tolt who owns a rental house. It's empty right now. Irene said she'd pay me back if I had to front you any monies. She graduated you know, has a job." I did know, she wrote me and told me she had landed the job of her dreams in a hospital ward catering to babies. "She's a nurse now. Mmm, mmm, that Irene she is quite a woman." He stared ahead lost in thought. "You like Tolt?"

I thought about my mom and the garden in our back yard and how every time she dug up a carrot she held it up in her dirty hand, turned it to and fro and said, "You like carrots?"

"I think I will," I said, looking down at baby Emma's little red lips.

"I'm William. I'm your landlord. Rent is 400.00 due at the first of every month and the utilities, well, they're on, but put them in your name on Monday okay?" He was short, with white paint stained coveralls. His cheeks were rosy pink and his eyes a clear blue.

"William, I think you'll like this little lady and her baby. They come recommended to me by a dear, dear, lovely friend, whom I am hoping someday will be my wife." He looked at me and smiled as wide as the river. "Surprised?" he asked me.

"A bit. That's nice. Irene deserves some niceness."

"She doesn't know yet, so this is our little secret."

"Hmm," William cleared his voice, looked at me appraisingly. "Here's the key." He handed me a gold key. It hung from red yarn that had been woven into a braid. Our hands touched. I saw him alone on a porch swing, rocking, holding a pipe and staring up at the stars, a nice vision.

"I am paying first and last for this little lady," Irene's suitor said.

"I…well, I don't know what to say, how can I thank you, um…?"

"Frank, name's Frank. Don't thank me, thank Irene, this is her money; she's paying me back. I love that lady!" Frank handed an envelope to William and set my few belongings on the front porch of the little house. He turned with a wave and climbed into the tan Impala, his forehead glistening in the sun.

I loved the little house. It had a living room with balding grey carpet and a small kitchen with a dining area covered in tired linoleum. From the kitchen was a back door with a small landing and two concrete steps going down to a small concrete patio in a fenced backyard. There was a beautiful tree in the back yard with a twisted trunk that stretched to the sky. From the kitchen there was a door that led to a large bedroom, and down a narrow hall was another smaller bedroom and a bathroom. It was perfect. It was small and compact and luminous at the same time. The sun came in perfectly from the available windows and I knew now what I had been missing all that time I was traveling, running. I had been missing this, a house, a place with lightness, a place to be, a place to laugh and cry and keep dry. I let Emma wander and mark the walls with her tiny handprints.

I walked to a pay phone that night and called Irene. Her hello was tiny and tired. "Irene, it's me, Rosalene."

"Oh honey, I'm so glad to hear your voice. Thanks for the letters."

"I moved Irene, I want you to know. Frank moved me this morning."

"Oh, yes I heard he might. That was nice of him. Write me with your new address."

"He likes you, you know."

"I know."

"Irene, do you think they are still looking for me?"

"Honey, I haven't seen anything since that one small article in the paper. I think you are okay to use your own name. I need to send you the birth certificate for the baby."

"Yes, that would be good. Irene thank you so much, you have saved my life."

"Yes, I imagine I have. Rosalene, everyone deserves a chance to make it, don't you think? Look how long it took me to get my chance. I didn't want you to have to wait that long."

I cried on the phone and clutched the receiver. A vision came to me. Irene and Frank surrounded by flowers, a swimming pool in the background. They were holding hands and Irene was feeding Frank a strawberry, laughing at him as he took it in his mouth. "I see you Irene, on a trip with Frank."

"Am I having fun?"

"Yes, you're laughing."

"I guess I'll go then. He asked me to go to Hawaii with him in June."

"How is Miss Alexandria?"

"She is in a care facility right now. She fell and broke an arm. She's driving the nurses crazy, telling them their futures. She told one of them to get a divorce quick because her husband was cheating on her. Sure enough, he was doing the dirty with her sister!" Irene laughed. "Well I've gotta go honey, I'm working a double tomorrow."

"I love you Irene."

Dave came by the house two days later, his red pickup loaded to the brim with his belongings. "I'm heading to Oregon," he said.

We made love on a wool blanket on the living room floor while Emma played with spoons and pans in the kitchen.

"I love you Juniper," he said, stroking my cheek as he laid beside me. "I can't take you with me. I have a girlfriend there."

"I know," I said. "It's alright." And it was. My body was vapor and if I closed my eyes people and places could pass right through me.

The town of Tolt was small, ten blocks in one direction, five blocks in the other, with the state highway intersecting the middle. The river ran through the front side, then shifted course to the backside of town, then ran back around to the other end. It was surrounded by timber, everywhere you looked there were trees as tall as a hillside and the town was full of loggers. Emma and I sat in the 2x4 restaurant in the afternoons so we could smell the delicious scent of woodchips as the loggers entered for coffee or drinks in the bar at the back.

"You want more coffee Rosalene?" Mazzie asked me, one hand on her hip, the other holding a full pot of coffee.

I used my real name now, now that I had a birth certificate for Emma and Irene had seen no more news of the "runaway girl." "Sure," I said and watched her fill the heavy porcelain cup.

I learned where the food bank was and the clothing bank, and I wondered how to make my next month's rent.

"You go get welfare," Mazzie told me. "You head down to Bellevue on the bus and you sign up at the government's office and maybe, just maybe you get some money from the daddy of that cute little girl there." She pointed to Emma who sat up tall and pointed at her own chest.

"EEEmmmaaa," she said, pointing to herself over and over.

I rode the bus to Bellevue, found the social services offices and filled out a two-inch thick pile of paperwork. Emma played with the grimy toys in the corner of the waiting room. When I was done a lady with bleached blonde hair piled on top of her head welcomed me into her sweltering office.

"Is it hot in here?" she asked, crinkling up her forehead.

"Yes."

"Oh, the central heating, you have to get used to it. Rainy day huh?"

The rain was coming down in torrents, pelting the high window in her office. "Let's see now…" She clicked her teeth now and again as she read through my paperwork. "We can give you four hundred dollars a month, tickets for groceries, food stamps, so to speak, and free medical and a dentist for the little girl. Who is the father? It says here unknown, but a lot of women do actually have a pretty clear idea. If you do, well that is an income source for the state you know."

"No."

"What?"

"I mean, no, I don't know who the father is."

She laughed, the nameplate on the desk said her name was Deirdre Lovely. "It is still the age of Aquarius is it not?"

My rent. My food. Emma's food. Nothing else. I made it work. I managed to find folks getting rid of a sofa and chair; a kitchen table came my way, and slowly a bed, a bedside table, a dresser. All mismatched, all lovely. I babysat once in awhile and dated a lot of men who were willing to take us out to eat or buy us groceries, buy me cigarettes and wine. Since I saw their auras I was able to avoid the ones with the dark brooding personalities. And I knew impermanence, never, never let yourself get attached to love.

One day at the library I sat in the big comfy corner chair and read the Seattle city newspaper while Emma played with the basket of blocks. On the back page was a large ad sponsoring bracelets for the Prisoners of War and the Missing in Action. The war was still going strong.

"May I borrow your pen?" I asked the male librarian. I wrote down the phone number for the agency and called from the phone booth at the grocery store later that day. The paperwork came in the mail.

Names and names and names of men who were missing, unaccounted for, dead or dying or bleeding from the soul somewhere. Michael's name was on the third page. My heart stopped, it listed his regiment, the date he was recorded as M.I.A. and "still unaccounted for" written under his name. I registered and received a bracelet in the mail the next week. They gave you random names, you couldn't choose. My missing in action boy was Dusty Livingston. I wore the bracelet, morning, noon and night, I never took it off, and I let it turn my wrist black. I thought about him, Dusty Livingston, what he must have looked like. I felt his tragedy and sometimes wept as I twisted it around on my wrist.

One day I called information from the phone booth at the 2 x 4 and asked for Michael's parent's number. Emma sat in the booth coloring on a waitress pad with crayons. Mazzie gave them to her to play with along with a giant hot chocolate with whip cream. My hands were sweaty. I dialed. It was early afternoon, maybe his mom worked; maybe she was out shopping. She answered.

"Hello?" Her voice was clear and curt.

"Mrs. O'Reilly?"

"Who is calling please?"

"My name is Juniper. I am a friend of Michael's."

A long silence fell.

"Mrs. O'Reilly, I was a really good friend of Michael's and well…I know he is missing in action and I know how you must be suffering and well…I wanted to tell you that he has a daughter."

The phone went dead. The dial tone buzzed loud in my ear, the phone weighed down my hand and made my wrist ache. I replaced the receiver and looked over at Emma. She was stirring the hot chocolate with a yellow crayon.

Two years later they found my missing in action boy. His body was flown home on the 25th of March. I took off the bracelet and placed it in a small painted box next to my bed. Dusty Livingston. Michael; my Michael. Sometimes I dreamed of him and in my dreams he spoke to me and told me how beautiful his daughter was. He was right; she was a beauty of the earth. She turned four and on her birthday I held her hand and we looked at cloud shapes, giving them strange names. While we were touching I had a vision of her falling from the backyard tree. I yelled for her and ran to catch her, but I could not reach her in time. Her arm landed in an odd shape, twisted at the wrong angle from the elbow.

"No climbing that tree," I said.

She looked at me, her green eyes slanting in the sun. "No!" she said.

"That's right."

When she was eight I had a vision of her falling from the monkey bars on the playground at school. She fell atop her head, blood coated her hair and she laid still on the asphalt pavement. For two weeks I watched from the fence, called her to me on her recesses, so I could remind her not to climb the monkey bars.

"I know, you told me," she said firmly through the fence. "Stop following me."

I did readings for a few select people in my kitchen. It held magic for some people, especially men. I could see it in their eyes. I read for them and they fell in love with me, thinking I had the power to make their lives turn out all right. I though, felt powerless. All the things I saw and all the things I should be able to prevent, but how can one person make people change their actions to prevent their mistakes, misfortune and mayhem? Many nights I laid awake, smoking cigarettes in bed, wishing I had no sight. Seeing things was a curse. Seeing auras, that was a gift, but the sight of people's future was a weight heavier than my own body. One night I dreamed of Ling. We were in his aunt's restaurant at the back table with the Chinese lady who read the sticks. "She sees us married," Ling translated to me. "She sees you having my baby. I love you…touch me," he said, reaching across the table for me. I tried to lift my arm and reach for him, but my arm was too heavy. I could not reach for his outstretched hand.

"I can't reach you," I shouted, "come closer!" I cried in my dream and Ling and the Chinese lady moved further and further backward, floating away from me. They were laughing. The Chinese lady held her sticks in the air and yelled in Chinese.

"I bet you wish you could see!" Ling shouted to me and laughed, tossing his black hair back. I awoke in a pile of sweat. I downed a small tumbler of stale whiskey sitting next to the bed.

Sometimes I told the men I slept with what I saw and sometimes I didn't bother. They weren't staying around so it didn't matter. If I read for them I gave them the absolute truth. I never lied or left out information. I rarely saw death, but once when I was reading for Ned, sweet Ned, I saw his brother's death. "It's okay," he said. "That's nature." Ned never believed in the cards.

Ned became attached to Emma. They went on "nature walks", as Ned called them, and often times I would find them stargazing in the back yard. Emma was tied to nature like an embryo to the womb. She was like that the minute we landed at the trailer in the woods. She heard every bird whistle, every squirrel's chatter and noticed the changes in the weather before they showed themselves. Nature to me was something to be survived.

"Mama, rain," she said to me one afternoon. The sky was cloudless. Forty minutes later the rain came in torrents, forcing us into the house. I looked at her with amazement.

Ned taught her to track animals, he taught her to identify the calls of the birds. "That's a jay," she said one day after we heard a loud screech in the backyard. One afternoon Ned and I were lying on the bed. I was stroking his hair, half asleep.

"Emma has the skill to read nature you know. She's probably always had it, but now she knows she has it. She is a white witch." He looked at me and winked. I already knew that.

Ned was my deer. My soft, strong, sure footed deer. If I were to pick a father out of the sky for Emma, or for myself for that matter, I would pick Ned. He was good in bed too, and many a night we made love until dawn.

I saw Ned's future in the cards and I wept. I knew he would leave no matter what, whether I told him what I saw or not, the outcome would be the same. Would I follow him? I was too afraid to leave my little home; afraid I would end up a wanderer again. My little home was all I had. It was my greatest treasure.

When Ned left six months later a hole opened inside of me and a black gust of wind flew through the window and filled it right up.

Nothing helped until Carlos; Carlos, my infinite playmate. The hole though, never completely healed over, and the darkness stayed. It grew without me knowing it. I had so many holes when the wind blew at my chest; it went right through me to the other side.

"Conchita, sometimes you look so sad." Carlos nuzzled me and spoke in my ear. His accent tinged his every word.

In the summers when Carlos landed in my lap we drank, we danced, we smoked, we played Spanish music and laughed, our bodies swayed across the living room carpet. I was Carlos' beautiful carnival prize. Every morning he told me he loved me and every night he told me I was beautiful. He came and went, like everybody else, but that was okay, others took his place when he was away. Men were my diversion from survival, from the consistent struggle to pay bills, keep Emma safe and keep my visions from destroying my own mind. My visions grew stronger and stronger. It had gotten to the point where even a casual bump at the market would set off a vision. A woman grabbed my forearm one morning at the post office. "You dropped a letter," she said. In that instant I saw her jump from a bridge, and fall with her arms outstretched into a fast running river.

"Don't do it," I said staring into her sad brown eyes.

"Don't do...what?"

"You know. I can't stop you, but think about it really hard. It is not just you leaving, it's them being forced to stay without you."

Her hand flew to her mouth and she dropped her mail.

I saw things with men too, but the lovemaking and the excitement of a new audience washed away some of the distress, the responsibility.

The day Emma graduated from high school I took off all my clothes and stood in front of my plastic framed full-length mirror naked. I looked good, a little saggy near the bottom of my abdomen, right about where Emma had blossomed seventeen years earlier. My legs looked okay, my pubic hair still red and my breasts were large enough to be noticed, but not too big to be hanging down yet. I turned around and looked at my back, it was nice. It was long and slim and I liked the way my scapula shaped my shoulder area. My red hair hung below my breasts, a few silver strands caught the light. I started to sing. "Little girl going to town, take a pony, don't fall down and when you ride on horseback dear, remember I am always near..."

It was one of the lullabies Dave had sung to Emma in the rusty trailer years ago. I closed my eyes and smelled the wet grass and damp pine needles. I heard the soft river tumbling over the rocks. I was there. "Dave," I whispered.

I sat on the balding carpet and cried.

Sometimes I felt like my cup was full, like I couldn't hold one more vision or one more piece of information about someone. Yet, sometimes I felt as wide as the ocean, like I could hold the world in my head.

Carlos and I were on the back stoop one hot night in July. He smoked a cigarette, passing it to me every two drags or so. He touched my hand lightly, sending a shiver through my breastbone. I saw him, in a car, a black car, someone else was driving and it was raining outside, raining in torrents. The car swerved in a puddle and hit the side rail with a sick thud and the shrill scraping of metal on metal floated across the road like a flock of crows. The car penetrated the rail and rolled, over and over. I heard Carlos scream my name into the black sky. His body flew from the car like a ragged doll, limp and twisted until it landed, mangled, hanging from a tree. I stared at him hard, memorizing the lines around his eyes, his crooked lips, the way his hair fell upon his cheeks. I went to bed and didn't care if I got up or not.

Chapter Eight: Kimmy; The Wheel of Fortune

Emma took off with Jesus to work the carnival. I was left alone. I became obsessed with trying to contact my mother. I walked to Roalene's house three or four evenings a week and begged her to do a ritual to contact my mother. I needed her. I dreamed of her every night. The dreams woke me, leaving me sweaty and sticky. I dressed and walked to the edge of the cemetery with my flute. The cool night air wrapped me in a blanket of sorrow. I closed my eyes and played and played, my fingers dancing over the keys. When I opened my eyes they were dancing; the spirits of the graveyard; dancing in their flowing mourning clothes, dancing on the moon kissed breeze.

"Save me," I whispered.

My days were spent swimming at the river, trying to avoid Carl and trying to walk past the bathroom without picking up the razor. I hadn't cut myself for three days, but I wanted to. The blood was gratifying, a testament to the fact that I was still alive inside.

Rosalene answered the door. "Can we do it tonight?" I pleaded; my hand on the screen door was shaking.

"Kimmy, you need to stop torturing yourself. If your mom wants to contact you she will, you don't have to muster her up." She raised a hand to my hair, stroked my braid. "And stop cutting yourself."

"How did you know? Did Emma tell you?"

"No honey, I saw red in your cards, I felt it. That's why I kept calling you day in and day out. I finally gave up, you never answered the phone."

"I'm sorry." I hung my head. "Please Rosalene, help me."

"Not yet," she said, and she took the screen door from my hand and shut it tightly.

I didn't have to work. Carl gave me everything I needed. I had money, food, all the clothes and jewelry I could want, but no conversation. We talked about the weather or the birds in the yard, or the neighbor's annoying dog, but not much else. Never, never could we talk about my mom or the rape or the way I felt when the razor touched my skin. I cried at night wishing I could tell Carl, but he was made of stone. The town was empty, especially with Emma gone. One morning after I heard Carl's truck leave, I stripped off all my clothes. I wanted to cut myself one last time. I wanted to mark myself, give myself a brand to represent my suffering, so that every time I looked in the mirror I would remember. My body looked milky white. My hair matted from sleep, hung past my shoulders. I grabbed a razor blade from Carl's medicine chest. It was cold and solid. I held it to the light. The steel was beautiful, reflecting and gleaming. I held the blade against the side of one of my breasts and closed my eyes. I simultaneously pushed and pulled and screamed aloud when the blade cut my skin. Blood pooled on the vanity in front of me, bright red and slow dripping. I doubled over the sink and sunk my teeth into my lower lip. An amazing sense of relief washed over me. No one could hurt me as much as I could hurt myself. The phone rang. I ignored it.

When my breast stopped bleeding I clumsily bandaged it and walked to the 2x4. I was hungry, but too worn out to make my own lunch. Marsha was there. Familiar sounds welcomed me and I slouched into a booth by the window.

"What happened to you?" Marsha asked.

My hand went to the side of my breast. "What do you mean?"

"I mean; you look like hell's daughter. Look at your hair. Shit Kimmy, is something wrong?"

"I've been going to the river."

"Uh huh."

"I've been trying to get better."

"What? Are you sick?"

"Yea."

"Oh god. I know who can help you. Here look at this, I'll be right back." She dropped a menu in my lap.

Marsha came back with a water glass and a tall blonde guy in a chef's coat.

"This is Steve. Steve, this is Kimmy Franklin."

He bowed at the waist. "Nice to meet you."

"Same." I touched my matted hair.

"Steve here has a mom that does natural medicine and he can help you. Well his Ma can, so Steve, you take a little break and sit with Kimmy for a minute and Kimmy, you tell him what's wrong with you. I'll get you the soup, it looks like you need it." She walked to the kitchen leaving Steve standing next to the table. He folded his long legs into the seat across from me. He looked square at me. His eyes were large and brown like a deer. I played with my napkin.

"You don't have to tell me anything," he said. "Marsha's always trying to fix everyone. She is like a sorceress." He smiled. His teeth were nice. "You are very pretty."

I put my head in my hands and groaned.

"That bothers you?" he asked.

"Yes, that bothers me, because I know I look like shit. I don't usually look like this, I'm just, well…I'm just…" I looked out the window and watched a lady across the street help her toddler maneuver the sidewalk. One hand held the babies tiny hand, her other hand was out, ready to catch the baby if he fell.

"I've gotta go back into the kitchen. How about I take you to dinner sometime? Somewhere nice. Like in Bellevue. I know this Italian restaurant where they play jazz on the weekends. The food is very good. Would you like to go with me? Then I can see what you really look like, although I can't imagine it gets any better than what I am seeing right now."

I looked into his soft eyes and thought about him touching me. Would I like that? I shivered. "Yes, that would be okay. I'm not much into jazz though."

"We can sit far away from the music; Friday night then? I'll come by your house at six. Tell me where you live."

"Marsha knows."

"Oh. Okay. Thanks Kimmy. Oh, by the way, you can tell me on Friday if you want help from my mom. She is a genius." He gave me a wave and walked back to the kitchen, his long legs carried him there in four steps.

I went home and took a nap on the green couch. I covered myself with the brown afghan, even though it was eighty degrees out. I fell asleep and dreamed of a forest. It was dark in the forest and the birds were calling my name in different rhythms, confusing me. I turned this way and that way, but I could not find the right path. Steve appeared from behind a tree. "Take the dirt path Kimmy, the one closest to the earth." I walked closer to him. I could almost touch him. The birds began to laugh. "You'll never make it," said a wicked blue jay, larger than a baby buggy. "You're a bad, bad girl," the jay said and then he laughed, showing rotten gnarled teeth inside his oversized beak. I awoke in a pool of sweat, breathing heavily. My breast ached.

Friday night Steve came and picked me up. I was watching for him from the window so that I could meet him in the driveway, but before I could open the door, he had bounded up the walkway. "I want to meet your folks," he said.

"I don't have folks." He stared. "I mean I don't have a mom."

"I don't have a dad. Well, he doesn't live in this state anyway. My mom left him. Let me meet your dad."

I turned from him and he followed me into the kitchen where Carl was sitting at the table drinking a glass of water from a Welch's grape juice jar and reading the paper. "Carl, this is Steve. We're going out."

Steve stuck out his big hand and shook Carl's hand. "Nice to meet you Mr. Franklin."

"Pleasure," Carl said.

"Okay, let's go." I drummed my fingers on the kitchen table. "See you later."

"How about those Mariners?" Steve asked.

"Oh yeah, that last game was a doozie, never thought they had it in them. I used to watch the Oakland A's and think the same thing though. You never know when a ball team's gonna change their stride."

"It's nice when they get off of that losing streak," Steve said.

"Let's go Steve. Goodbye Carl."

"You kids have a nice time and nice to meet you Steve."

In the car Steve looked at me and said, "You call him Carl?"
"Yes."

"Oh." He paused, backed out of the driveway, "I like him."

"Yeah. That's the most he's talked in a year."

I had worn a low cut tight black dress so that Steve could stare at my cleavage, but he didn't. He stared at the marble statues in the corner of the restaurant, at the "beautiful presentation" of the salad and at the amazing lines of the stand up bass. He talked about Italy and his trip there as a boy with his mother. "I don't remember much, just mounds and mounds of the best spaghetti I had ever eaten."

Halfway through the main course he said, "By the way, you look breathtaking."

I choked. "Thank you," I said between coughs.

We shared a dessert. We each had an espresso coffee. The coffee was dark and bitter, but Steve seemed to love it. He ordered a second. "I love this place. It feels like a part of me. I must remember something about Italy in my bones. We were there four months after all."

"What does your mom do?"

"She's a naturopath. She studied in London and in Italy. She left my dad when I was very young, so she took me to Italy with her."

"What is a naturopath?"

"It is a doctor of natural medicine. Not widely accepted here, not like in Europe, that's why she's studying to be an acupuncturist now. Needles. She uses needles to heal you. She thinks that is the new western trend. She feels it is compatible with what she already does."

"Sounds like voodoo," I leaned over the table toward the dessert, squeezing my cleavage together. Steve looked away.

"Speaking of voodoo, I've heard you play your flute before." Stillness washed over the table. "I stood beside the cemetery once and listened." He cleared his throat. "Well, more than once. I get off late you know, and I walk that way on my way home. It was an accident the first time and then I must admit I looked for you every night after that." He lowered his eyes. "It's like a dream. Have you ever tried out for the symphony?"

I laughed.

He drove me home and walked me to the door. "Thanks," he said. He touched my forearms, and then stepped away. "You are a lot of fun." With that he turned to go.

"Is that it?" I asked his retreating back.

"Oh yeah, I'll call you." He threw it away over his shoulder as he lumbered his tall body toward the car.

Steve was confusing. Days later I went to the 2x4 and he looked excited to see me, ambling up to my table and sliding in beside me. "Hey, what're you doing in here with the sun out there?" he asked. He elbowed me in the ribs.

"I came in to see Marsha. She's having a party tonight. Do you want to go?"

"Maybe I'll come after work. I close tonight, I don't get out of here until after midnight."

"I'll meet you there," I looked at him sideways, gave him a sexy smile.

"Okay," he looked toward the kitchen, barely glancing my way before sliding away.

Marsha's house was full of people. Some I knew from school, a few I recognized from the 2x4 and a lot of people I had never seen before. I felt shy. I found Marsha and she handed me a joint. "Here," she said, "a little party popper for ya."

"Thanks." I sat in the corner of the living room on an overstuffed red chair. It was draped with a yellow and orange fabric, shimmery and light. I ran my hands over it and it felt exotic and warm. There were matches on the table in front of me so I lit up and settled back into the cushions so I could watch the party. I felt something at my shoulder; someone had sat on the arm of the chair, a gorgeous blonde green-eyed guy with wisps of curls in his eyes.

"Mind if I watch your lips drag on that joint because I find it incredibly sexy?" His voice was like a loud purr.

"Hmmm, I guess not. Do you want a drag?"

"If it's been on your lips, yes." He grabbed the joint and took a long hit in slow motion. "Mm, you taste sweet. I'm Jake."

"I'm Kimmy."

"That's a cute name. Here," he passed me back the joint, "get nice and high."

I felt myself relax. The noise of the party and the warm body beside me was comforting. "I'll get you a beer," Jake said. Time stretched itself out and I got higher and higher. "Hold out your hand," he said. He placed a beer in my hand, wrapped my fingertips around the bottle. "I like you," he whispered in my ear. "In fact I'd like to eat you like a strawberry."

I laughed, beer flew out my nose and I laughed harder. I wiped it on my sleeve and melted into the red cushions. Marsha came by with a mirror loaded up with lines. She stopped in front of me and I leaned forward, put the straw in my nose and inhaled through one nostril, holding the other shut. "Ah," I said. "Thank you."

She held the mirror for Jake and he did the same. He stood up and kissed me on the cheek, "I'll get you another beer."

I was fucked up, but I liked it. I felt okay, better than okay. Jake came back and pushed me over on the cushions so that he could sit beside me. He snaked his hand up the back of my shirt and rubbed my shoulder blades. I left my body and floated above myself, I watched as he felt up the front of my shirt with his other hand. I sat with the beer, took timid sips and stared into a pot and coke induced abyss.

"I don't know Jake, I've been through a lot."

"We've all been through a lot baby." He nuzzled my neck, ran his tongue around my ear. I was dizzy.

"Jake, I don't really know you and I think that maybe..."

"Maybe we should get to know each other. That's right baby. Let's go in the bedroom, you want to lie down?"

"Yes, I do want to lie down, but..."

"Come on," he grabbed my hand and helped me stand up. I looked around the room and tried to find Marsha, but the room was wavy and hazy with smoke. Faces swam in and out of focus. "It's okay baby." He led me to Marsha's bedroom. It was dark. He moved aside coats on the bed and pushed me down on my back. He stood over me and unbuttoned my shirt. He opened it wide, revealing my lace bra. He lowered his head into my cleavage and began to nuzzle me between my breasts.

"Jack, Jake, whatever your name is, I don't want...stop doing that, I got stuff going in my mind and...." I tried to push his head away.

"You heard her!" A loud voice came from the doorway. A square of light fell across Marsha's bed.

Jake stood up, pushed back his wisps of hair. "Who the fuck are you? Get out of here!"

It was Steve. Steve walked to the bed. He pushed Jake to the side causing him to stumble against the wall. "Come on cupcake, time for you to go home." He buttoned my shirt and picked me up like a baby, cradling me in his arms. He carried me out of the bedroom and into the main room where the party was still going on. "See ya Marsha," he yelled out. "Thanks a lot." He carried me out the front door and into the night. The stars were twinkling and the day's heat lingered in the air. "Don't do stuff like that," Steve said. "You are like a siren. You put men in a trance. Don't you know guys hunt for girls like you? You have to keep your head on."

I didn't understand what he was saying. I let my head fall back and watched the stars. He walked me all the way home, cradled in his arms like a lost kitten. That night I dreamt of my mom, she and I riding on a ferry together. We were at the front of the bow, sitting on curved benches, looking out at the churning water. Neither one of us spoke. She turned to me and smiled, I smiled back and the sun hit us just below the chin and warmed our hearts. She was with me. She reached over and took my hands, caressing my fingertips over and over.

"Look for yourself," she said. She pressed her hands to my heart.

I awoke in the morning on the couch in the living room, the afghan tucked around me. I had one shoe on, one shoe off and the makeup stuck to my face made it hard to open my eyes. It was like a dream, the party, and the cute guy, getting handled. I closed my eyes and tried to remember his name. I gave up. I did remember Steve carrying me in the moonlight. I sighed. I rolled off the couch and peeked in Carl's room, he was gone. My head hurt.

Steve called later. I heard the clanking of dishes in the background. "Just making sure you are okay this morning," he said.

"Yeah. Yeah, I'm fine. Urr, thanks for walking me home."

"I didn't walk you. I carried you. There is a big difference between the two. Well, that's all. I'll talk to you later." He hung up the phone and I stood with the receiver in my hand listening to the dead space.

My day was empty. My life was empty. Time stretched before me like an earthen tunnel, dark and lightless. I had to get out of the house.

In the afternoon I walked to the 2x4 and ordered coffee from Marsha.

"You have fun last night?" she asked.

"Sure," I stirred the white cream into the black liquid, the spoon singing against the porcelain cup.

"You want to come over tonight? I'm having a poker party. All you need to bet with are your clothes." She tossed her hair back and laughed.

"I best not, I seem to be having a hard time keeping my clothes on as it is. Is Steve coming?"

"I don't know, but I'd love to see him without his clothes on."

"I hear you talking about me." Steve walked up behind her and placed a large hand on Marsha's right shoulder. "I do look good naked."

Marsha laughed. "They all say that. I gotta get moving. See you tonight if you decide you want to come."

"Maybe we could go on a walk when I get off work tonight."

"What time is that?" I asked.

"Midnight. We'll take a midnight amble about town, how about it?"

"Okay."

He knocked lightly on the door at midnight. We walked the streets of Tolt. "I love looking into people's living rooms at night and guessing what their life must be like. Sometimes I make up imaginary stories about them," he said. He reached for my hand. "Look in that room, those people are still up watching television. I bet they're watching Johnny Carson. They just sent the grandkids home and this is their alone time. They've been married fifty years. He's a retired plumber. She was a teacher. See, see how I make stuff up?" We walked to the river and sat on a log. I took off my flip-flops and scrunched sand between my toes.

"Do you want to kiss me?" I asked.

He turned and stared at me, cocked his head. "Not now."

I stood up and faced him. I pulled my shirt over my head. I had not worn a bra so the moonlight touched my nipples.

"Don't," he turned his head away.

"What? Don't you want me?"

"I want you Kimmy, so much. Just not your body, not now." He turned and looked at me, full in the chest. I hoped he would give in, reach out stroke me; love me. I wanted him to love me. I wanted to feel something. "What's that cut? Who did that to you?"

"I did that to me." I bent down and picked up my shirt. I covered my chest. The tears came, hot and fast down my cheeks, hitting my bare shoulders. They were cold in the moonlight. "You don't have to touch me. Just walk me home now."

"Kimmy, you don't understand. I would love to touch you. I would love to run my hands up and down your body; I mean, your body is perfect. Just look at you, you are wondrous, but that is not the part of you that I want to love first. I want to love this." He pointed his index finger to my heart. I felt his heartbeat through his fingertip. It penetrated my skin, my tissue, and my bone. It touched me deep between my breastbones. "I am in love with your music, I followed that sound until I found you at the cemetery. I want to know that melody. I want to smell it, to taste it. I want to drink it up. I want those sounds in my own soul. I want to know what makes a girl play like that. That's what I want first." My tears turned to a sob, not a light sob, a keening moaning sob. I dropped to the sand and cradled my head in my hands, my shirt falling to the earth, my insides falling out all over the river rocks. It hurt worse than the cutting. I was on fire. Melting.

Steve stroked my hair, "I'm sorry Kimmy. I'm sorry."

Chapter Nine: Emma; The Magician

Mama rolled back over and wrapped herself tighter in the blanket. I sat beside her, studying my hands, the curves of my knuckles. I felt the wrinkles in my palm, the coolness of my fingernails.

"Mama, talk to me. Mama!" I dug my fingernails deep into the wrinkles, making pink indentations. "You are not dying. What makes you think you are dying?" Silence. "Mama!" Minutes upon minutes passed. She didn't change shape. No sound came from her. No movement came from her. I left the room closing the door behind me.

Jesus set down my bags and talked in beautiful Spanish to Carlos. They stopped when they saw my face.

"What is it Emma?" Jesus asked.

I looked out the window; the sky was blue, small clouds draped about like laundry drying on the line. I thought about the river, about Kimmy's abortion. "She says she is dying." Jesus stood still for a moment. He wrapped himself about me.

"She has been saying that now for five days. That is why I called you Emma, I don't know what to do. She won't go to the clinic with me," Carlos said. "All I can do is pray. I need you."

I sat on the battered sofa, the one with the beautiful prayer shawl thrown across it. Mama found the shawl at a shop in Seattle. It was an altar cloth of orange and black and gold with lion statues and lotus flowers. "Won't this look good on that ugly plaid couch?" she said as she held it up in the light of the shop. It had been thirteen dollars, two bags of groceries.

"What are you going to do Emma?" Jesus asked.

I called the health clinic and talked to the nurse. She knew me, she knew mama. She had given me all those shots in the butt as I was growing up. "Do you want to make an appointment for her Emma?" she asked.

"She won't get out of bed." Silence. "Look, Nurse Jacobs, could you ask the doctor if he'll come over?"

"We don't really do that sort of thing."

"I know, but, she...she says she is dying." My voice caught. I couldn't get any breath in.

"I'll have him call you."

Carlos made burritos. The house smelled of garlic and cilantro and sweet soft tortillas. I heard the crickets chirping behind the house. It warmed my bones, which were cold enough to crack despite the hot weather. I looked in on mama six times. Each time she was curled in the exact same shape.

"She doesn't move," said Carlos, "not unless she sits up to eat or drink whiskey or smoke a cigarette."

The doctor called back early in the evening. "I'll be over at eight Emma," he said. He knew mama. His daughter had been over several times to have her cards read when she was deciding on a college. She decided to forgo the college plans and headed to New York to be an artist. "She had the most creative cards in her draw I had ever seen," mama said.

The doctor was early. I let him in the screen door. The sky was beginning to soften. He smelled of disinfectant soap and aftershave.

"Dr. Cordoan, this is Carlos and Jesus." They shook hands.

"I'll see your mother now Emma."

I opened the door to the bedroom and turned on the light. The glare made the room look even shabbier. I pulled back the sheet over the window, letting in some of the pink and orange colors of the sky.

"Do you want me to wake her for you?" I asked.

"No," he said. "Why don't you just leave us for a bit? I will wake her, talk to her, take her blood pressure, and that sort of thing. I think privacy is best."

I shut the door behind me.

Jesus and I sat on the front porch and watched the sun relax. Jesus and I smoked. Carlos paced in the dead grass.

"I carry her to the bathroom you know," Carlos said. "She doesn't even remember to go. I tell her."

"Thanks for doing that," I said drawing tight on my cigarette, holding my breath as long as I could.

"Emma," the doctor's voice was deep coming from behind the screen, breaking the evening spell, "can I see you all now."

We sat at the round kitchen table. Carlos traced water rings with his brown finger.

"I just need to clarify a few things before I tell you what I think. Now, has she shown any signs of vomiting or diarrhea in the past week?"

We looked at Carlos. "No," he said.

"Has she had any fainting or dizzy spells? Any shortness of breath?"

"No," Carlos said.

"Any crying jags, loss of memory, confusion?"

"Yes!" he said, excited that he could agree.

"Emma, Carlos, Jesus; I have to tell you that Rosalene is suffering from a severe depression."

"Thank god," I said. "Thank god she's not dying."

"Oh, but she is."

"You just said she wasn't."

"No. I said she was in a severe depression." He flexed his hands in and out, in and out. "And a person in a severe depression, if they believe they are dying, they can will themselves to do just that."

Carlos cleared his throat, "So her sadness could carry her to the ghosts?"

"Most definitely," said the doctor.

"I don't understand, I mean she doesn't care about anything. I mean look at how she lives!" My breath was short and fast. "Men just careen through here and she doesn't give a shit. She just lets everything fly to the wind; she doesn't even remember to buy groceries. I do everything. I even have to remind her to pay the bills! I have to tell her when the landlord's coming, I cut the grass, she never fixes the sink, I mean what does she have to worry about? She doesn't care about anything! She never even got me up for school like most moms do! I don't get it..." I stood up and paced around and around the table, my breath coming even faster. "She doesn't get like other people. She's not like other people; I mean this can't be right. You must be missing something. She probably has a bug or something, are you sure she's not just sick?" I grabbed hold of the chair; I felt the room grow watery.

"I'm sure."

He left us with a prescription, a drug I couldn't pronounce and didn't understand. "Something to help her relax. No more whiskey," he said.

"But it is the only thing that makes her breathe right," said Carlos.

"No more," said the doctor, he opened the screen. "I'll be back in a couple of days. I will try to get an associate over here. She's a counselor."

And then he was gone; the screen door bounced shut and left us in the quiet of the house. Carlos sank onto the couch. "It is my fault," he said. His shoulders shook, "I could not love her right." He cried big tears that landed on his hands and his lap.

"Carlos, I'm sorry about what I said. About all the men, I didn't mean it the way it came out, I…"

"No, Emma. You are right. I already knew that, but what Rosalene and I have together, well, it is magic. Like the carnival, it disappears but then comes back again and again, like magic." He looked at me and his eyes were tired. "I will play music."

The sounds of Spanish music followed me as I went out back to smoke. The sky was turning a blue black. It was twilight, the time of day when the veil between light and dark was the thinnest. The time when everything was impossible and possible at the same time. I was sure she was faking. She constantly had to be the center of attention. It didn't matter what I did, or how far away I went, she commanded me, and everyone else for that matter, to be her fucking audience. And if she willed herself to die I'd kill her.

The next morning I woke to Jesus twisted about me. We were on the single mattress; the sun was soft in the sky. It was going to be a hot day, you could tell by the stillness of the clouds.

"What are you going to do today?" he asked. "I want to know so I can think about it when we are not together anymore."

"I have to go to the 2 x 4 and see if I can get my hours back. Mama's not working so I'll have to pay the rent."

"I will send you some money."

I looked at Jesus, at the curve of his jaw, the dark soft hairs at the top of his jaw line. I started to cry. "I will miss you so much."

"I know." He held me tighter.

Jesus left early, Carlos packed him burritos and coca cola and he drove away in the truck with the tiger on the side. I cried. Carlos looped an arm on my shoulder. "He loves you Emma, he will be back. Life is like that, come, go; come, go. Everybody's going somewhere. Just be in love when you are together, that is all you can do."

Carlos said he would take care of mama so I took off to the 2 x 4. I didn't even look in on her; I just had to get out. I walked to the restaurant in my flip-flops and an orange skirt. It was already hot and I wished I had brought a hat. The town looked the same, smelled the same, a blend of asphalt and river water and good soil. I took in a big breath and when I reached the back door of the restaurant, it flew open and made me jump. Joe the cook came out, all ready to light up. He looked at me, dropped his cigarette, and picked me up in a big bear hug. "Ahhh!!!" he shouted, "I'm going to put you on the grill and eat you up! You look great girl, where the hell have you been?"

"I told Marsha I was going to work in Spokane for a while."

"She told me you'd married a sheik."

"Sort of, I went to work at a carnival with Jesus."

"Ah, the savior."

"Yeah."

Joe looked me up and down then up and said real soft, "I missed you. No one else likes to smoke with me. Here," he said, extending the pack.

"That's a lie. Where's Marsha?" I asked. I lit the smoke, drew it in. I felt my shoulders relax.

"She's off today, it's the new girl, Candace. I call her Wandy Candy. She's a real whiner. 'The food's too hot, the food's too cold, my feet hurt, the smoke is bothering me, the glare from the windows hurts my eyes,...waaah waahhh wahh'."

"Whoa."

"Yeah, that's what I say, put the fucking brakes on that one. I'd fire her ass, but the boss lady likes her because she's always early for her shift."

"Huh."

"She's a kiss ass. What are you doing back?"

"My mama's sick. I'm gonna have to pay the rent. I came to see if I could get my hours back."

"I'm sure you can," he stamped out his cigarette with his grease stained shoes. "Mazzie expanded the little bar in the back. You could always bartend. It's just a bunch o' lettin' guys look down your shirt, then they give you a tip."

"Great. Seen Kimmy?"

"Yea. She's been around a bit. She seems a little quiet."

Kimmy. I had to see her. "Is Mazzie here?"

"Yea. I gotta get back in anyway."

I followed him through the back door. The sounds were the first thing that hit me. I closed my eyes and melted into them, the clatter of plates and glasses, the sizzling of the grills, and the soft crackling of the coffee pots. My edges softened.

"Emma," Mazzie greeted me with a bar towel in each hand. "I missed you. How's your mama?"

"She's sick Mazzie."

"That's why I haven't seen her around town lately. You look good though."

"I need some hours back."

"Doesn't everyone. The mill is phasing out its last plant. I've got so many loggers on the chopping block it makes me wanna cry, it's good for bar business though. You come tomorrow night. I'll have you sling beer 'til a waitress shift opens up. You're not twenty one, right?"

"Uh…close." Not really.

"Got fake ID?" she asked.

"Uh…yeah."

"Good, just make sure you have it on you. Mum's the word. What else are you doin' now?"

"I don't seem to be doin' anything. I feel like I'm going nowhere really."

"Where's there to go?" she laughed. "Be here at seven, and bring your ID."

Kimmy's house looked the same from the outside. I was twelve again, pitching stones at her window. The yard was manicured and the driveway swept clean. I knocked on the door. No one answered. I knocked again. No one answered.

"Kimmy," I shouted. Silence. "Kimmy, it's me Emma, open the door."

I heard shuffling behind the door, a creaking. A crack in the door opened and Kimmy's face appeared.

"It's you," she broke into a smile. "I thought it was someone tricking me, but it's really you. Thank god! I have missed you so much." She threw the door wide and grabbed my wrist, pulling me into the house. Everything looked exactly the same, the same green couch, the same seascape above it and the same small stack of logs next to the fireplace. I drank it in, feeling safe and trapped at the same time. Kimmy hugged me and she smelled like mama's room. She tightened a red bathrobe about her, looked down at her slippers, and touched her tattered hair. "I look like crap huh?"

"Uh…do you want me to lie?"

"Yea."

"You look great, best ever." We laughed.

We sat out back at a table in front of the sliding glass doors on her small patio. Two squirrels zigzagged through the grass.

"When did you come back?" she asked.

"Yesterday. I came back early. I was in Spokane with Jesus working the carnival."

"I know, the 2x4 is the place for the news, you know, you don't have to tell me anything."

"Joe didn't seem to know."

"He's always in the back, he can't hear anything."

"Mama is sick."

"I didn't know that. What's she got?"

"Nothin'. Well, something. She's depressed. She thinks she's dying."

"Heavy." Silence. "Yea." She played with the sleeves of her robe. "I know how your mom feels. That's how I feel."

"Like you want to die?"

"Like I'd love to die." I hugged her and she started crying, her narrow shoulders shook against me.

"Let's get out of here," I said. "Get dressed. Let's go to the river and take all our clothes off."

She looked at me with her pretty blue eyes, her lashes tinged with tears. "Okay."

We walked to the river, away from people and sounds and took off our clothes. The river was cold. It ran cold year round, coming off of the mountain pass. We gasped and choked for air until our bodies got used to it and we relaxed into its breath. A bald eagle circled overhead.

"It is beautiful," Kimmy pointed to the sky. "Why do I always need a man?"

"I don't know. I know why I do. I need a father, it's the closest thing I can find, I guess."

"I need a mother," said Kimmy. "Mothers are the ones that are supposed to prepare you for this kind of shit."

I snorted.

"Let's go see your mom," Kimmy said, after we had toweled off.

The house was quiet. Carlos was on the back porch reading a book. He was talking to himself. He didn't hear us until we were right beside him.

"Oh, I recite poetry to myself. Practices my englese."

"Nice. It sounds really nice," I said. "Where's mama?"

"Same place."

In the kitchen the crock-pot was going, steaming the windows. "Chorizo stew," Carlos said. He opened the door to mama's room. It smelled like dirty dishes. "I gave her a bath this morning. She will get in the tub, but you have to wash her. Remember that Emma."

"Great."

Kimmy and I went into the bedroom; I pulled back the sheet on the window.

"Hey Mrs. J. It's me Kimmy."

No movement.

Kimmy looked at me, shrugged her shoulders. "I just wanted to come by and see you." She tried to make her voice cheery.

Mama groaned.

"What's wrong mama, are you okay?" I rolled her over. Her eyes barely opened, they were opaque and bloodshot. "Mama, talk to me."

"Emma," she reached up, touched my cheek. "I'm sick."

"I know mama. What can I do for you?"

"He's on every corner Emma. I can't get away." She licked her dry lips.

"Who's on every corner mama?" I asked. Kimmy made the crazy sign with her hand.

"Death. I see Michael on the corner, everyone who's ever left me, except my father. I can't find him. I can't see him through the fog. The tule fog, it's so thick." She was quiet. "I've reached my line Em, the line, the fill line that says when it is enough. I can't take another drop. I'm really tired."

Silence, breathing, birds chirping. "You've got to get up mama, you can't stay in this bed."

"I don't want to get up. Carlos is leaving isn't he?"

"Yes, soon."

"Yes. He's going to die Emma. I saw it." She rolled back over and pulled the quilt around her.

Kimmy motioned for us to go. We closed the door softly. "Shit," she said, "she's a mess."

"Yea. At least she talked to me. She moved. That's something. Who is Michael?"

Kimmy shrugged. "What are you going to do?"

"Doctor Cordoan is sending over a therapist lady…he said."

"Oh, she'll come tomorrow," Carlos yelled from the back porch. He always over heard my conversations. "I leave in seven days you know Emma. I don't want to, I have to go to make the money. Jesus and I we go to Bellingham, then Canada. We have to get the most out of the summer before it goes you know."

"I know." My hands were tired, even my fingers. My feet hurt.

"I'll try to help you Emma," Kimmy said. "I'll talk to my dad, he owes your mom one."

"You? You feel like dying, how can you help mama?"

"It will take my mind off it. If you worry about someone else dying you don't have as much time to think about your own death. I'm just happy you're back. I've been so lonely. Don't leave again Emma, not for a while. Promise."

"I promise."

Carlos and I fed mama. She was like a small child eating stew off of the spoon. She dribbled water on herself when she drank.

"Want to sit outside mama? It's starting to cool off," I asked.

"No. All I want to do is sleep. And bring me some whiskey, straight up, no ice."

"The doctor said no booze," I said.

"Get it," said Carlos, rubbing mama's feet beneath the blankets.

She drank three shots, and then fell asleep. That would've put me to sleep too. I left for work.

My shift at the 2x4 was easy. Pouring beers, wine, a few orders from the kitchen. Joe was gone for the night. This cook was tall and reedy with soft blue eyes. His adams apple stuck out. "I'm Steve," he said. "Are you new?"

"No. Recycled," I said grabbing an orange slice on my way through to the dishwasher.

I gave a last call at ten to two, like Mazzie had told me. I went down my closing list. Washed all the glasses and vacuumed the popcorn off the carpet. I emptied and rinsed the ashtrays and stocked the beer for the next day. I tried to get the customers out so I could count and stash the money. One guy would not leave. He kept staring at me. I went back to the kitchen. Steve was taking off his apron, the grill looked shiny and bright.

"Uh, Steve right?"

"Yea."

"Could you help me get this guy to go home? I gave last call," I said. "I'm closing up, but he just sits there staring at me."

"Ah, another lost soul."

"How do you know?"

"Because I'm one."

He sauntered into the bar on his long legs. He gently put his hand on the big guys elbow, stood him up and softly guided him toward the door. Steve took him all the way outside, patting him lightly on the back. "See ya good buddy," I heard Steve say. Then he locked the door.

"Thanks." He had been so gentle.

"Anytime," Steve said. "I've got to walk you home. Mazzie said if you didn't have a ride I had to walk you. Too many deranged loggers and mad spotted owls."

I counted the till, counted my tips, forty-seven bucks. I stuffed the money down my shirt and grabbed my bag. Steve locked the door.

The moon was just a sliver, but it was bright and there was a big beautiful star beside it. It lit up the asphalt road. "That's Jupiter," Steve said.

"Oh god, you're not an astrologer are you?"

"No. I just read a lot."

Our feet were soundless on the pavement. The night was very still, not even a cricket.

"Joe said you have a sick mom."

"Yea."

"My mom is a doctor. Well sort of."

"I'll keep that in mind." I didn't want to talk about mama. I didn't even want to go home. "Hey Steve?"

"Yea?"

"Want to go to Marsha's? She's always partying at this time."

"I don't know. Is Kimmy going to be there?"

"I don't think so."

"That's good. I think she might not want to see me just yet," he said.

"Kimmy? Why…?"

Steve shook his head and gazed up at the night sky. "I love her."

Marsha greeted us on the gnome steps. She held me for a long time. I smelled the patchouli oil on her skin. "God, I missed you," she said.

Marsha gave us each a beer and put Steve's long legs up on a soft cushion on the coffee table. "You got legs that long honey, you've gotta get tired."

He laughed. Marsha got out her rolling papers and fresh weed. "I don't smoke," said Steve.

"Good," Marsha said, "that's good. More for me and Emma."

"You smoke?" Steve looked at me, the question in his eyes.

"I try not to stop myself from doing anything," I said. We all laughed.

Marsha quizzed Steve. Steve didn't grow up in Tolt. Lucky him. He and his mom moved here so she could learn a new type of medicine. He said the northwest was big for her kind of medicine. She commuted all the way into Seattle. She taught classes at a private college when she wasn't studying.

"What kind of medicine?" Marsha asked. "Because I have had this crink in my neck for over two weeks now. Does she give pain meds?"

"Not that kind of medicine," he said.

Marsha put on jazz. She sat in front of me on the floor so I could rub her shoulders. "I'm going to go visit your mama," she said. "I want to get my cards read."

"She's sick. Real sick. She thinks she's dying."

"Aren't we all? We start dying the minute we're born. I'm going to visit her anyway."

The next day the counselor came. Her hair wound around her head until it ended up in a tight bun at the top. She wore loose cotton clothes and a big strawberry-colored moon necklace. I had a bad feeling.

"My name is Sansha," she said extending her hand. Her nails were red.

"I'm Emma." I hadn't showered and I still smelled like the bar from the night before. Carlos, luckily, had a shirt over his tank top. He ran to greet her, grabbed her hand out of mine.

"I am Carlos. So nice that you could come. We are so worried about her."

"Okay," she patted the top of Carlos' hand. "Let me talk to.... Rosalene, is it?"

"Yes," Carlos said, leading her to the bedroom.

"I'm afraid we haven't really been able to clean up in there." I cared what Sansha would think, I didn't know why. I felt embarrassed for mama. I felt like the kid at school who had no lunch money.

Sansha turned to us at the door, "I would like to see her alone if that is alright with you."

"Perfectly," I said. Carlos looked nervous.

"Let's go smoke," he whispered. We went out back. I heard quiet voices from the bedroom. I hoped she could get mama to talk.

A half an hour passed. We watched the blue jays. "Jesus called last night, asked where you were," he said. "I told him, 'you don't think she's gonna sit here and mope around for you', only in Spanish of course. He said you were too pretty to mope. He really likes you Emma. I tried to warn you."

I laughed. "Too late."

"We are going to leave next Monday. I am sorry to leave you. You have to look after your mama. I will teach you. She needs to eat. You have to feed her. She looks a million miles away, some days not." He paused, gazed into the steamy sky. "And you have to bathe her if she will not. You will have to get someone to help maybe, maybe not. Kimmy maybe. Maybe her. Let her smoke and drink whenever she wants; it helps her. I read her poetry from books in Spanish, ahh that you cannot do." He laughed. "I worry about her so much. How can the joy go out that fast? You know in my country we say you are possessed by an evil spirit when this sort of thing comes. I just don't know."

I said nothing. I didn't want to take care of her, but I was going to be stuck. I didn't want to be the responsible one. I stared at a robin, big and fat and thought about college. I wondered what that would be like, to be at college, to be free and going somewhere, anywhere.

"Hmm," Sansha cleared her throat. She came into the back yard, clutched her notebook to her chest. "I have reviewed your mother, your…," she looked at Carlos, "lady friend. It is my opinion that she be hospitalized."

"What?" I asked, my voice rising high.

"She should be in an institution where she can be monitored, have therapy and proper medication. She looks terrible."

"That's why we called the doctor!" Carlos said.

"Well, I have paperwork in my car so I will get that and we will make the necessary arrangements. Do you have insurance?"

"No," I said. "We don't have insurance."

"Oh." She paused, shifted her weight nervously. "You will have to watch her from home then. But, understand, this is like a suicide watch. She is dangerous to herself, not with her actions, but with her thoughts."

"Like what?" I asked.

"I cannot divulge patient therapist conversations, let's just say she has had a breakdown. Life got to be a load she could no longer carry and she cracked; for some it can be a very large crack."

"How do we put her back together?" my voice caught.

"That is different for everyone. I will talk to Dr. Cordoan and see what kind of arrangements can be made that the state will pay for. In the meantime, feed her well; make her eat if you have too. Don't let her get dehydrated. Encourage her to get up and get some air and exercise. Let her talk whenever she feels the need. Give her these." She extended her hand to me; she had a bottle of pills. "It is Valium and it is great for taking the edge off of things." She laughed. It sounded like the kind of thing Kimmy and I needed. "Oh," she said, pursing her red lips, "no alcohol or cigarettes if you please, prescribed medicines only. Well okay, she can smoke, but no alcohol, especially with the Valium. Oh! That would really do her in!" She laughed again, her bun bobbing in the sun. "Well, you may never see me again, but then again you may, so good luck with it all." She turned abruptly, shut the screen door, and headed through the kitchen.

"What did she say?" Carlos asked. "Are we sending Rosalene away?"

"Mama won't go away because we don't have any money for that."

"Good, sometimes poor is good." He walked in the house. I heard him go in the bedroom. I heard mama crying.

At the 2 x 4 I switched with Darlena, one of the older gals, the bar shift for her late waitress shift. Mazzie didn't want to take too many chances with me in the bar. "You never know when the liquor inspector is coming," she said. Although Marsha said he hadn't been around in over a year and the last time he had come, she told him how sexy he was and he turned as red as a marinara sauce.

"Don't drop this," Joe said, he passed me a giant T Bone steak through the order window. T Bone was the special, with a baker or mash and a salad with ranch or blue.

"Emma," Marsha waved me over to the coffee station.

"What?"

"You know Steve, the new guy?"

"The cook?"

"Yea."

"Well," she looked around, "Kimmy has it in for him."

"What!"

She cocked her head at me. "I think she digs him!"

"You think? She either does or she doesn't."

"She does. She really likes him, I can tell. I like how he's all quiet and stiff."

"Stiff?" I asked.

"Yea, he's not all smarmy and gooey like most guys. He's well, he's..."

"He's got manners?"

"Yea," she cried, "that's it! I find that incredibly sexy. Look out, table nine is giving us the wave."

Midnight came, we were off. Marsha and I and Joe had a cigarette in the back.

"Let's have a drink in the bar," said Joe.

"No," said Marsha. "Let's go to my place."

We did the usual, flopped around on the silky over sized cushions, lit incense, took tokes of pot and rubbed each other's feet. Joe was very good at the foot rubs.

"Best day?" Joe asked.

"Ah, easy," said Marsha, "the day my dad showed up at the house with a new doll for me, all wrapped in tissue with it's own basket and bottle of fake milk. She wore a pink and white gingham dress and said 'maaamma' when you turned her over."

Joe looked at the ceiling. "Eighth grade when the girl with the pig tails down to her butt followed me to the drinking fountain and laid a big kiss on my cheek as I was taking a drink. I almost chipped a tooth. I loved her. Her name was Darla Farrington. I'll never forget Darla. Pass me a beer. Emma?"

"I don't know." I thought softly. "I guess the day when Ned and I sat in the back yard and took chalk and drew pictures on the pavers for an hour while the sun went down in the sky. I really felt like he was my dad that day."

Marsha said, "You should call him."

"No, I can't."

"Shut up." She looked at me serious.

"Not while Carlos is here, it would break his Cuban heart. He's always trying to look after me, in his own sloppy way."

"Yea." Marsha got up to stretch. She lifted her arms high above her head and made a groaning noise. "He's sexy."

"Marsha," Joe started in, "you think every one's sexy."

"Not you Joe."

Joe looked hurt, hung his head. Then he lunged for her, tackling her to the ground in a brother sister type tussle. They laughed and I wished the night would stretch into days.

Mama wasn't getting any better. I tried to ignore the whole thing until Carlos called me into the kitchen the next night.

"Emma," he said in a whisper, "you're working tonight?"

"I worked this morning Carlos, why?"

"I need you to come into your mama's room and bring that little table." He pointed to the end table with the chewed up edges.

"Why?"

"Your mama wants her cards read and I cannot do that. You, you have to do it. You have seen it so many times, I know you can do it."

"Unh uh. No way. I'm going out. Tell her to read her own damn cards. I'm going to Kimmy's and then, well, I don't know."

"Emma," Carlos grabbed my wrist, "this is important. You must do this. She has been begging all day."

I stared at him and said nothing.

"It could make her better, you know how she believes everything those cards say to her," he said pleadingly.

"Fine. I'll do it, but I don't know what the hell I'm doing and I'm going to hate every minute of it. I hate those fucking cards!"

"Shhh! She'll hear you. Just do it for your mama and do your best. You must always do your best."

"You and Jesus and your philosophical bullshit. Sometimes I just like to do my worst."

"Shhh!!!" He shushed me angrily.

Carlos carried in the side table. He already had the cedar box out and mama's silk cloth. Mama was curled up, her back to me, her spine like a snake under her t-shirt. Her hair was matted.

"Don't you brush her hair?" I asked him.

"I try, she cries."

Carlos turned on a lamp, because even though it was early the windows were still covered in dark sheets. I felt the walls coming closer; it was hard to breathe.

"What am I supposed to do?" I asked Carlos.

"I don't know, do what she does. You have seen it so many times, just copy."

I laid the silk over the table, opened the wood box and picked up the cards, wrapped in the white silk handkerchief. Carlos woke mama, she sat up and her hollow eyes searched the room for me. When she saw me with the cards I saw a light, small but shiny in her pupils. She smiled at me. She loved those cards.

"Oh, baby, you will read for me. I want to know when I will go." Her voice sounded shaky.

"I don't think I can figure these things out mama. You have to help me."

"Shuffle them then let me cut them. I am going to cut them three times, so I can have a true reading for myself. Ask the cards my time of death and they'll answer. We all start dying the day we are born."

"No," I looked at her defiantly. "I will not ask that. If you make me ask that I am leaving."

"Okay, just read them for me. Lay them out." Her head listed to the side, it took all her strength to keep sitting up. "Carlos, you must get a white candle."

He jumped up like he'd won a million dollars and began rummaging about the room looking for a white candle. He found one, set it on a dirty plate, lit it with his silver and turquoise lighter and sat at the edge of the bed, one hand on mama's covered thigh. They looked at me expectantly.

When I unwrapped the cards, I hardly felt any weight in my hands. They were as light as meringue, and instead of being cold like a normal deck of cards; they were surprisingly warm in my palm. I shuffled them, walked them to mama's bedside; she cut them once, then cut them again, then cut them a third time.

"Now lay them out into a cross," she was whispering now. "I am not scared Carlos."

"No, you are my brave pony."

I laid the cards out. I hoped Kimmy was home. When I was done with this I would need a good hit of pot. I should have had a hit before I came in.

"Slowly," she said. "It's all in the intention."

I intended to get the hell out of there. The cross was laid.

"Turn over the center card, around which all else will come to pass."

I turned over the center card. "It's a wheel with creatures around it."

"The wheel of fortune," mama said. "I have made my bed, now I must lie in it. Top card."

"A hunched over man with sticks."

"Ten of wands, hmm," she said. "Now the bottom card."

"A scroll with a hand and a pencil."

"The beginning of my journey, I knew it. Side card." "Two people dancing, upside down."

"I must make all my apologies," she started to cry. "Turn over the last one Emma."

"A woman with a flock of flowers."

"The Empress reversed…that does not fit. I don't understand. The light. The rejoicing. No, that is wrong. In two days, I want another reading. Now take the cards and hold them over a bowl of salt to purify them, and then wrap them back up. I have to go back to sleep now. Tell Miss Alexandria I missed something."

"What?" I asked mama. No response. "What did she say, Carlos, what did she say?"

"I don't know. She says all kind of strange things."

"Is she going to die?" I asked Carlos quietly. Mama had rolled back into a ball.

"Yes, baby," her voice was muffled.

I did the salt bowl, held the cards over it and almost dropped them. I wrapped them in the silk cloth and put them in the cedar box. I was done. I tried to get the hell out of there, but Carlos stopped me at the door.

"Emma, Jesus will be here next Saturday. We leave for Bellingham on Monday. You have to look after your mama, do you see?"

"You mean; can I do it? Is that what you are asking? Are you asking me if I can look after her, read her fucking cards and work and pay the rent and try to have a normal life, is that what you are asking?"

"Yes."

"I doubt it."

"Emma, I grew up in a family of ten kids, four bambinas, six bambinos. My mama she did sewing for the rich, both white and Cuban people. One day at the market, I saw a man spit on her. He spit right on the middle of her back and called her "washer woman". I took care of my brothers, my sisters and my mama because I am oldest. There are not so many of us left, but the ones who are not lucky, who do not have money like me, I send it to them. My mama, she died when she was forty-four, not because she was sick, you see, because she was tired. She could not go any further down her path. So, yes, I know you can do it."

I could feel the heat seeping into my face. My eyes filled with tears. "I'm sorry. I'll try." I opened the door and walked down the cement path, my steps as heavy as stone.

I went to Kimmy's house.

"I think she's dying. She thinks she's dying. She looks so thin and…sick. I need help Kimmy. I can't do it. Help me."

There was a pause. I could hear her breathing. "Of course I'll help you. I am you and you are me." She held up her palm, the blood sister palm. I held up mine and we pressed them together.

"Thanks," I said, my tears fell to the front of my shirt making long patterns in the gauze.

It was after midnight. My shift was done; Marsha's shift was done. We were at the river dangling our feet off a rock, into the cold running water.

"Smell," Marsha said. "Just smell that. There is no smell on earth like the smell of that river. It gives eternal hope to all things."

"That would be nice." I had been depressed all night, waiting on people and feeling envious of their happy lives. Wishing, always wishing that mine was somehow different.

"Let's go back and get Steve; he should be done by now." We walked the dirt path back, Marsha's ponytail dancing in the moonlight. Steve was emptying his last grease bucket and wiping his hands on his apron when we walked in the back door.

"You ladies back for more?" he asked.

"I guess you could say that," Marsha said laughing. Then she stopped and looked at him with her softest eyes. "Come to the river with us, Steve."

"Okay."

We waited for him to say goodnight to the bartender, hang up his apron and lock the back kitchen door.

"I like the way you close up," Marsha said.

"Thanks," he beamed down at her. "How's your ma, Emma?"

"Not good."

"What's she got?"

"The doctor and the psycho lady said she is suffering from severe depression. She says she's dying."

"The mind can kill you," Marsha said.

"And she said the same thing you did, Marsha, which is weird."

"What's that?" she asked.

"She said she started dying the day she was born."

Marsha laughed, "I know, I know."

Steve cleared his throat, slowed down his stride to match ours. We took two steps to his one. "Would you like me to ask my mom about it? I mean in all confidentiality. I wouldn't have to tell her it was you or anything. Would you?"

"Yea, I guess. And Steve," I said, "you can use my name, there're no secrets in this fucking shit town. Well, not any that you can keep anyway." I laughed, finally. Steve gave me hope. Maybe it was the sure height of him, or maybe it was his calm nature. The water called us down the path to its shore.

"All the maidens are out tonight," Marsha whispered, slipping her arm through mine. "That would be me and Emma." She laughed, I laughed, Steve whistled.

"I am a lucky guy!" he exclaimed.

Friday Carlos cleaned house. I watched, sulking. I was tired and hung over.

"Why don't you help me Emma?" he asked, yelling over the Spanish music he had on the turntable.

"I'm tired. I'm hung over. I don't feel like it."

"Why?"

"I called the doctor to renew her prescription," mostly because Kimmy and I stole some of her Valium, "and he said he needed to come back out, but couldn't until next week. You know why? It's because we don't have any money, that's why. The people with the money get the doctor first. You know what I mean. I told him that he shouldn't put us off that way, that I waited on his family every week in the 2 x 4 and that he knew how hard I was working. And you know what he said?" I was yelling over the music, he turned it down.

"What Conchita?" he was dusting in his white tank top and cut off Levis.

"He said he treats all clients the same, no matter what their circumstances. He is a liar."

"Maybe he tells the truth. Maybe he's just busy."

"Yea, well you always think the best of people. People make me sick."

"You know what I think?" Carlos said.

"No, what do you think?"

"I think you need to close your eyes and thank the Mother Mary for the things that you have here."

"Right."

"Help me change your mama's sheets."

The room was still dark. He talked to her like a baby. "Darling, Carlos is going to take off these sheets, let Carlos wash them." He saw me reach for the light switch. "She does not like the light, Emma."

"I don't care, it's like a tomb in here."

"It's okay baby," he was whispering, mama stirred, moaning.

I left the switch alone and instead I took the black sheets off the window. The light came tearing in, illuminating all the dust and dinginess. I opened the window, the birds were singing. You could hear a lawn mower and kids laughing from a neighbor's backyard.

"No," Mama said. She covered her eyes with her hands. "I don't want to see the light, it hurts."

"Mama, these curtains…sheets are filthy. They will make you sick."

"I am sick."

"I am washing them. I'll hang 'em back up when they're done." Although I was thinking I would probably leave them off. If I didn't go to the laundromat right away, they would sit in the hamper. She would get used to the light. It would be good for her.

"Carlos, baby, bring me a drink."

"Yes, baby girl." He left the room in a hurry.

"Mama, we need to change your sheets, can you get up?" I got near her, she smelled bad. "When did you have a bath last?" Carlos reentered, his hands full of two tumblers and a bottle of Jack Daniels. "When did she have a bath last, Carlos?"

"I don't remember. It was a while ago."

"She smells."

"It doesn't matter Emma," she said in her scratchy voice. She took a shot of whiskey in one swallow. "When the spirit world greets you, you always smell divine whether you are a prince or a beggar."

"Well you definitely smell like a beggar. I can't stand it and come Monday I am in charge of you so you are going to be clean."

She looked up at Carlos with doe eyes. "You are leaving me?"

"Yes, I must Conchita. I will be back in winter, when the ground has had its first freeze, I will be done."

"I'll be gone by then Carlos. You will have to see me in the other world when you pass. Promise me you will look for me."

"I promise, my rose."

"Mama! Stop that! Stop talking like you are dying, goddamn it! Carlos, make her stop!" I was steaming, burning. "You are not dying. You are depressed. Do you hear me, depressed, because you've never taken any responsibility for anything! You just live willy-nilly any way you fucking want to and when everything goes to shit, it's too much for you, because you can't take responsibility for a goddamn fucking thing, least of all your child! Look at me, I haven't done a goddamn thing with my life and you think that's great! 'Just be in the present and read the fucking cards and everything will be okay'. Well, it's not. I'm a big fat zero. You go through spells and visions and all the while reality sneaks up on you like a rattlesnake and poisons you. You need to grow up and face it, face the fucking demon. Get up!" I was holding the black sheets in my hands. She looked at me blankly. "Get up!" I was sweating. Sweat ran down my breastbone, between my shoulder blades.

Carlos stood still. He stared at me. He was as still as mama and the stillness stretched as wide as the river. The clock ticked and ticked and finally mama let out a sigh.

"I think you should go Emma. I will change the sheets. I will give her a bath," Carlos said. Tick. Tick. Tick. "Come back in a while when things are different." Tick. Tick. Tick.

I went straight to Kimmy's house. I was a witches' cauldron, I bubbled with poisonous brew, waiting to boil over.

"What's going on?" Kimmy asked me. She was in her robe again; she had dark circles of mascara under her eyes.

"I can't take it anymore, Kimmy." I flopped down on her couch, threw my legs on the coffee table, knocking magazines to the floor. She bent to pick them up. "I can't do it. Carlos is leaving. Mama says she's dying. I can't take care of her. I don't even fucking believe her. Jesus is leaving with Carlos as soon as he gets back. I'll be alone to take care of this woman. I can't do it."

"She's your mom."

"Yea, that's the problem. That's always been the problem."

"What are you going to do about Jesus?"

"What do you mean?"

"I mean," she twirled a piece of her hair, jutted a hip out, "are you going to start seeing other people. He's leaving and all."

"No. Why would I do that? I love Jesus."

"Yea, but he's leaving. You'll have nobody."

"You're just like her," I laughed. "You and mama, you're the same. You can't be without a guy. Always spreading your legs for somebody. Well that's fucking great isn't it? Look what it's gotten mama." My words spilled out of my mouth like acid; they burned everything they touched. "I'm not like you guys, I don't go around spreading my legs to make myself happy. I can be alone. I just can't take care of her alone. That's what I meant." Silence filled the room. "You and mama are fucking great you know, you're always falling in love with some cock or another. I couldn't live with myself if I was like that."

Kimmy's head drooped. "I can't live with myself either."

"You can't help me. Sometimes even best friends can't help each other." I looked at Kimmy, got off the couch and left.

I felt hot, like I had a hundred degree fever. I burned from my diaphragm outward. The heat flowed through my arteries and filled my extremities with hatred.

When I got back home the house was quiet. Carlos was out, probably to get cigarettes or more whiskey for mama. I opened her door. Marsha was lying on the bed spooned around mama and her quilt. The clock ticked behind me. I shut the door quietly. I wanted to roll a joint and get out of there, but before I could finish, mama's door opened.

Marsha's hair was ruffled, "I love her." She sat across from me at the kitchen table. "You don't get it Emma." She looked at me hard. "I really love her."

"Yea." I licked the joint to seal it, rolled it between my fingers and smelled its sweetness.

"She told me some things."

"Yea," I said. I didn't want to know. I decided to light the joint.

"She told me about your dad. She thinks she killed him you know."

"What? She hardly knew my dad. He was with a circus or something, a lot like Carlos." I felt my breath catch. I put the lighter down and rolled the joint harder between my fingers.

"No. He was a waiter at an Irish restaurant in Seattle. She said he was a beautiful Irish boy. He joined the war. She tried to stop him you know, because she had seen it. She saw him die." She leaned her body across the table and lowered her voice. "She knew he wouldn't make it back. But he went anyway and well, he died; in Vietnam; in the war."

"You're lying." My fingers shook. "She's lying, that is shit. She would have told me. My dad is alive in some other country. He didn't want anything to do with me." I took a long toke, but I could hardly hold it, my chest was wrapped tight.

"Your mama tried to stop him, she told him not to go, but he wouldn't listen." Marsha tapped her fingers on the kitchen table. She stared out the window; she sighed. "He never knew about you. She never told you about him because she thinks she killed him. In her mind; she murdered Michael; your father. She didn't want you to know she had murdered your dad."

"You fucking believe her?" I stood and paced the kitchen.

"Yes."

"Fuck." I took a deep breath, looked up at the stained ceiling. "First I don't have a father, then I don't have a father. What is the difference?"

"The difference is you don't have a father who didn't want you, like my dad, he never wanted me. You have a father who died; who never had a chance to want you. He never knew your mom was pregnant."

"Why did she tell you all this?"

"Because she is dying. Because she thinks the same thing is going to happen to Carlos and it is so heavy she can't hold it in her heart any longer."

"She has always been a liar." I looked at Marsha, but I couldn't bring her into focus. I looked around the room and nothing came into focus. I was floating, looking down at myself. I watched my body walk to the door, leaving Marsha behind with her head in her hands.

I navigated myself to the river, my only savior. I laid down on my back on the bank, my face turned to the open sky. The rocks hurt me, jabbed at my bones. I felt the vibration of the rushing water through the stones, the curving of the falling water, back and forth, over and under. My tears made their way in torrents to the river and the river careened back into me. I closed my eyes and let it fill my insides. I had a dad. He had a name. He didn't know me, he didn't know of me. I would never know him. Mama never told me. I hated her for that. She thought she killed a man she loved. Of course, she thought she did it; it was always about her. But it wasn't. He died, he died for something he believed in; it had nothing to do with her. He went to war and fought for something he believed in. Why didn't she tell me? I watched the clouds and thought about a belief so strong you would die for it. What did I believe in? What was I willing to die for? My family? What family? I loved mama, but I also hated her. The only thing I believed in was nature, the water, the seasons of the wildlife; the patterns of the birds and the path of the currents. I was willing to die for that. For a patch of forest, or a curve of the river, I would fight to the death. I was born of the trees and made of the water. And I had a dad, a dad who might have wanted me, who might have died for me, if only he would have known me. Mama would die for me. She would make a production of it, but she would, I knew she would and Carlos, I think he would die for me too. Carlos; Carlos who lost a girl and me, who lost a dad. Maybe I could be Carlos' lost girl and he could be my lost dad. Go figure, the carnival man. The guy with the gold tooth and the pony tattoo, that's who I got for a father. Love her or hate her I had to save her. I had to see Steve and ask about his mom, I had to ask him to help mama.

Chapter Ten: Rosalene; Death

I dreamt of Michael three nights in a row. Each night the dream was the same. He was in a boat on the river, his body upright and majestic; he was a great blue heron at the bow. I called to him from the shore and he turned, looked at me for an instant; his eyes the blue of beach glass. He looked away to the jungle behind and I waved and shouted, "Michael, get down," but he didn't hear me, the shot rang out and Michael's shape changed. The sound of death was so loud; it sent ripples downstream to the sea. I awoke covered in sweat, tears on my cheeks. I became dreamless after that, for four nights I did not dream at all, then I lost track of night and day and began to dream again, the dreams became my escape.

They came in and out of the room, Carlos and Emma and the others. I talked to them little, I wanted to be left alone with my dreams. My dreams became precious. I had dreams of Ling and the lights and magic of Chinatown. I had dreams of Megatross and the peaceful farm with the smells of the earth, burritos and wood smoke. I wrapped my arms around myself and I was back in Window's kitchen. She stroked my hair; I felt the wool of her sweater on my forehead. I was in the van with Miguel watching the hills drift. I felt peaceful and safe. I was at the Irish restaurant watching Michael wait on a husband and wife, their faces aglow with appreciation. He looked at me and winked. My heart swelled, then my belly. I was pregnant and then I was with Irene. She was cooing in my ear, one arm around my shoulder. Dave was singing into my ear on the other side of me, sweet melodies of love and rest. Madame Alexandria was reading my cards. I drank tea from a china cup. My mom waved to me from across the street. I was sitting in the yard, our yard, the yard back home. Home. She smiled and I waved back to her. I was with Ned at the round kitchen table; he smiled at me. "I love you," he mouthed to me in silence. Carlos was there too, dancing in the background. He smoked a cigarette and swung his hips in time to the music. His gold tooth flashed in the light. The light, the light was everywhere, warming my bones. But they drew me back over and over. "Mama",

"Rosalene", they called me and wanted me to eat and sit up. All I wanted to do was dream. I was tired of surviving. Couldn't they see that I just wanted to dream?

"Mama," Emma shook me.

I opened my eyes a slit; she was standing before me. She looked like a ghost. I barely made out the outline of her body. "Leave me," I said.

"Mama, there's someone here to see you. Someone to help you."

Next to Emma stood a woman, a tall woman with graying brown hair and deep hazel eyes. She bent over and looked at me, studied my face. Her eyes were flecked with green and gold. I tried to focus. I knew her. I recognized her aura. It was very pretty. She was a seer, like Madame Alexandria. My lips were dry. "What do you want?" She had come for me; I knew it. It was time for me to go. "Am I dead?"

"No," she laughed and her voice sounded very pretty. "I came to work on you. Are you familiar with acupuncture Rosalene?" She didn't wait for an answer. "I stick needles in your pressure points. I open up your energy channels, your wind gates. Do you trust me Rosalene?"

I did. "Yes," I whispered.

"Emma, I need matches and a small bowl of water and a bowl for incense and after I get set up you can dim the lights."

I fell asleep and dreamed and when I awoke a beautiful scent surrounded me. Sandalwood and eucalyptus and other woody textures filled the air. I had needles in my arms, my legs, my hands, all over my body. I was Frankenstein in frankincense. I felt relaxed, comfortable, like I was floating on water. I fell back asleep. When I awoke the second time the needles were gone, the window was slightly open blowing in the fresh scent of the night. I was thirsty, terribly thirsty. I was alone in the room. "Can," my voice came out quietly, "can I have some water?"

The door came ajar and the tall woman entered. She had a glass of water in one hand and a towel in the other. She helped me sit up and I drank half of the glass of water, choking as it went down my parched throat. I laid back down and she put the towel on my forehead. It was cool and moist and I floated toward her.

"You have some major blockages. I can feel them. I think I may have helped," she sat next to the bed.

She had a crooked nose and one of her eyebrows drooped. Her eyes were like a doe's eyes. "You see things don't you?" I asked her.

"Yes," she said.

"How do you do it?"

"What do you mean?"

I turned my head to the wall. "How do you see awful things and live with them? I just can't. I can't do it anymore."

"I try to focus on the good things I see."

"I saw Carlos and he died; then I died."

"Yes, I understand. I don't see as much as I feel. I feel first and then a picture comes into my head. I saw my ex husband once, in a terrible accident with a band saw. It was awful. Blood everywhere. I warned him and so far, nothing. Maybe someday it will happen, but I like to think maybe somehow I moved fate just a little to the right."

"I'm so tired."

"I'll come back tomorrow. We'll get your energy back. Do you trust me?"

"Only you. And I'm not sure why. I know you."

"Yes."

She left me in the cool room and sleep came easy. I slept for twelve hours without dreaming and when I awoke Carlos was laying next to me, curled around me like a caterpillar in a chrysalis. "Carlos," I woke him.

"Hmmm?"

"Carlos, I love you."

The woman's name was Rita May. Rita May came the next day and then twice a day, morning and night for a week. She brought needles and scents of beauty, cool towels and herbal patches of warmth. Carlos fed me soups of vegetables and tofu.

Emma stayed away. "Where is she?" I asked Carlos one night.

"She is angry. She is scared. She doesn't want to lose you in her heart."

I thought about my mom. From the moment I lost her, my life became a state of survival. I survived the streets, the people and the elements. I slept under bushes, in rusted out trailers. It was me against the world always. Even now I tried to survive, feed Emma, collect the food stamps and the welfare, find the part time jobs, pay the rent, pay the heat, feed myself, find love, fight the visions. No wonder I was so tired. I couldn't fight anymore.

"Carlos, I saw you die; in a car accident, in the rain. Someone else was driving, you went around a curve and you...Carlos; you died. You left me."

His eyes went wide. They searched my face. "Okay. No car in the rain. I will not forget." He buried his body next to mine. He held me.

"You're my last hope. Everyone else has left me. They are always leaving. I could not stop Michael, I tried Carlos, but I couldn't save him. I tried."

"I must leave too Conchita, but there is one big difference."

"What's that?"

"I always come back."

Carlos left two days later. Rita May kept coming. "Don't you have school?" I asked her.

"You're part of my internship now," she said.

I fell in love with Rita May. She rarely spoke. She didn't need to. She said everything with her hands; her incredible healing hands. I wanted to get out of bed. "Is Emma here?" I asked.

"She and Steve and Kimmy are in the kitchen."

"Who's Steve?"

"That's my son. That's how I came to be here. Steve and Emma work together at the restaurant. One night she came to the restaurant. She fell to the ground in front of him, cried and begged him to save you and herself. He called me and I came that very night."

"Thank you." I took a deep breath.

"She thought she was losing you."

"She was."

The next time I awoke, Emma was in the room. She and Rita May were talking in the corner, the moonlight brushing their faces.

"Let's try this. Close your eyes Emma," Rita May was whispering, holding Emma's hands. "What animal do you see?"

"I see an owl."

"What color do you see?" Rita May asked.

"I see white." Emma's eyes opened.

"I knew it. You have the Native healing in your bones. The owl is the healing totem for your mama's condition and white is the healing color. I think you are an instinctive healer my girl."

"I am?" Emma smiled wide.

"Emma," Rita May bent her head close to Emma's so their heads were almost touching, "what do you want to do?"

"Right now? Nothing."

"No, I mean, what do you want to do, you know, when you grow up?"

Emma laughed. "Grow up. That's a strange thought. I don't know if I can get out of here. The river, the trees, I'm tied to them somehow. It's all I have."

"You could be a forest ranger."

I saw Emma's face lift. I saw the thought form inside of her, growing. "Yea, yea, something like that. I'd like that. Getting paid for following squirrel tracks, protecting the trees. I could do that, either that or something like Ned is doing."

"I can help you get into school. You have an advantage because you're economically struggling and have no father."

"Yea." Her head drooped. She sighed. "So being poor and following all those squirrel tracks might pay off?"

I closed my eyes and feigned sleep until they left the room.

When they were gone, I sat up and worked my way out of the bed. I walked to the bathroom and in the mirror I saw the strangest sight. It was me, but it wasn't me. I was wearing a disguise, a layering over myself. A layering that I could peel; shed like a reptile skin. I was underneath this ugly wrinkled layer and I wanted to come out. It was me, Rosalene. "Let me out," I said.

That night in my dream a great wind flooded my body. It began in the soles of my feet and traveled up, filling my sternum with pure clean air. The wind wasn't just wind, it was a spirit flying through me. I recognized the smell of her, the light floral scent of her, like rosewater. It was Miss Alexandria. "Wake up Rosalene," she moaned inside of me, "wake up."

The wind filled my throat and passed to my head. It filled my ears, my eyes, and my nose. I was about to explode with the enormity of it when it suddenly exited through the top of my head, spilling into the room, illuminating everything that it touched.

"I need you," I cried.

"You have me," the wind cried as it circled about me.

I awoke and sat straight up in bed. I called her name, "Miss Alexandria? Miss Alexandria? Where are you?" I heard the wind outside, a branch brushed against the house. I fell back on the bed and smiled. She loved me. She'd been watching me. I wasn't alone. She would help me carry the weight of my visions, of the psychic truths I was born to witness. I had never been alone; I just thought I was.

I was still very weak so Rita May had cooked dinner. Steve was there, sitting in a kitchen chair, his long legs splayed out into the center of the room. Kimmy sat to my right on the couch, one of her hands on my forearm. She looked very pretty and smiled at Steve a lot. "I'm going to marry her one day," Steve said pointing his finger at Kimmy and shaking his head yes, up and down, up and down. Kimmy's smile lit up the kitchen. Emma set the table. Kimmy got up and lit two white candles in the center of the table, beautiful pillars in cut glass candleholders.

"Those are from Carl. He was worried about you. You saved his life once Mrs. J.," Kimmy said.

Did I save Carl's life? Could I have saved someone's life? Was I capable of that? I didn't know. Rita May had saved my life.

The phone rang. Emma answered. "Mama it's for you, it's Carlos."

"Carlos?"

"Feeling better Conchita?" His voice sounded scratchy and far away. There was a hum on the line.

"I am Carlos. I'm out of bed."

"I knew. I prayed to the Mother Mary for you. Jesus prayed for you; I asked him to pray."

"Thank you Carlos."

"I am calling to tell you something. It is raining hard here, so hard the streets filled with water. It is so much it cannot drain. We closed the carnival early and two men from the crew, they invited me to drive up North to eat and drink and celebrate the day, but I remembered Conchita. I remembered what it was you said. I did not go with them." He paused. "They both died Conchita." He began to sob over the phone.

"What?"

He paused and found his voice again. "Can you hear me? They died, both of them. I had only known them a few days, they came from another city and joined their rides with us, but now...." He stopped short and I heard him begin to cry again. "You were right and now it is my life that is spared because of you Rosalene. If you had never said a word to me, I would have gone in that car without thinking in my head. I am coming home. You are all I want. I love you Rosalene."

We were both crying into the phone, miles away, joined by tears. I had saved Carlos' life. He wasn't going to die. I had moved an instant in time. Me. Rosalene. The mixed up woman with the haunting visions and the heavy gift, I had done it. If you can see the future can you change it? I had asked Miss Alexandria that years ago and now I knew the answer. I couldn't save Michael, but I saved Carlos.

"I can't believe it," I said.

"Yes, it is a miracle. Jesus will stay for me and run things, he can do it all on his own, I know. I will see you in five days my lovely bird."

I put the phone on the hook and turned. The room looked different. There were colors everywhere, beautiful colors. The red of the wine and the pasta sauce, the yellow light shining through the window, the white pillars, Kimmy's rose lips, Emma's green eyes, Steve's golden hair. I smiled.

"What Mama?" Emma asked.

"Carlos. He is coming home. He didn't get in the car, the car I saw him in; the car that crashed in the rain. He stayed behind. They didn't make it, the two men in the car died, but Carlos stayed behind. I saved his life...."

Silence filled the space between us. Emma dropped her head. "I'm sorry people died in the car."

"I saw it. I saw it. It was horrible. The car hit a tree. It swerved in the rain." I started to cry again. Emma put an arm around my waist and laid her head on my shoulder.

"You saved Carlos, and you tried to save Michael, my father. It wasn't your fault, you know. He was willing to die for what he believed in. It wasn't you mama," Emma looked at me with her green eyes, eyes the color of the forest.

"Let's celebrate! Here's to saving lives!" Rita May broke the sorrowful spell.

The smell of lasagna filled the air, garlic and cheese and heavenly tomatoes. The back door was open letting in the twilight. The frogs croaked and the grasshoppers sang and I rejoiced. I had my visions, I had my curse, but I had survived. I had Emma. I had Miss Alexandria always, and Carlos was alive. I was alive.

AT THE TABLE

"This is the last time Kimmy. Are you sure you want to do this?"

Kimmy grabbed Steve's hand. "I have moral support. Let's do it."

Rosalene lit the candles; the room was dark save for the circles of light given off by the white pillars. Steve's face glowed in the yellow light.

"Close your eyes and hold hands, palms up." Rosalene began to rock and she chanted, low and beautiful. The sound was animalistic, a beautiful rolling sound. Emma closed her eyes tight and wished she was at the river. Kimmy closed her eyes in anticipation and Steve kept his open, trained on Kimmy and her translucent skin.

"I'm here Kimmy," Rosalene's voice lilted.

Kimmy kept her eyes closed tightly. "Where mom? Where are you? I need you."

"I am beside you. Feel my hand and I am looking at you right now. You are so beautiful. I see you from the inside out. I'm in your heart. You are my girl, you are my love." Rosalene's lips moved with precise articulation.

Kimmy opened her eyes and looked beside her. Emma was on one side, her eyes shut tight, slouched in her chair. Steve was on her other side; his eyes open, gazing at her as if she were the finest piece of china ever made, the finest flower, the finest hour in the finest piece of history. "Oh mom, I love you so. I have been waiting for you for years. Thank you." Kimmy dropped Emma's hand and grabbed Steve's hand with both of hers. "Thank you. Thank you."

Rosalene's head dropped forward, and came close to hitting the table.

"Mama?" Emma called her quietly.

Rosalene's eyes opened slowly. "I can't do it again Kimmy. It's too hard to cross over. It takes every ounce of strength that I have. This was my last try. Did you see her or feel her? Did you hear her?"

"Mrs. J. you don't have to do it again. It worked. I heard her and I'm not alone anymore. I have everything I need. No more cutting Mrs. J., I promise." Delicate tears stained her cheeks.

"Good," Rosalene said.

Emma banged her hands on the table signaling the finality of it all. "Good, now let's all go to the river and take our clothes off. Time for some real hocus pocus!"

Rosalene laughed. Kimmy laughed and put her arm around Steve's shoulders. The kitchen filled with a soft melody, the song of a flute. The moonlight entered the room and spilled across the top of the wooden table, illuminating every pencil mark and every scar that had ever been made.

Printed in the USA
CPSIA information can be obtained
at www.ICGtesting.com
CBHW021414271024
16407CB00005B/19